CRIME LORD'S CAPTIVE

CRIME LORD SERIES, BOOK 1

MIA KNIGHT

COPYRIGHT

DEDICATION

To my dogs who put up with my odd hours, emotional outbursts and love me anyway.

1

"Do you have to go?" Morgan asked her boyfriend.

Jonathan grinned as he wrapped his arms around her. "Gonna miss me?"

"Yes." She couldn't shake the ball of dread in her stomach.

"I have to travel for work," Jonathan said as he stroked her back. "I haven't gone anywhere since you moved in, but I can't put it off any longer. Three months is a long time."

"I know."

Jonathan brushed a kiss over her mouth. "I love that you want me here, but I have to go. If we moved to the West Coast, I wouldn't need to travel as much."

Morgan's stomach jittered. "I like it here in Maine."

"Then we'll stay in Maine," he said.

Jonathan leaned down and gave Morgan a deep kiss. She clutched handfuls of his jacket to prolong the moment. She didn't realize how much she depended on him until he announced his business trip. It was just her luck that her boyfriend was an IT consultant who had to travel for work.

Jonathan pulled back, eyes warm. "At least I know you'll be here waiting for me."

Morgan gave him a weak smile. "Yes, I'll be here. Hurry back to me."

Jonathan shouldered a laptop bag and pulled up the handle of his small suitcase. He opened the door and paused to look back at her. "You're going to be okay, right?"

He doesn't need this, Morgan thought and felt guilty for making him worry about her. "Yes," she said and tried to sound confident.

Jonathan blew her a kiss before he walked out of the apartment. Morgan stared at the closed door for a long minute before she forced herself to get a move on. She could survive a week on her own. She was alone for two years before she met Jonathan. He traveled a lot for work, so she had to learn to deal with his long absences.

Morgan went through her morning routine as the world slowly began to light up outside her window. She styled her long honey blond hair into a French twist and smoothed a hand over her conservative black skirt and white blouse. Morgan surveyed herself in the mirror and was satisfied with her image. She looked competent and boring. Morgan did everything in her power not to draw attention to herself.

Her phone chimed, signaling it was time to leave for work. She grabbed her bag and gave the tidy apartment a cursory glance as she walked out the door. Morgan walked two blocks to the bus stop just in time to see it pull up to the curb. She claimed the seat she always did and scanned the faces on the bus out of habit.

Morgan tried to shake off her unease as she entered the bank and was greeted by her co-workers. *Just another day*, she reassured herself. Morgan put her things in the break room and began her daily routine of setting up her desk and counting her money.

It was an uneventful day, which reassured Morgan that she was overreacting to Jonathan's absence. She felt restless and on edge, but a call from Jonathan on her lunch break made her feel better. Morgan had become very attached to Jonathan since they started dating a year ago. Jonathan's easygoing personality was a balm to her uptight one, and she couldn't wait for him to come home. Before Jonathan entered her life, she had been a nervous wreck. Now, she felt a little more like her old self.

Morgan left the bank at the end of the day, walking briskly as the sun set. She reached the bus stop precisely on time and leaped up the steps with a nod to the driver. Her normal seat was already taken so she settled for an aisle seat and tried to settle her nerves, which were taut now that night had fallen. Jonathan would be back in six days. No big deal.

Morgan hopped off the bus and approached her building, climbing two flights before she reached her apartment. She knew her neighbors by sight but none by name, and that's the way she liked it. Morgan glanced both ways as she unlocked her door and swiftly entered. She knocked the main light switch with her elbow, set her keys and purse on the stand beside the door, and froze.

A man sat on a stool in her kitchen. As she took a step back and slammed into the door, her mouth opening to scream, he shook his head in warning. The small gesture made the scream die in her throat. Morgan stared at the man in the black business suit with an awful sense of doom clawing at her throat. He had merciless black eyes and a scar through his left brow.

"Lyla, come away from the door," Blade said.

Lyla. She hadn't heard that name for three years. Panic grabbed her by the throat. Her past couldn't be sitting in the apartment she shared with Jonathan.

"It's a good thing your boyfriend is away. I had orders to kill him," Blade said calmly.

She took two unsteady steps forward. "Jonathan has nothing to do with this."

Blade cocked his head to the side. "You think not?"

"I've been gone three years," she rasped. She thought she was safe.

"Yet here I am." Blade withdrew a phone from his pocket. He swiped his finger over the screen and jerked his head at her. "Come, Lyla, say hi to Gavin."

Nausea churned in her stomach as she watched Blade dial. She was torn between running or snatching the phone to break it into pieces. She did neither. Instead, she watched with her heart in her throat. Even though she knew running would be pointless, she took a step back.

Blade's eyes narrowed into slits. "Don't, Lyla."

She heard the threat in his voice and froze. She was well acquainted with Blade, Gavin's personal bodyguard. Blade was unflinchingly loyal to Gavin and would carry out any task, legal or illegal.

"Blade, please," she whispered.

Blade gave her an unreadable look before he focused on the phone in his hand.

"She's here. Come, Lyla, Gavin wants to talk to you," Blade said pleasantly.

Blade turned the phone toward her. Gavin Pyre looked back at her. Her heart thumped so hard in her chest she was afraid she might have a heart attack. Gavin hadn't changed.

He wore a deep V-neck shirt that showed off his defined chest. He was otherworldly handsome with shoulder-length black hair and stunning amber eyes. Gavin's intense gaze skewered her. The boyish charm he used to fool everyone into believing he wasn't dangerous was alarmingly absent.

"Lyla."

Her name rolled off his tongue. The sound of that deep voice, the one that haunted her dreams, made her take a step back in self-defense.

"You're more beautiful than I remember," he said.

She shook her head wildly. "Gavin. Please, don't," she said in a choked voice.

"Why, Lyla?"

She shuddered and whispered, "What do you want?" Gavin wouldn't send Blade to track her to Maine after three years for a friendly chat.

"*Why*, Lyla?"

She didn't answer. She couldn't. Three years did nothing to lessen the impact of his presence. She didn't realize she was moving until she hit the kitchen counter.

Blade followed her with the phone. She turned her face to the side to avoid eye contact with Gavin who watched her silently.

"Come back to me, Lyla," Gavin said quietly.

"No," she choked out and glanced at the screen in time to witness Gavin's expression smooth into unyielding lines. Dread morphed into full-blown terror as she witnessed the change. She knew how ruthless Gavin could be.

"You might find this interesting," Gavin said coolly as he disappeared off the screen.

Against her will, she eased forward to get a better look while her mind tried to process what she was seeing. A man bound to a chair. His face so swollen and disfigured that she wouldn't have been able to guess his identity, but she recognized the bloody crucifix around his neck. She clutched the countertop for balance as her head swam.

"What have you done to my father?" she whispered.

"He's been stealing from me," Gavin said as he strolled into her line of sight. Gavin pulled a gun out of his waistband and pressed it to her father's temple. Her father came alive, bucking at the ropes, eyes rolling madly. She felt her world tilt sideways as she listened to her father's stifled screams through the gag.

"Gavin, no!" she cried as she took the phone from Blade who let it go easily enough. She held the phone between shaking hands, willing Gavin not to pull the trigger.

Gavin raised a brow in mock surprise. "You care if he lives, Lyla?"

"I have money," she said and tried to keep the phone steady as her hands shook like crazy.

"You have half a million?"

The bottom dropped out of her stomach. "Half a million?" she whispered, aghast. Her father was a fool. She didn't have more than five thousand in her bank account, and that was because Jonathan didn't let her pay rent. Maybe she could get a loan—

"Your father knows the consequences of stealing from us," Gavin said.

Everyone knew not to fuck with the Pyres. The Pyre men weren't known for being merciful. They were hard, cruel, and calculating.

"What are you willing to do for him?" Gavin asked.

She broke out in a cold sweat. Gavin knew what she would say. "I'll do anything," she whispered.

"Blade will bring you to me," Gavin said.

"Gavin, I can't—"

"You want your father to live?"

She couldn't speak, so she nodded.

Gavin lowered the gun and walked toward whoever held his phone. Gavin's face filled the screen. Her breath seized. The force of his personality reached through the phone and grabbed her by the throat.

"Didn't you miss me even a little bit, Lyla?"

She wanted to hurl the phone and make him disappear. Gavin's voice was soft and seductive as if he wasn't blackmailing her and hadn't just held a gun to her father's head! She glared at him mutinously, and his expression darkened.

"Blade tells me your boyfriend is out of town. Count yourself lucky, or you would have come home to a bloody surprise." Before she could react, he continued in a much calmer tone. "Go with Blade. Don't give him any trouble. Come to me, Lyla, and I'll let your father live."

The screen went blank, and her legs gave out. She crumpled to the kitchen floor, hyperventilating.

"We don't have time for this," Blade said impatiently and hauled her up. "The jet is waiting and so is Gavin."

"J-jet?" she wheezed, mind whirling.

"Pack what you need. You have ten minutes," Blade said shortly.

Her life just turned upside down, and he was giving her ten minutes? She ran to the bedroom and slammed the door. Three years, she'd been on the run. Three years, she planned every step only to end up caught. In a matter of minutes, Gavin crushed the normal life she'd built into tiny pieces. She wanted to believe that Gavin was lying about her father stealing half a million, but she knew better. Her father had a gambling problem and Gavin didn't make idle threats. He would kill her father if she didn't go to him.

Blade pounded on the bedroom door. "Five minutes."

She wanted to curse, cry, and rage, but she didn't have the time for such a luxury. Blade was here to carry out Gavin's wishes, and he would do whatever it took to see it through. She snatched a handful of clothes off the hangers and shoved them in a duffel before she grabbed a piece of notebook paper and began to write. She didn't need a crystal ball to know that she would never see Jonathan again.

Jonathan,

I will never forget what you've done for me. You're an amazing man. I'm sorry for leaving like this. I hope you find a woman worthy of you.

Morgan

The pen shook in her hand. She stared at the name she'd scrawled. She had been Morgan for three years, but a new identity hadn't been enough to stay hidden. She hadn't told Jonathan she was on the run from Gavin Pyre. Morgan had a fictional background that didn't include a former relationship with the crime lord of Sin City.

"Open the door, or I'll break it down," Blade ordered.

Lyla unlocked the door and barely avoided being hit when it slammed open and Blade charged in. He saw the note immediately. He read it, sneered, and tossed it on the bed.

"You're lucky I came instead of Gavin," Blade said.

Lyla said nothing as he grabbed her duffel.

"Anything else?" he asked.

She lifted her chin. "Is it true? Dad stole half a million?"

"Your dad's always been a dumb shit," Blade said and towed her toward the front door.

She dragged her feet to buy time, terrified to leave the safety of the apartment and the life she'd built for herself. "But half a million?"

"He's a greedy fuck."

She managed to wrench out of his hold and stood in the middle of the apartment, wringing her hands. "What does Gavin want with me?"

Blade surveyed her coldly. "What do you think?"

Her throat began to close. "He's going to kill me for running from him?"

Blade snorted as if her fear was unfounded. "If he wanted to kill you, I would have done it."

That didn't reassure her. Maybe Gavin wanted to do the deed himself. "Why now? Why after all this time?"

"You'll have to ask him that." Blade opened the apartment door. "Let's go."

Lyla's eyes brimmed with tears as she looked around the apartment that had become her short-lived haven. For three months, she allowed herself to believe in a happily ever after with a good man. What would Jonathan think when he discovered her note? The only way she could ensure her past didn't touch Jonathan was to leave without a trace. Jonathan was no match for Gavin Pyre.

Lyla followed Blade out of the apartment and found a taxi waiting at the curb. Blade held the door open for her. Lyla stopped, racking her brain for a way out of this, but in the end, she had no choice but to get in. She and Blade sat side by side in silence. There was nothing to say to one another. Blade wouldn't reveal anything that would help her. Lyla focused on keeping her roiling stomach under control.

The taxi dropped them off at a private airstrip where a Pyre jet waited. Lyla paused, eyeing the sleek black and gold jet. Blade ushered her up the steps where a beaming flight attendant greeted them with warm cloths for their hands and champagne. Lyla took the cloth before she collapsed into the nearest seat and closed her eyes. To be surrounded by such luxury would thrill most people, but Lyla knew it was a gilded cage. A heavy pressure on her chest made it hard to draw in a normal breath. There were no other passengers on the jet aside from her and Blade. She tried to act as if she were sleeping, but knew she didn't fool Blade. She felt the impact of his stare.

Lyla tried to wrap her mind around the fact she was going back to Las Vegas and Gavin Pyre. Her body tingled with fear as she conjured up Gavin's face. Cold, beautiful, cruel. Once upon a time, she loved him with every fiber of her being. She would have done anything for him, and then Gavin shattered her heart into pieces. Self-preservation made her run.

Lyla turned her face toward the window to hide the tears she couldn't hold back. What did Gavin want from her? Why use her father to force her back to him? How would she pay off her father's debt? The thought filled her with mind-numbing terror.

Lyla saw The Strip appear, a city in the middle of the desert. She spotted several Pyre Casinos, towers of gleaming black with a bold stripe of gold. Despite the fasten seat belt sign, Lyla lurched out of her seat and barely made it to the bathroom in time to vomit. The flight attendant handed her a miniature bottle of mouthwash, which she took gladly. Even after two ginger ales, her stomach rocked as if she were seasick. She hadn't been able to eat a thing.

Blade gave her an amused look, clearly enjoying her fear. He was in a better mood now that they were here. An unexpected storm in Chicago had delayed them. Blade had several terse conversations with Gavin who was clearly displeased. Lyla wished the delay had been for days instead of hours even as the suspense of not knowing what lay in wait consumed her. She hadn't been able to sleep and was now sick with exhaustion. She muttered prayers under her breath as the plane landed and taxied. When it came to a stop, she didn't loosen her death grip on the armrest. She held her breath as the door of the jet opened, expecting Gavin to barge in. Blade impatiently unbuckled her seat belt and shuffled her toward the door, ignoring the flight attendant's appalled gaze. Lyla was too tired to elbow him in the stomach for his rough handling.

Lyla stumbled down the stairs, looking around wildly for Gavin, but he wasn't there. Her hands were clammy despite the warm wind that tugged hair out of her ruined French twist. Blade put her in the back seat of the private car waiting for them and sat up front with the driver. Because of the solid partition, she couldn't hear them, which put her on edge. Now what?

Las Vegas had changed little since she left. The stark desert landscape was a far cry from Maine's rocky coastline, lighthouses, forests, and lakes. They drove out of the city to a mansion surrounded by red mountains. This place was as familiar to her as her childhood home. Passing through an

electronic gate into the inner courtyard, she eyed the armed
guards patrolling the grounds. The car rounded the fountain in the drive and stopped. Blade opened her door. She
took his hand because she didn't want to fall on her face,
and still had some pride left. Blessedly numb, she walked up
the steps into the foyer and stopped. She took in the familiar
white marble floors and open floor plan of Gavin's mansion.
It was alarmingly quiet.

"Gavin's at work," Blade said shortly. "You want something to eat?"

Lyla shook her head. Blade took her arm and led her
upstairs.

"What about my father?" she asked.

"Gavin will talk to you about him."

"But how do I know he's alive?"

"You don't," Blade said as he opened the door to a room
and pushed her in. "I'm locking the door from the outside. If
you need anything, use the phone on the nightstand."

Lyla's skin stretched tight as she surveyed the master
bedroom. It hadn't changed since she'd picked out the
sheets, drapes, and cream carpet. She and Gavin spent
countless hours making love in this room.

"C-can I wait for him in another room?" *Anywhere* else.

"No."

Blade closed the door and turned the key in the lock.
She waited until his steps retreated down the hallway before
she tried the door. Yes, locked. Lyla stared at the bed as if it
would come to life and swallow her whole. The girl who
once inhabited this house, this room had been so naïve, so
trusting. Lyla wasn't that girl, not any longer. She retreated
to the window seat, looking out over the property.

Gavin's compound was ten minutes away from any sign
of civilization. He was paranoid and liked his privacy. Even

though she couldn't see it, she knew he had an Olympic size pool in the backyard and a monstrous garage that housed luxury cars. Lyla knew a secret route to get out of the mansion in case of an attack and the location of Gavin's safe house in New Mexico.

Tears slipped from her eyes. She was in Gavin's world again—a dangerous world swimming with violence, money, and sex. She wanted no part of it. Damn her father for putting her in this position.

Lyla paced the room like a caged animal, taking in the walk-in closet, opulent bathroom, and familiar surroundings, which made her want to scream. Lyla dug her nails into her arm, willing herself to wake from this nightmare. She couldn't be in Las Vegas, in the room she once shared with Gavin. What did Gavin want from her? She had no idea how he interpreted her escape three years ago. She suspected he would make an effort to find her, but thought he would have given up by now. Did he renew the search when he found out her father had embezzled money? Was she here for punishment?

Sick with worry and exhaustion, she settled on the window seat and wondered how long Gavin would make her wait. Gavin now knew the measures she took to remain hidden. She paid an exorbitant amount to have a new identity created. She had a birth certificate, social security card, and driver's license declaring that her name was Morgan Lincoln. Her identification passed muster in five states. She traveled as far as possible from Nevada without leaving the country. She took low profile jobs and kept to herself until Jonathan. She didn't know how to protect herself from his friendliness and warmth. For a short time, she believed she could live a normal life. Now, she was back in hell, awaiting judgment. By now, Jonathan would know something was wrong. Would he come back early? Would he believe she'd willingly leave him?

Lyla moaned and stretched out on the window seat. She dozed in the sunlight streaming through the window as a tear slipped from her eye.

2

LYLA LAY AGAINST A WARM CHEST. She looked up at Jonathan who wore an unusually somber expression. They were in bed in their apartment. Sunlight poured through the window, but the apartment was curiously silent. She sat up and brushed a hand through his short-cropped hair. Something niggled at the back of her mind, but she pushed it away so she could focus on him.

"What's wrong?" she asked.

"Why didn't you tell me about him?" Jonathan asked.

Lyla retracted her hand. She had no doubt who Jonathan was referring to. "How did you find out?"

"He called. He says he wants you back."

Lyla tried to move off the bed, but Jonathan gathered her in his arms. She was surprised by his strength as he lay down and settled her beside him.

"Do you want to go back to him?" Jonathan asked gently.

"No!" she whispered, clutching fistfuls of his shirt. "Please don't make me."

"You want to stay with me?"

"Yes."

"Then we'll figure this out," Jonathan said.

She relaxed fractionally, willing herself to believe him. "We can?"

"I have connections," Jonathan said and brushed her hair back from her face. "I'll do anything for you, Lyla."

Her heart swelled. Jonathan, her gentle knight. She was safe with him. Lyla's hands went to his chest. She needed him. She was so damn cold. Desperate to feel his hot skin against hers, she ripped the front of his shirt and heard buttons bounce across the floor.

"Lyla," he began, but she covered her mouth with his.

She had never been so hungry or desperate for touch and comfort. She tore off her clothes and plastered her naked chest to his. She moaned at the contact even as he ripped her underwear. She felt the snap of fabric on her inner thighs and then cool air a moment before his fingers pressed into her. Even as his aggression made her hot, something about it struck her as odd, but she couldn't think past the inferno consuming them. She drank from his lips to wash away the taste of fear. His fingers burrowed into her channel, making her dizzy with need.

"I need you," she said as she trailed kisses over his face. "Don't let me go."

Jonathan suddenly pinned her beneath him. He spread her thighs and pressed the head of his cock over her slick lips.

"Do you want me, Lyla?" he rasped.

"More than anything," she said, reaching for him, needing him inside her. She needed Jonathan to claim her, to make her believe she was his and no one else's.

"Lyla," he moaned a second before he slid inside her.

The burn of pleasure rocketed through her. She paused to savor the moment. Here, something was different as well, but she couldn't think when she was so full of him and his mouth devoured hers. He was dominant and animalistic, taking her as he never had before. Pleasure burst through her, eclipsing fear and replacing it with ecstasy.

"Do you belong to me?" he asked.

Lyla tossed her head back as he sped up his thrusts. He was going deeper than he ever had, as if he could sense her desperation and need. Instead of his usual gentleness, an edge of violence to his lovemaking made her wild.

"Lyla, promise me."

"Promise what?" She was having a hard time concentrating. Why did he want to talk now? She was so close—

He stopped moving. "Promise you won't leave me again."

"I never left you," Lyla said and rocked against him, desperate for relief.

"You did," he growled.

Lyla's breath stalled in her throat as a sliver of fear cut through the ecstasy. She tried to push away, but he kept her in place with heavy, deliberate thrusts that made her moan through clenched teeth.

"You'll never leave me again," he decreed.

Lyla opened her mouth to argue, but the climax hit so hard and fast that she wasn't prepared for it. She let out a high-pitched scream as he pounded into her. Jonathan's face began to distort. Even as Lyla reached up and raked her nails along Jonathan's back, she realized it was too broad and muscled. Confusion and panic clouded her mind. She blinked furiously as the orgasm faded and reality smacked her in the face.

Lyla wasn't in her apartment in Maine with Jonathan. She was in Gavin's master suite in his home, and he was fucking her. Gavin's harsh breaths filled the room as he thrust into her, amber gaze spearing hers as he neared his climax. Through the dim light of a nearby lamp, Lyla could see he was fully dressed in a gray suit, his shirt ripped down the front with just his pants undone.

"No!" Lyla screamed and tried to get away, but she was pinned beneath a solid body that definitely wasn't Jonathan's.

"I missed you so much."

Gavin brushed kisses over her face, even as she tried to avoid his mouth. Gavin's face darkened, and he planted himself to the hilt.

"You're mine," Gavin hissed a moment before he climaxed, flooding her with his sperm.

She dreamed of escaping him, only to wake and find him fucking her. Lyla began to shake uncontrollably as he hovered over her, not saying a word. The familiar scent of his cologne made her stomach lurch.

"How could you do this to me?" she whispered and then pounded his chest and screamed, "Get off me!"

"Lyla—"

"No, let me go!"

Gavin flipped her onto her stomach and rested his full weight on her. Lyla turned her head to the side so she could breathe and dug her nails into the rumpled sheets that smelled of them. Enraged and helpless, she beat at the mattress and tried to buck him off with no luck.

"Don't," he warned in a lethal voice.

"You raped me!" she seethed and tried to bite him.

"You wanted me," Gavin said against her ear, causing her to shiver. "As soon as I put you in bed, you reached for me. You ripped my shirt and told me you needed me."

"I was dreaming, you asshole!" She didn't get wet for *him*; she was dreaming about Jonathan. That's why her body responded, right? Lyla stiffened when Gavin's cock slid between her legs again.

"You recognize my touch even in sleep, baby girl."

"No!" She tried to dislodge him, but he controlled her easily. This couldn't be happening. "Please, Gavin."

His hands moved over her, just as they had in the dream. "Do you know how many times I dreamed of having you beneath me like this again?"

"You can't do this to me! Stop, Gavin!" She sobbed as he moved inside her.

"I can do anything I want to you," he said and brushed achingly light kisses along her wet cheek. "I own you, Lyla Dalton."

Lyla buried her face in the sheets as he fucked her. Her body betrayed her, welcoming him and clutching at his cock. Gavin groaned into her hair and moved faster.

"You won't escape me this time," he said, hands stroking her body, overloading her senses.

She shook her head, unable to speak as he climaxed again and came with a triumphant shout that she was sure his security could hear. Lyla hated that her body demanded its own release. Didn't her body know that she hated him? The moment Gavin eased to the side, she rolled off the bed and ran to the en suite bathroom.

"Lyla—" Gavin began, but she slammed the door.

Lyla stepped into the shower and turned it on full blast. She scrubbed her body vigorously, trying to erase his touch and scent. How could her body respond to him? How had her dream merged seamlessly with reality so that she thought she was having sex with Jonathan instead of Gavin? She crumpled to the ground with her hands splayed on the floor as she wept. What did Gavin want from her? Was he trying to punish her? If he wanted to make her feel dirty and violated, he'd succeeded. The shock finally caught up to her, and she sobbed uncontrollably.

"Lyla."

She felt a draft as Gavin opened the shower door. At any other time, she would have been mortified by the whimper that escaped from her lips, but she was too far gone to care. The impact of seeing him after all these years was like a punch in the gut. The young, slick boss in training was gone. His hair was longer than she remembered, and his body had a layer of muscle that made Jonathan look like a boy going through puberty. Gavin crouched in front of her and brushed wet hair back from her face.

"Don't cry," he ordered roughly.

She stared into his beautiful eyes framed by dark lashes and had the suicidal urge to punch him. Gavin narrowed his eyes and shook his head.

"Don't, baby girl."

She hated that he knew her so well, even after all this time. Was she that predictable? Had she learned nothing since she left him? Her mind skittered as she tried to figure out how to handle him. "Leave me alone."

Gavin picked her up with a show of effortless strength that scared her. He settled her on a seat built into the shower and squirted shampoo into his hands. Before she could avoid him, he began to massage it into her scalp. The familiar smell of her favorite shampoo startled even as it soothed her. Lyla sat like a broken doll as Gavin bathed her. Lyla felt as if she were in an alternate reality. This couldn't be real. She couldn't be here with Gavin. She didn't have sex with him, and he couldn't be bathing her as if he had every right to. Lyla retreated into her mind because she wasn't capable of digesting what was happening.

Gavin cleaned himself before he stepped out of the

shower with her. He engulfed her in a soft cashmere robe and sat her in front of the vanity as he toweled her hair and brushed it. She was blessedly numb and didn't say a word. She examined Gavin in the mirror as he tended to her. The man in the mirror was a far cry from the man she fell in love with. Back then, Gavin had been arrogant and charming and possessed more power than one person should. Most people never witnessed the darkness in him since he was so good at disguising it. Now, it was on full display as if he didn't bother wearing a mask these days. Although he was tending to her as efficiently as a maid, power emanated from him and kept her still and quiet before him. Once upon a time, she loved him without reservation, but she had been a fool, and it took her four years to realize she was living a lie. Her emotions were a tangle of nostalgia, rage, fear, and betrayal. She loathed him yet a small part of her still believed he was the boy she'd fallen in love with. How could she love and hate him at the same time?

Gavin seemed harder and colder than she remembered, and it scared her. Gavin was so familiar yet ... not. How much had he changed in three years? Lyla reminded herself that Gavin had never been anything but gentle with her, but she knew that could change in a heartbeat. Lyla didn't realize she was crying again until Gavin crouched in front of her. He cupped her face between his hands and brushed her tears away with his thumb. Piercing amber eyes moved over her face.

"Don't cry," he ordered softly.

"I don't know how to stop," she whispered and began to shake.

Gavin gathered her in his arms and carried her into the bedroom. Panic infused her, and she began to struggle as he settled her on the bed.

"I'm not going to fuck you again," Gavin said.

Lyla took him at his word and curled into a ball on one side of the bed. There was an awful silence, and then arms pulled her back against a large body. Lyla made a distressed sound and tried to get away, but her limbs were weak with exhaustion and shock. She could feel his body heat through the robe, which reminded her of the dream and how she had ripped "Jonathan's" shirt, desperate to feel his skin against hers. Her eyes scanned the floor and stopped on the buttons scattered over the carpet. She moaned and covered her face with her hands. No wonder he fucked her. She'd practically begged him to do it. Within hours of being in his vicinity, he'd fucked her twice. What did this mean? Guilt clawed her insides. She was in love with Jonathan, yet Gavin made her come and played her body as easily as if she'd never been with another man. She hated herself.

"I want to see my dad," she said. She wouldn't be able to rest until she saw that he was alive. Gavin was underhanded enough to use her father to bring her back and still kill him for embezzling half a million.

"Tomorrow," Gavin said.

"No." Lyla rolled and braced herself to face him. "I want to see him."

Gavin stared at her for a long moment before he rose. "He's downstairs."

Lyla's heart lightened a bit. She slipped out of bed and belted the cashmere robe, which was too large for her. Gavin pulled on a pair of jeans and black T-shirt. She didn't comment as he put a gun in his waistband.

"Come," he said and opened the door.

Lyla held her breath as she passed him. She stopped in her tracks when she saw movement at the end of the hallway. She flushed with mortification as Gavin ushered her forward. The guards were expressionless, but she knew they had heard their boss fucking her. She looked like the weak female they assumed her to be. In this world, women were bought and sold to the highest bidder. And none was more powerful than Gavin. She tasted bile on her tongue as Gavin led her down the staircase and to the basement, the only area in the house that had been off-limits to her.

Lyla's damp palms slid along the iron railing as she walked down the steps that led into the basement. It was chilly down here, and the smell of blood was overwhelming. The basement had no windows, just endless concrete. Florescent lights revealed a figure in the middle of the room tied to a chair. Blood splattered the floor around him, and he wasn't moving.

Lyla shoved past Gavin to reach her father. She clasped his head between trembling hands. His face was swollen, discolored, and grotesque. His nose had been broken, and his lips were ripped from being pummeled against his teeth. Unfocused, dark brown eyes opened.

"Dad?" Lyla said urgently and snapped, "Gavin, untie him."

"Do it," Gavin said, and Blade appeared with a knife.

Lyla glared at Blade as he cut the ropes. Her father tipped forward. She fell back on her ass as she took his full weight.

"He needs a doctor," Lyla said as she held her limp father in her arms. He moaned pitifully.

"No."

Lyla glanced back at Gavin who had his arms folded across his chest.

"The price for stealing is death. Healing naturally from his beating is small recompense for what he owes me."

Gavin narrowed his eyes at her. "Don't look at me like that, Lyla. You know how our world works."

"Your world," she shot back.

"And you're back, so it's *our* world."

"I came back to pay his debt, not stay here permanently."

"You saved your father's life by coming back to me. I think it's fair to say a life for a life."

Lyla went cold with fear. "Life?" Was he going to kill her? Torture her? Turn her into a prostitute?

"Lyla?" her father croaked.

Lyla turned her back on Gavin. "It's me, Dad."

Dark brown eyes focused on her. "You shouldn't have left."

The venom in his voice battered at her.

"You ran off, leaving your mom and me to fend for ourselves, you selfish bitch ..." he ranted, blood trickling out of his mouth and over her pristine robe.

"That's enough, Pat," Gavin hissed as he appeared at Lyla's side. With one quick, ruthless shove, Gavin caused her father to topple backward. Lyla heard her father's head smack the concrete. She tried to go to him, but Gavin jerked her against him. "Your daughter is the only reason you're still breathing."

Lyla was sure her father was unconscious. The way his limbs were bent at unnatural angles made her stomach heave. She fought Gavin's hold, but he easily controlled her. Her father moaned. She dug her nails into Gavin's arm, but he didn't budge.

"If she stayed, I wouldn't have had to borrow money from you..." her father garbled through a mouthful of blood.

"Borrow?" Gavin asked in a dangerous voice.

"She used to give us half of the allowance you gave her

every month." Her father's voice took on a whining note. "I've had a hard time paying the bills."

"You think I don't know how much money you gamble away every week?"

Gavin's rage was ice cold and even more terrifying than Lyla remembered. She wanted to tell her father to shut up, but he wouldn't listen to her. He never had.

"I thought if I could just make more money, I could hire my own investigator to find Lyla for you and—"

"Shut your mouth," Gavin said, and her father went silent. "The only person you care about is yourself. You never cared for Lyla. The only time you remember she exists is when you need money."

Gavin pushed Lyla behind him. She stumbled, and Blade steadied her. Gavin crouched down and grabbed her father's face with one huge hand and squeezed.

"Gavin, no!" Lyla tried to go to her father, but Blade wrapped an arm around her waist to stop her from interfering. Lyla was close to hyperventilating. She knew what Gavin was capable of.

"Don't you ever talk to Lyla like that again," Gavin said in a calm, even tone. "Even if your stupidity brought her back to me, deal or not, I'll end you."

Gavin released her father who turned his head to the side and coughed up blood, which splattered the already stained floor. Gavin rose and turned. His expression darkened when it fell on her. Blade released her instantly. Gavin grasped her hand. When she fought him, he hauled her over his shoulder and carried her upstairs into his beautiful home that was untouched by the horror in the basement. Gavin didn't stop until they were back in the master suite. He set her on her feet with a jarring thud.

"Your father is a piece of shit," Gavin said as he took off her robe, which was stained with her father's blood.

Lyla didn't agree or disagree. Gavin pulled her into the bathroom and washed her arms with warm water and took care of himself before he conjured up another cashmere robe and slipped her into it.

"You hungry?" Gavin asked.

Lyla shook her head. Had she expected her father to change since she left? Wasn't distance supposed to make the heart grow fonder? Fuck that shit. Apparently, that didn't apply to her father. Even after all these years, she hadn't earned a crumb of his affection. He had always loathed her. Even sacrificing her life for his didn't inspire any warm emotions in him. After Jonathan's gentle caring, her father's disgust felt like a slap in the face. Did her father know why she was here? Even if she'd known that her father hadn't changed, she still would have come back for him. He was her father—a liar, gambler, thief... and her downfall.

"I have work to do," Gavin said abruptly.

Good, she thought. She needed to be alone.

"If you need anything, let me know." Gavin pointed at a cell phone on the nightstand. "My number is speed dial one."

Lyla nodded. When he moved toward her, she went rigid, but that didn't stop him from cupping her face and giving her a quick kiss. She didn't react. He rubbed his thumb over her bottom lip and searched her face. What the hell was he looking for?

"I wish the circumstances were different, and that you came back to me on your own, but I'm glad you're back," he said.

Lyla didn't respond. Gavin gave her another kiss before

he walked toward the door. He opened it, paused, and turned.

"No contact with anyone from your old life," Gavin said, face hardening. "That's done now. You don't want anyone to get hurt, do you?"

How could he go from protector and lover to threatening her? Lyla glared at him, but he didn't back down.

"You're back in my world, under my rules. You disobey, and I'll know. You got me?"

Lyla nodded.

"I'll see you soon," he said and left.

Lyla wanted to lie down, but she couldn't bear to sleep in a bed that smelled of their lovemaking. By fucking her, Gavin severed her tie with Jonathan irrevocably. Did he do it on purpose? By staking his claim on her through ties of the flesh, he separated her from her old life and brought her back into his. There was no going back. She could feel it in her bones.

Lyla stretched out on the window seat again and stared out at the moonlit grounds. There was a nagging ache between her legs. Why did her body respond to Gavin as if he were her soul mate? Lyla covered her face with her hands and moaned in self-loathing. She thought of her father and how he blamed her for his financial woes. He had always been greedy, but half a million? He was a bastard, but she loved him enough to leave her safe life behind. A small part of her had always feared that coming back would be inevitable.

3

"LYLA."

A hand stroked her hair. The touch was so gentle that she smiled before she opened her eyes. But as she stared up at Gavin, her new reality snapped into place. The smile vanished from her lips as Gavin brushed a finger down her cheek.

"This is the second time I've found you on the window seat. You got a problem with the bed?"

"No," Lyla lied and sat up, fixing the robe that had come undone. She flushed under his regard even though he was more familiar with her body than Jonathan was.

"You must be hungry. The clothes you brought are old and tattered, so Blade got rid of them. Your old clothes are still in the closet." He gestured to the double doors. "Get dressed, come down to the kitchen, and we'll talk."

Lyla slid off the window seat and winced as her stiff muscles protested. She didn't say a thing as she went to the closet and disappeared inside to escape his probing eyes. The closet was exactly as she had left it. One wall dedicated to outrageous heels while the other walls held racks of designer label clothes. These clothes belonged to a different person—someone who didn't have a care in the world. Back then, she didn't give a second thought to using Gavin's money or care that she was glorified arm candy. That felt like a lifetime ago. Lyla ran her hands over the fashionable, edgy garments and fought the urge to tear the closet apart. What would be the point? It wouldn't change her circumstances, and she had to find out what plans Gavin had for her. Last night, he had said a life for a life. Surely, he didn't mean forever?

Lyla chose one of the most conservative outfits—a long, skintight black skirt that had high slits on both sides and an electric blue crop top. She gave the wall of shoes a cursory glance before she chose a pair of strappy black heels. When she emerged from the closet, Gavin was gone. She took a deep breath and went into the bathroom to look for an extra toothbrush and paused. Last night, she'd been too distraught to examine the countertops. Now, she saw that, just like the closet, her perfumes, lotions, and makeup from her other life were here as well. She looked at herself in the mirror. She was pale, and her light blue eyes were bloodshot from exhaustion. Lyla didn't feel like herself in the bright, revealing clothes. For three years, she tried to blend in, and now she felt exposed on so many levels. She reached for the makeup and sifted through the shimmery eye shadow, lip gloss, fake eyelashes, and playful lipstick shades. More reminders of the frivolous life she once had. Lyla settled for mascara, ChapStick, and lotion.

When Lyla left the bedroom, she half expected to see guards outside the door, but to her surprise, the hallway was empty. It made her skin prickle with alarm. Was Gavin planning to do something that he didn't want them to witness? For a moment, she thought of making a run for it. Her muscles tensed, and her heartbeat accelerated. The front door was so close... Common sense reasserted itself a moment before she heard footsteps and Gavin appeared.

"There you are. Come, breakfast is ready," he said.

Lyla took a deep breath before she started downstairs, her heels clicking on every step. Gavin's eyes moved over her, and he looked pleased, but Lyla averted her eyes as she passed him. An assortment of breakfast foods filled the marble island in the kitchen. Despite recent events, she was starving. She made a bowl of oatmeal with fresh cut strawberries, a bagel heavily smeared with cream cheese, and a plate of sausages. She carried her food to the table and ignored Gavin who sat beside her. She refused to let his stare unnerve her. He didn't eat, which either meant the food was poisoned or he had eaten earlier. Lyla set out to demolish everything in front of her. Gavin said nothing and waited patiently.

"Do you want more food?" Gavin asked as she finished.

Lyla shook her head.

"Look at me."

Lyla clenched her teeth before she obeyed. Today he wore a blue shirt with the first two buttons undone and no tie beneath a black suit jacket. His carefully styled hair framed his attractive face, and he was freshly shaved.

"Do you want to see your mother?" he asked.

Lyla's hands fisted on her lap. Was this a trick? "You'd let me see her?"

"Of course."

She searched his eyes. "Why?"

"I want you to be happy here."

"What?"

"Why do you look so surprised?"

Lyla folded her hands on the table and braced herself.

This was the moment of truth when she learned what her future looked like. She met his eyes and asked, "What am I doing here, Gavin?"

He frowned. "I want you here."

"For how long?" she asked, her heart threatening to beat out of her chest.

He didn't answer, and her palms dampened as anxiety slid through her veins. Gavin watched her like a wolf daring its prey to make a move. One wrong step and he'd eat her.

"I can give you what money I have and make payments," she said.

"I don't need your money."

"Then why?"

When he reached out and captured her chin in his hand, she resisted the impulse to jerk away. She was extremely vulnerable and at his mercy. She hated the feeling of helplessness that filled her, making her want to lash out.

"I can buy, bribe, or steal anything I want," Gavin said.

It was true. Knowing the power he wielded kept her still and silent.

"Your dad stole a chunk of change he didn't earn and pissed it away. If he won, I would have charged him interest."

Which meant he'd known about her father stealing and allowed it to continue until he saw an opportunity to use her father's betrayal to his advantage.

"In the end, your father's stupidity and greed worked in my favor. I wanted you to come willingly—"

"I didn't," she snapped, and he tightened his hold.

"I have the manpower to have you watched day and night, but I need more insurance than that." He leaned forward until he was only inches away. "And I have yet to discover how you escaped me the first time. Do you want to enlighten me?"

"No." She would take it to her grave.

"No matter," Gavin said as if he didn't care, but she knew better. "Your love for your worthless father gives me the insurance I need that you'll do what I say, when I say. Isn't that right, baby girl?" His thumb stroked over her lower lip.

She wanted to bite, but was too busy sifting through his statement. "And how am I supposed to pay off my dad's debt?"

"I told you."

He had? Lyla frowned, and his eyes flashed.

"I want what we had."

Lyla jerked out of his hold and surged to her feet. She clutched the back of the chair and tried to keep herself from shouting. "What did we have, Gavin?"

"A great life together."

She wanted to slap him. "I don't understand you! You have women begging to give you blowjobs. What do you need from me that you can't get from them?"

"There's no one like you."

She wanted to tear her hair out. She released the chair and began to wave her hands as she paced around the kitchen. "There are hundreds, no, *thousands* of women like me."

He said nothing, and she wondered if pride made him act impulsively. He didn't really want her. He wanted a submissive woman who doted on him. That wasn't her, not any longer.

"I want *you*, Lyla."

She shook her head. "You *had* me, Gavin. I wasn't enough for you." She gave him a sugary sweet smile while her blood began to boil. "Or did I imagine you having an orgy in the club?"

"I told you that was a mistake."

"And there were dozens of *mistakes* before I found out!" she shouted and turned away from him to regain her composure. How could she be so mad after all this time? She thought she had put it behind her, but seeing Gavin in the flesh and having him say he wanted what they had made her chest burn.

"That's over."

"Yes, it is," she agreed and desperately tried to rein in her temper. Why were they even having this conversation? Oh, yeah, because he wanted things to go back to the way they'd been three years ago when she was a naïve fool. "I'm not the same person, Gavin. Whatever you think you'll get from me... I can't. Within a month, you'll be back to your old ways. Maybe I can pay off Dad's debt another way. Maybe I can—"

"No."

She turned as Gavin rose and stilled when she saw his implacable expression.

"I took you for granted," Gavin acknowledged as he slowly rounded the table and closed the distance between them with deliberate steps. "I didn't want to change. I admit that. I liked having you in one section of my life and the business and girls in the other. I had it all, and then Min fucked up when he let you into the club without checking with Blade first."

"It was kind of hard for Min to check with Blade when he was getting sucked off by two women," she said and glared at him. "I can't believe you shot Min. It wasn't his fault!"

Gavin shrugged as if it wasn't a big deal, and to him, it wasn't. Gavin grew up in the cutthroat underworld. He learned to fight, fuck, and deal before he hit puberty. Gavin wrapped a hand around the back of her neck and plastered her against him.

"I thought you'd been taken by one of my enemies. I thought you'd been killed." His eyes hardened. "How could you, Lyla?"

"I wanted out," she said. Her heartbeat accelerated as Gavin's energy began to pulse in the air around them.

"I was tortured by thoughts of what my enemies did to you before they killed you. Three years of regret and then my investigator finds you in Maine with a different name, working as a bank teller." His eyes raked over her face. "And living with another man... a fucking nerd. You let another man touch you, make love to you? How could you do that to me?"

"You expect me to be faithful after you cheated on me?"

Gavin's eyes flashed with rage. Gavin lifted her off her feet and shook her like a rag doll.

"What does he have that I don't, Lyla? You leave me for a guy who makes fifty thousand a year? Who I could beat to a pulp?"

Lyla struggled to get free, but Gavin didn't seem to notice. His eyes blazed with fury, and his hands were moments away from crushing bone.

"Your life belongs to me. No other man is allowed to touch you."

Lyla trembled in his grasp. "Gavin, you're hurting me."

"And you hurt me!" he shouted and shoved her away from him.

Lyla staggered back and hit the glass door that led into the backyard hard enough to make it bow and shudder in its frame. She shook like a leaf. She knew what Gavin was capable of. The night before she left him, she witnessed him kill a man with his bare hands. He was a savage beneath the polished veneer, and could kill her easily. His ragged breathing filled the kitchen. She bowed her head and waited for him to come after her, to finish her off.

"Don't push me, Lyla. I'm so fucking angry with you. Look at me."

She was too afraid to raise her head. Suddenly, he was right in front of her, and once more, his hand shot out. She screamed as his hand closed around her throat. She wrapped both hands around his wrist and struggled to get away.

"When I tell you to do something, you do it!" he shouted in her face. She closed her eyes against the sight of him. "You don't leave me, Lyla. Do you understand me?"

She nodded because she couldn't speak.

"Open your eyes."

When she didn't obey, his hand tightened in warning. Her eyes popped open.

"Tell me you understand."

"I-I understand," she whispered as his hand threatened to cut off her airflow.

"Tell me you won't leave me."

A tear slipped down her cheek. "I w-won't leave you."

He grabbed her lower lip between his teeth. She moaned and tried to turn her face away, but he increased the pressure and bit. She tasted blood, and more tears slipped down her face. When he released her, a trickle of blood slipped down her chin. He glared at her as if he hated her and was debating whether she was worth the trouble. She held her breath.

"You belong to me," he stated without emotion as if she was an object he was claiming ownership of. "You try to leave me again, I'll hunt you down and make you watch as I slaughter everyone you love. Then, I'll make you pay."

Lyla couldn't conceal her horror. In the four years they were together, Gavin never touched her in anger. He had been so gentle with her, so caring. With everyone else, he was a beast, but he always reined it in around her. Now, it was on full display, and it made her tremble.

"Your place is by my side. You listen to me and follow my rules. You don't have the freedom you had last time. You check in with me for everything. You understand?" At her slow nod, he stepped back. "Go upstairs and fix your face. Then I'll take you to see your mom."

Lyla lurched into motion, making a wide circle around him as she left the kitchen on unsteady legs. She walked upstairs, focusing hard on putting one foot in front of the other. When she reached their bedroom, she closed the door and stood there for a long moment, mind racing. If she stayed, he would kill her. But there was nowhere to run where he couldn't find her. Even though he suspected his enemies had killed her, he hadn't called off the search. He meant every word he said in the kitchen. He would kill her family if she ran again. He didn't make idle threats.

Lyla walked into the bathroom and stared at the blood and mascara smeared over her face. Her swollen lip was still seeping blood in a steady stream down her chin. Her arms ached where he grabbed her, and her neck began to darken with bruises. With shaking hands, she wet a washcloth and wiped her face.

The bedroom door slammed open. Moments later, Gavin appeared in the bathroom doorway. He leaned on the doorjamb and watched her with brooding eyes. Lyla clutched the washcloth between shaking hands and waited for more punishment.

"You kill yourself, and I'll make your family wish they were dead, you got me?" he asked.

Lyla gave a jerky nod.

"Hurry up," he snapped.

Lyla nodded again and finished wiping away the mascara. There was no chance of concealing her ravaged lip, and she had no idea what other things lay in wait for her. She didn't bother to reapply mascara. She turned to Gavin, head bowed. He snatched her hand in his, and she swallowed hard to keep her breakfast down. Gavin grabbed the cell phone she had yet to touch and slapped it in her hand.

"You keep this on you at all times," he said.

He led her downstairs and pulled her out of the house. No less than fifteen of his men were waiting for them. The men lounged on the steps and around the large fountain in the middle of the drive. Lyla dropped her head to conceal her swollen lip as Gavin opened the passenger door of his silver BMW. Lyla buckled herself in, clutched the phone between her hands, and stared straight ahead. Gavin spoke to Blade for several minutes before he climbed into the driver's seat. Lyla leaned against the passenger door in an effort to gain more breathing room. The small space made her feel claustrophobic. Gavin sped off his property toward the automatic gates that opened at his approach. Neither of them said a word. When Lyla couldn't stand it a second longer, she rolled down her window and took a deep breath to stop herself from vomiting in the expensive car. Gavin didn't object as he navigated the freeways.

The Strip didn't look as alluring in the daytime as it did at night. The Strip was Gavin's playground. She wanted to stay as far from it and Gavin as possible. She wanted to believe this was a nightmare she would wake from. When he drove up to her parents' house, of its own

accord, her hand reached for the door handle. She was out
of the vehicle before it stopped. Lyla ran to her family
house and raised her fist to beat on the door, but it opened
before she could. Her mother stood in the doorway. She
leapt forward and embraced her mother before she could
see her face.

"You're home," Mom whispered in her hair.

Her mother smelled of garlic and sesame oil. It stirred
up bittersweet memories. Lyla held her tight, wishing she
were a child again when everything was simple.

"Mrs. Dalton."

Gavin's voice broke through her hysteria. Lyla stiffened
in her mother's arms. Would Gavin beat or slap her mother
around to punish her further?

"Gavin, thank you for bringing my daughter home,"
Mom said, voice choked with emotion.

"No problem," Gavin said. "How's your husband?"

So her father was here, being tended by her mother.
That was good news, but how dare Gavin ask about her
father's health as if he wasn't responsible for his state? Lyla
wanted to scream.

"I finished stitching him up a minute ago," Mom said
pleasantly and patted Lyla on the back as if she were a
newborn.

"I brought Lyla by to reconnect. You don't mind if I leave
her here while I go to work?" Gavin asked.

"Of course, not! I'm glad to have my baby back."

"Good. I need to speak to her before I go."

"Of course," Mom said and loosened her hold, but Lyla
didn't let go. "Lyla? Gavin needs a quick chat."

She didn't want to lose touch with her mother even for a
moment. A large hand touched the small of her back, and
she stiffened. Remembering the strength in that hand as it

wrapped around her throat, she released her mother and whirled to face Gavin.

"Leave us," Gavin said without looking at her mother.

"I'll be in the kitchen, Lyla," Mom said.

Her footsteps faded, leaving Lyla to face Gavin in the foyer of her parent's humble home.

"You don't touch my mother," Lyla said. She wasn't sure where this burst of defiance was coming from when she felt so emotionally and physically battered, but she knew one thing. She would die before he lay a finger on her mom.

"There's no reason to hurt your mother," Gavin said.

But there was a reason to hurt *her*?

"I have to go to work."

Lyla nodded. Good. She needed time away from him to think.

"Blade will be outside along with several other guards. You're not allowed to leave here. I'll be back to pick you up."

Lyla nodded again and took a step back. Before she could walk away, Gavin grabbed her arm in the same place where she was already bruised. She hissed in pain. He instantly switched his grip to her elbow. He looked down at her discolored skin and brushed a thumb over it.

"I didn't mean to hurt you," he said quietly.

He cupped her chin and lifted her face. Gold eyes swirled with conflicting emotions. The maniac who attacked her in the kitchen was nowhere in sight. If she hadn't witnessed it for herself, she would have thought it was a hallucination. Right now he was the cool businessman and appeared to have all his emotions under control.

"You make me feel..." He shook his head. "*Everything*. You make me crazy."

Lyla tried to ease away, but he tightened his hold.

"Be a good girl," he said and kissed her forehead before he released her.

Lyla didn't bother to watch him leave. She turned on her heel and walked toward the kitchen. Her mother stood at the stove, stirring something in a pot. She wore white capris and a tight shirt that showed off her carefully maintained physique. Lyla was a mirror image of her mother. There was no sign of her father in her.

Mom turned. When she got a good look at Lyla, she dropped the wooden spoon, which skidded over the tiles.

"Lyla, what happened?" Mom whispered.

Bile rose, and this time, she couldn't stop it. Lyla turned and ran to the nearest bathroom where she retched. Her mother held her hair and murmured soothingly as Lyla gagged until nothing was left in her stomach. Mom mopped up Lyla's face with a warm rag and dabbed at her lip, which began to bleed again.

"Brush your teeth," Mom ordered as she pulled an extra toothbrush from the cabinet, and Lyla did so.

Her mother led her back to the kitchen where she guided Lyla into a chair and made peppermint tea for them. Mom sat in the chair facing Lyla and tapped the top of her clammy hand.

"Tell me everything," Mom said.

4

Lyla wrapped trembling hands around the hot mug. She was shaking too badly to pick it up but was grateful for the soothing smell and warmth. She surveyed her mother's platinum blond hair cut into a chic bob that framed bright blue eyes. When Lyla lived in Las Vegas, she rarely visited her mother after she moved in with Gavin. She had been too busy primping or partying.

"I'm sorry," Lyla whispered.

"For what?"

"I shouldn't have left."

"Why don't you tell me why you did," Mom prompted gently.

Lyla rotated the cup between her hands. "Carmen and I went to Malibu, a girls' trip, but I missed Gavin and came back early to surprise him. I caught him having an orgy at a club."

Her mother showed no sign of surprise. Gavin was a Pyre, and this was Sin City, after all. The people of Las Vegas were as jaded as New Yorkers.

"I shouted at him, made a scene. I lost it." Lyla had a

vague recollection of smashing glasses and belting a prostitute across the face. "I drove home, and he met me there. He
apologized and told me it would never happen again. I
wanted to believe him, but I asked if this was the first time
he cheated on me. It wasn't." Lyla finally felt steady enough
to sip tea. It coated her dry throat and warmed her from the
inside out. "That week he bought me a new car, jewelry,
more clothes. He told me we would go on a trip, just the two
of us."

Her mother listened without saying a word. There was
no condemnation or anger on her face, just calm
expectancy. Lyla buried these memories deep down and
refused to think about them until now.

"One night, Gavin said he had to do something before
bed. I was suspicious, so I snuck past a guard and followed
him to the basement. One of his guards was tied to a chair.
Gavin beat the crap out of him and injected him with something to force him to stay awake. The guard had fed information to the cops. Gavin questioned him and then beat
him to death with his own hands in front of his men. I left
the next day."

Lyla felt sick, so she drank the rest of the tea, hoping it
would banish the awful taste in her mouth. She witnessed
Gavin systematically rip this man apart. She hadn't been
able to eat for a week after.

"I got a new identity and moved a lot, kept under the
radar. I met a great guy in Maine."

Lyla's voice broke, and her mother reached out and
squeezed her hand.

"We just moved in together. He's so good to me ... I came
back to my apartment and Blade was there. He showed me a
live video of Dad. They told me he stole half a million.

Gavin told me I would pay the price for Dad's debt. I arrived yesterday."

Mom got to her feet while Lyla sat at the table, staring into space. She had always known that Gavin was involved in shady shit. His father owned casinos, hotels, and clubs on and off The Strip. Parts of Gavin's job were legit and other parts weren't. Lyla turned a blind eye to it until she watched that guard die a slow, painful death. She couldn't take her eyes off Gavin that night. She had seen him angry, but the detached, emotionless way he continued to beat the man chilled her to the bone. He never raised his voice, never lost control. The way he dealt out punishment that night made her realize she couldn't live this way any longer. She couldn't get it out of her head that if she ever made Gavin that angry, he would do the same thing to her. And the kitchen incident this morning confirmed her fears.

"Here." Mom set a sandwich in front of her. "It's only peanut butter. Your favorite." When Lyla made no move to touch it, she said, "You'll feel better."

Willing to oblige her mother, Lyla took a bite.

"I warned your father about stealing from the Pyres." Mom leaned against the counter and wrapped her arms around herself. "I suspected he was stealing from them. I knew it meant his life when they caught him, but he wouldn't stop. He's addicted to gambling, always has been, always will be. I knew when Gavin's men showed up what it meant." Tears sparkled in her eyes. "I never thought I'd see him again, and now you're both here."

Lyla tried to respond to her mother's watery smile, but she couldn't.

"I know you don't want to be here, but I'm glad you came home to save your father's life."

Mom loved her father beyond all reason. The same way Lyla had once loved Gavin. Her father was brilliant with numbers and had never been able to stay away from gambling. He would go through a streak of luck and then shower her mother with gifts before he hit a bad streak and everything went to hell. Her father had struggled to keep a job because of his addiction until he became an accountant for the Pyre Casinos when she was seventeen. She visited her father at work one day and met Manny Pyre, the CEO of Pyre Casinos and Gavin's father. Lyla felt an instant connection with Manny. Despite her father's warnings, Lyla dropped in on Manny throughout the summer and helped with minor administrative tasks. During her senior year, he hired her as a personal assistant. She shadowed his every move when she wasn't in school. Manny introduced her to Gavin, and the rest was history. Despite the fact Gavin was eight years older than she was, they began to date, much to her father's displeasure. It took her a year to realize something wasn't right with the business. Gavin never talked about it, but she wasn't stupid. Gavin moved her into his mansion, and she quit her job at Pyre Casinos to become a kept woman. She slipped her mother part of the allowance Gavin gave her when her father was on a bad streak. Life was good... until it wasn't.

Lyla stared at her mother who had yet to address the darker parts of her story. Although it had never been discussed, they knew the Pyre fortune had a dirty side. As an unspoken rule, it was never discussed.

"Gavin's going to kill me." The words burst out of her mouth before they materialized in her head.

Her mother waved a dismissive hand. "He won't."

Lyla stared at her mother and gestured to her injuries.

"What did you do?" Mom asked with a thread of accusation in her voice.

Lyla surged to her feet and didn't notice the mug totter off the table and shatter when it hit the ground. *"What did I do?"*

"Gavin loves you," Mom said in a consoling tone. "He wouldn't have hurt you unless you made him angry beyond reason."

"So it's my fault I look like this?" Lyla demanded. Her mother always stuck up for her father, and now, it seemed she was sticking up for Gavin, the man responsible for her father's nearly comatose state. "Did you *not* hear me say that he cheated on me and killed a guy with his bare hands?"

"He's a Pyre," Mom said as if that dismissed Gavin's sins. "You should be grateful he still cares for you. You have to keep him happy, Lyla, for all our sakes."

"I should be grateful," Lyla repeated dumbly. She should be grateful Gavin was so furious that she left three years ago that he wanted to punish her? Her world was caving in around her, and her mother was figuratively clapping her hands in delight. The feeling of homecoming and safety faded, and the nasty taste of betrayal filled her mouth.

"You didn't mention how you escaped," Mom said casually as she stirred the pot on the stove.

Lyla went cold as her intuition pinged. Her mother would tell Gavin who helped her escape, and Lyla had no doubt that person would die.

"I have my own connections through the Pyres," she said mildly and got to her feet. "I want to rest."

"Of course, honey. Let me—"

"No, Mom, I got it," Lyla said and escaped upstairs. She went to her old bedroom and found it untouched. The room smelled musty, but she didn't care. Lyla collapsed on the bed and heard her father yelling in pain from several doors

down. Lyla covered her ears with her hands, buried her face
in her pillow, and screamed.

———

Lyla must have dozed off because when she woke, someone
was straddling her middle. As she lost her breath and transi-
tioned from sleep to frightened wakefulness, the person
grabbed her by the shoulders and shook her while
screaming a torrent of profanities. Lyla opened her eyes and
tried to focus on her assailant as her head snapped back and
forth. She reached out for leverage and encountered bare,
silky skin. The person stopped shaking her and bounced on
her tender tummy. Lyla finally recognized the slim woman
on top of her and couldn't hold back a delighted shriek. Lyla
wrapped her arms around her cousin and hugged her tight.

"Bitch, you roll back into town and forget to call me?
What the fuck?" Carmen demanded, voice thick with tears.

"Got back yesterday," Lyla said, voice muffled by
Carmen's surgically enhanced bosom.

Carmen released her and sat back on Lyla's thighs.
Carmen wore a fire engine red dress that barely covered her
ass with large cutouts on the sides. Her blond hair had fine
streaks of fuchsia, and her face looked airbrushed, it was so
perfect. Carmen's eyes flared as she took in Lyla's bruised
throat, arms, and scabbed lip.

"What the fuck happened to you? Who hurt you?"
Carmen leaped off the bed and didn't bother to brush her
dress down to cover her girly bits. Carmen braced her legs
apart like a superhero ready for takeoff, gold glitter hooker
heels shining in the light. "I'll tell Vinny. He'll kill whoever
did this to you."

"Vinny's going to kill his boss?" Lyla asked sardonically and gingerly touched her swollen lip.

Carmen's eyes bugged comically wide. "Gavin did that to you?"

"Yeah."

"But Gavin loves you. He's been looking for you for years—"

"And he's pissed enough to beat the shit out of me," Lyla said and brushed a hand over her tender throat.

Carmen flushed with rage. "What the fuck? What else did he do to you? I'll kill him myself!"

Carmen's overprotectiveness loosened something inside Lyla. Unlike everyone else in the business, Carmen was unrestrained and passionate. Her husband, Vinny, was Gavin's cousin. When they were younger, they double dated the Pyre men. That seemed like ages ago. Carmen was two years older than Lyla was and a Las Vegas native. Carmen showed Lyla the ropes when her family moved from California when she was eight. They had been inseparable ever since. Carmen's father, a second-generation enforcer for the Pyre family, helped Lyla's father get the accounting job at a Pyre Casino when they hit a rough spot.

"I've missed you," Lyla said simply.

Carmen's eyes filled with tears, and she launched herself at Lyla, knocking the wind out of her.

"I'm here. It's going to be okay. I promise," Carmen whispered.

Lyla clutched her. "I'm scared."

Carmen made a shushing sound and brushed Lyla's hair back like a mother would to comfort a young child. She took a deep, shuddering breath and took in Carmen's cotton candy scent.

"Do you know how he found you?" Carmen asked in a soundless whisper.

Lyla shook her head. Carmen pulled back and clasped Lyla's face between her hands.

"We're going to get through this."

Lyla didn't agree with Carmen's fervent reassurance. She felt as if she might shatter. She wanted to be anywhere but here because she felt unsafe, frightened, and desperate. She had nowhere to run, nowhere to hide, and no one to help. No one fucked with the Pyre family. You screwed them; they destroyed you. Whatever you did to them, they paid back ten times over. They were the crime lords of Las Vegas. The Pyres had a stake in every sinful desire you could dream up, and the manpower and money to make anything happen. Why hadn't she realized she was playing with fire?

Carmen tugged Lyla down so they sat side by side on the bed. She held Lyla's hand on her lap and said, "Now, tell me everything."

Lyla told her how she created a new identity, kept her head down, and about Jonathan.

"And Gavin knows about this guy you were living with?" Carmen asked incredulously. At Lyla's nod, she asked, "And he's still alive?"

At her fearful look, Carmen quickly reassured her that Gavin probably wouldn't bother Jonathan as long as she didn't piss him off. Lyla regained a little color in her face and told Carmen about her father's debt.

"Your father's always been a dumb shit," Carmen said.

In a quavering voice, Lyla finished her story by explaining what occurred in the kitchen this morning. Carmen's baby blue eyes were alight with holy fire.

"He doesn't get to treat you like this!"

"He can do whatever he wants," Lyla said and couldn't stop her shudder.

"Don't take this lying down."

"What do you mean?"

"Girl, you had him once."

"Yeah, me and a hundred other girls."

Carmen let out a disgusted sound. "You know what I mean. Gavin may have fucked around, but no man searches for their ex for three years unless he has feelings."

"Or an ego the size of Texas," Lyla countered.

Carmen tapped her long, pointed acrylic nails together. "I don't believe that. I still think he loves you."

"*This* is love?" Lyla said, gesturing to her bruises. "Aside from the fact that he *never* said he loved me, he beat the crap out of my dad and blackmailed me into coming back to him. That's fucked up, Carmen. This isn't a fucking romance novel."

"You have power."

"*Power?* Are you high?"

"He wants you. If Gavin wanted to kill you, he'd kill you. If he wanted to make you pay, he wouldn't bring you to his home, feed you, and then take you to your mother's house. Comprende?"

"Who knows why Gavin does what he does? He's losing it."

"Manny gave him the reins two years ago."

Lyla didn't care.

"Gavin doesn't take no shit. He's harder than Manny and ten times more ruthless. Vinny says he got worse after you left."

Lyla got up and paced her tiny bedroom. "Why? Gavin has a million girls to choose from. I'm nothing special."

Carmen hummed and wagged a finger. "*Girl*, everyone sees it but you."

"Sees what?"

Carmen braced her hands on Lyla's shoulders and gave her a small shake. "You're gorgeous."

"There are other girls more—"

"You're loyal, and you love with everything in you. You're strong. Strong enough to make it on your own without anyone's help. That probably pissed Gavin off the most." Carmen suddenly hooted and clapped her hands together. "Here he thought you'd been taken or would come back begging. Instead, he finds you after three years in Maine with another guy. Tell me that isn't funny."

"I have no idea what you're talking about," Lyla said.

"Well, I know and that's enough," Carmen said crisply. "You can make this work to your advantage."

She tried to stomp on the trickle of hope. "Carmen—"

"Listen to me," Carmen snapped. "I'm older and wiser."

Lyla took a deep breath. She was willing to try anything. "Okay. What do I do?"

"You make him crazy."

"Gavin *is* crazy."

"I mean, make him crazy for *you*."

"But I don't want him crazy for me. I want him to forget I exist and let me go."

Carmen looked crushed. "But you just got back."

"Carmen, I left for a reason." Because her ex was a serial cheater and possible serial killer.

"I know, but what if Gavin's changed? Would you consider staying?"

"How the hell did you go from threatening to kill him to asking me to stay with him?"

"I don't want you to go." Carmen sounded like a petulant

child. "I've missed you, bitch."

"I missed you too, but I'm a captive, *hello*."

"You're only a captive if you let yourself be. Captivate the captor," Carmen said with an exaggerated wink.

"What are you talking about?"

"Mama, use what the good Lord gave you." Carmen ran a hand between her legs, cupped her tits, and slapped her ass. "You look like a stripper and have the smarts to stay off his radar for three years. Use it to your advantage! Make Gavin your slave."

"He hates me, Carmen."

"It can't be all hate. He hasn't been the same since you left. Just try to get him to bed and see what happens."

Lyla clenched her hands into fists at her sides. "Done that."

Carmen's eyes nearly bugged out of their sockets. "You fucked him?"

"He raped me."

Carmen's eyes narrowed to slits. *"He raped you?"*

"I was having a sex dream, and when I woke up, he was in me."

"A sex dream? About Jonathan? Is he, like, a *hot* IT consultant?"

"He's cute."

Carmen didn't look convinced. "You love him?"

She and Jonathan never discussed it, but, "Yes," she said defiantly.

Carmen leaned in close and examined her suspiciously. "Like, *love him*, love him?"

"Yes."

Carmen gave her a somber look. "Lyla, there's no escape this time. The moment you started dating Gavin, you became Pyre property."

"That was years ago!"

"Doesn't matter. It's obvious Gavin will do everything in his power to make sure you stay put this time. Men like him don't let go of a good woman."

Lyla made an impatient sound. Men like Gavin... Maybe she could get Gavin hooked on someone else, and she could pay off her father's debt another way other than as his sex slave... or whatever it was that he wanted from her. Invisible walls were closing in. The urge to run was an insistent drum beat in her mind. Lyla jumped as someone knocked on the door. Her mother appeared with Lyla's cell phone in hand.

"It's Gavin. He wants to talk to you," Mom said.

Lyla's heartbeat went into overdrive. Before she could figure out a way to avoid the call, Carmen snatched the phone out of her mother's hand.

"Gavin, what the fuck did you do to my cousin?" Carmen demanded.

Fearing for Carmen's life, Lyla lurched into motion and tried to rip the phone out of her hand. Carmen shoved her away and continued to talk.

"Don't give me that shit, Gavin. If Manny sees her like this, he'll have a cow. What do you mean, it's none of my business? Of course, it is! She's my cousin." Carmen's heel tapped rapidly as she listened to what Gavin said on the other end. "No, I'm taking her out."

Carmen yanked the phone away from her ear. They could all hear Gavin shouting. Lyla shook her head wildly while her mother wrung her hands.

"Carmen Pyre," Mom said and tried to take the phone from her.

Carmen held up one finger and gave her mother a threatening look. Carmen put her hand over the phone and mouthed, "He needs to woo her back."

Lyla made a gagging sound.

Carmen put the phone back to her ear. "She needs some work done. Hair, nails, the works. We're going to have a girls' day. You can see her after." Carmen listened for a moment, and her eyes flicked to Lyla. "Okay, fine. Here."

Carmen handed the phone over. Lyla took it, afraid what hell Carmen created and how dearly she would pay for it later. "Hello?"

"Lyla?" Gavin bit out.

She closed her eyes against the sound of his voice and the memories of this morning. He wasn't the man she fell in love with. He wasn't a man she wanted to be around, ever. She learned to care for herself, to work for what she had. Now, she was reduced to a possession, a child who would be punished if she didn't please her master. She trembled with helpless rage. "Yes?"

A pause and then, "I should have figured Vinny would tell Carmen you're back. Do you want to go with her?"

"Yes." She needed to get out of this house and away from her mother who worshipped the ground Gavin walked on. Carmen stood up for her when no one else dared. She would stick with her cousin as much as possible.

"Blade will shadow you," Gavin said.

Lyla said nothing.

"I'll come for you after work."

Again, she didn't reply. What was there to say? He called the shots, and she did as she was told. That was what he wanted, right? A submissive doll to dress, fuck, and control.

"Lyla?"

"Yes?"

Gavin cursed and hung up. Lyla wasn't sure what that meant and didn't care. "Let's go," she said to Carmen who cheered.

"Lyla," Mom began.

Lyla kissed her on the cheek as she passed. "I'll see you later, Mom."

Lyla got out of the house as fast as possible, feeling better once she was in the sun. She paused for a moment to brush off the effect Gavin's voice had on her and saw Blade in the driver's seat of the SUV, ready to go. Gavin hadn't wasted time informing his security about their outing. Carmen put on a pair of pink sunglasses and jumped into a gold convertible. Lyla's lips quirked at the ridiculous car. Of course, Carmen would have a gold car. Lyla belted herself in and held on for dear life as Carmen drove like a reckless demon.

"You don't know how happy I am that you're back," Carmen shouted over the sound of the wind and traffic. "I mean, I know you don't want to be here. You never liked the way they do business, and it sucks that you saw the worst of Gavin, but that's the way it is. This is home, and if you want, I know you can be happy here again. You were before you found out about the other girls. You have the power to make sure that doesn't happen again."

Had she ever been happy here? It was hard to remember since the events that caused her to leave overshadowed the good. She didn't want to think about making a life in Las Vegas with Gavin. She wanted to believe this was a fucking mistake that would go away. She would be set free and then... Then what? She would reinvent herself again. She couldn't go back to Maine, to Jonathan. Not after this. Fucking Gavin made her feel like a whore. Was it rape if she had an orgasm? Her body welcomed Gavin back as if the time between had never been. Apparently, her body didn't realize that they belonged to Jonathan now. Well, *used* to belong to Jonathan—

"Are you listening to me?" Carmen shouted and narrowly avoided rear-ending a Ferrari. When the driver honked, Carmen flipped the bird and resumed lecturing Lyla about her new life. "Vinny adores me, and everyone knows it. I keep him topped up; you know what I mean? He's part of the underworld, but we're happy, girl."

"But I don't *want* Gavin!" Lyla shouted back.

"You wanted him once, and if you can overlook some things, he'd make a solid man. He'd provide for you and protect the fuck out of you. He would never take you for granted since you left him once already."

Carmen parked with a screech of her tires in front of a salon. She linked her arm through Lyla's, and they walked in with Blade on their heels. The salon played hip-hop music shockingly loud. Hairdressers wore the craziest wigs and hairstyles Lyla had ever seen. A large woman wearing a skintight dress and heels ran to them. She and Carmen exchanged air kisses before Carmen shoved Lyla forward.

"This is my cousin, Lyla. She's with Gavin," Carmen said.

The hairdresser's eyes widened. "No shit?"

"No shit," Carmen said solemnly. "She needs the works. Don't cut her hair and no dye or he'll have my head." Carmen gestured to Blade and the two other guards in the entrance. "Her bodyguards. She should be in their sight at all times."

"No problem," the hairdresser said. "I'm gonna give you to one of my best. Keenan!"

A muscled black man in zebra tights and a sagging tank top stomped toward them with a sulky expression.

"Keenan, she's with Gavin Pyre and needs the works."

Keenan lit up as if he'd been offered a million dollars. He kissed Lyla on the mouth and wrapped an arm around her. *"Girl!"*

"No kissing," Blade barked from the entrance, and the noise in the salon dimmed a bit.

Keenan blew Blade a kiss. "You got it, big boy."

"Trim, no dye," Keenan's boss ordered.

"You got it. Come, baby, and tell Keenan all about it," he said and ushered Lyla into the back of the salon to a private corner. "Let's condition that gorgeous hair. So did Gavin rescue you from a rough customer?"

"Customer?" Lyla echoed blankly.

"You're an escort, right? Gavin took you in?" Keenan gestured to her neck, lip, and arms. "Were you working for him and a customer got out of hand?"

Apparently, the salon catered to the Pyres and wasn't concerned how they made their money. The elite of Las Vegas were willing to get their hands dirty. Escorts, drug dealers, con men, strippers, and high rollers were the ones who rose to the top in this city.

Lyla wasn't sure what to think about Keenan's conclusion. Did she look like an escort? Did Gavin take in a lot of girls? Her stomach clenched when she realized he didn't wear a condom last night. He could give her an STD. Thank God, she had an IUD. She got her first one in her teens before she and Gavin had sex for the first time. She should have been a slut after Gavin so she would be immune to him now. At least she had been Jonathan's, even if it was just for a short time.

"No, I'm not an escort," Lyla said.

"Really? Stripper?"

She knew he wasn't trying to be insulting. "No. I've known Gavin since I was in high school."

Keenan looked like he might swoon. "*No.* You're high school sweethearts?"

Sweethearts? She didn't know how to explain what she

and Gavin were and was relieved when she didn't have to. Keenan spun a Romeo and Juliet tale in his mind. He drew his own conclusions, and Lyla allowed it. If only he knew how dark and twisted reality was.

With just a few sentences, she kept Keenan chattering excitedly about a range of topics, her least favorite being Gavin who Keenan had a major crush on. Keenan talked about Gavin's nightclubs and strip bars. It brought up memories of the night she found Gavin cheating on her. It made her stomach turn even after all this time. Why the fuck did Gavin bring her back? He didn't want her, not really. If she meant so much to him, he wouldn't have fucked around on her. He seemed genuinely contrite after she confronted him at the club. He told her the women didn't mean anything to him and that he wouldn't do it again. She hadn't made up her mind whether she would give him a second chance or not when she witnessed him murder that guard in his basement. That was her tipping point. Gavin should have forgotten about her and moved on. Every year that passed, she became more confident that she was free of Gavin, yet here she was.

Keenan chattered about his many lovers and their professions, which ranged from strippers to doctors, and interrupted himself to say, "I love your hair. I can't believe this is your natural color. Honey sunshine."

Lyla smiled at the description and watched as Keenan blow-dried her hair so it fell around her in shining waves. She couldn't deny that she felt like a million dollars. It felt good to let other people take care of her.

She gave Keenan air kisses and moved on to waxing. They waxed her bare (which was fine since she didn't have much hair anyway) and then started on her nails. Carmen chose a scarlet polish for Lyla's acrylic nails. Carmen

chatted with everyone while Lyla listened, not adding much
to the conversation. Everyone was friendly and dressed with
a seductive edge that reminded Lyla she wasn't in Maine. A
couple of days ago, she wouldn't have been mistaken for an
escort. Her crop top and skirt made her appear nun-like
compared to the salon workers.

She didn't know how to feel about her circumstances,
and her emotions were a jumbled mess. Any moment now,
she expected Gavin to burst through the door and beat the
crap out of her in front of everyone. The expression of
hatred on his face this morning haunted her. Even if he
decided to do something to her, no one would interfere
when a Pyre was involved. Carmen had some leniency, but
no one could stop Gavin from doing what he wished
with her.

When they finished, she and Carmen air kissed the
salon workers, and Lyla waited by the desk to pay.

"It's taken care of," Keenan said and gave her ass a smack
on her way out.

Blade looked like he wanted to say something but
decided against it when Keenan fluttered his eyelashes at
him. Carmen put the top up on her convertible so their hairstyles would last.

"Where are we going?" Lyla asked.

"My house. I told our cook to make something
fabulous."

"But what about Gavin?"

"If he wants to come, he'll come," Carmen said dismis-
sively. "You look great, by the way."

"I feel better."

"Great. Now, we're going to get dressed up for dinner and
figure out what to do with your life."

5

AN HOUR LATER, Carmen put the finishing touches on Lyla's makeup and stepped back. Lyla didn't look like Morgan Lincoln, conservative bank teller. She looked like a more sophisticated version of the Lyla Dalton who died three years ago. Carmen gave her the works with heavy eyeliner, fake eyelashes, lipstick, and enough concealer to take away the dark circles under her eyes. Carmen did an excellent job. Lyla looked well rested and luminous. The dark shade of lipstick concealed the worst of her bitten lip, and the black long-sleeve dress with a high collar covered her bruises on her arms and throat. Carmen topped it all off with a diamond bracelet that could pay half of her father's debt. Despite the fact they were eating at Carmen's house, they were dressed for fine dining. Carmen believed in always looking her best and, of course, accessories.

"There's my heartbreaker cousin," Carmen said as she danced in her five-inch heels. "Gavin is gonna jizz his pants."

"I don't want him to want me," Lyla protested.

"You're going to put Gavin in line. There's a reason they call us man-eaters. Men fear us."

Carmen posed in the mirror, showing off her legs and the indecently high slit on her eggplant dress before she turned and strutted toward Lyla, pouting her lips and making her eyes heavy-lidded. Carmen pressed a gentle kiss on Lyla's cheek and perched on her lap.

"You have to make him want you desperately," Carmen said in a throaty whisper that made Lyla's skin ripple with goose bumps. "You have to make yourself unattainable. You want him to work for your love and affection. Don't show fear or Gavin won't respect you."

"He's not the same man," Lyla said and then corrected herself. "Or maybe I never knew the real him."

"He's in there, Lyla. The good parts aren't gone, just buried. You can bring that out of him."

"How?" She didn't want Gavin's attention or desire, but if she had to deal with him, keeping him calm and not on the verge of bursting into fits of rage was where she wanted him.

"That's the best part," Carmen said as she stood and grasped Lyla's hand. "You just be yourself."

"Myself?" She didn't know who she was anymore. She went from arm decoration to a mousy bank teller. Being invisible became her goal in life and now... Who was she? A desperate woman fighting for survival. It didn't matter that she was dripping in diamonds and looked as if she hadn't worked a day in her life. If anyone looked deep enough, they would see her fear. Her future depended on how well she could play her part. Maybe Keenan was right. With her looks and dress, she looked like a high-end escort. Could she play the part of an escort? That had been her role before. She had no choice but to put on the best performance of her life.

"Even though you're a hot piece of ass, Gavin loved you for *you*. He could have picked anyone since you've been gone, but I swear to you, I haven't seen him with one woman."

Before Lyla could say she didn't give a shit if Carmen saw Gavin with one hundred women, there was a discreet knock on the door. A maid entered with downcast eyes.

"A guest, Mrs. Pyre."

"Thank you. We're ready," Carmen said.

"Gavin?" Lyla asked through stiff lips when the maid left.

"Probably. You ready?"

Lyla glanced at her reflection and said goodbye to Morgan Lincoln. Her eyes flashed with pain and longing as she thought of Jonathan and the simple life she left behind. What would Jonathan think if he saw her done up like a high-class hooker? Lyla shoved self-loathing to the side. She would deal with that later when she had time to wallow. Right now, she had a job to do.

They headed down the curved staircase. Carmen had decorated her home in bold colors and filled it with fine art, which included paintings, statues, and rare antiques. Carmen led her to the backyard, which had a beautiful infinity pool and a large dining table beneath a gazebo strung with white lights. A man got up from the table. Carmen and Lyla paused in mid-stride.

Manny Pyre, Gavin's father, wore a tailored black suit that wouldn't have been out of place on Wall Street. The top three buttons of his shirt were undone, giving him a rakish air. His shoulder-length white hair was combed into a slick ponytail at the base of his neck. Gold gleamed on his fingers and around his neck. Even at seventy, he was handsome. Despite losing some weight, Manny still possessed the physique of a much younger man.

Lyla's heart thumped rapidly. Even though she was glad to see her mom and Carmen, she'd been even more excited and terrified to see Manny. She had worked for Manny for a full year before Gavin asked her to be a kept woman. Manny was the father she never had, but what did he think of her leaving his son? Had he changed like Gavin? Did he loathe her? Lyla swallowed hard as she suppressed the urge to run to him.

"Uncle Manny," Carmen said and rushed forward. "I didn't know you were coming!"

"Vinny told me my daughter came home," Manny said, never moving his eyes from Lyla.

Lyla swallowed hard as emotion clogged her throat. From the very start, they had clicked. Manny called her his daughter when she and Gavin went on their first date. Back then, Lyla worried that Manny's pushiness would turn Gavin off. To her surprise, Gavin didn't seem bothered by his father's interference, and he fell in line with his father's wishes. After Lyla discovered he'd been cheating on her, she wondered if Gavin had dated her just to please his father.

"A drink, Uncle?" Carmen asked, sounding unusually nervous.

"No, I'm fine."

"I'll go check with the cook about the meal," Carmen said and left them alone in the backyard.

Lyla stared at Manny, the man she considered her father in every way but one.

"You don't have a welcome for me, baby girl?" Manny asked.

The pet name originated from Manny, and hearing it from him, she knew all was well between them. Lyla wasn't aware of her feet moving, but she managed to pull back a moment before impact so she wouldn't topple the older man. She wrapped her arms around Manny, buried her face against his chest and lost herself in his musky scent. The smell filled her with nostalgia and bittersweet memories. From the very start, Manny saw something in her that no one else had and took the time to nurture her love of learning. She tried to wrap her mind around the fact that Manny ordered the hit on the man Gavin beat to death in the basement.

Manny drew back and cupped her face in one large paw. "Let me see you."

Lyla tried to smile but failed miserably. Tears coursed down her face as Manny examined her. His thumb brushed her bottom lip. She jerked, and he tipped her face up to the light. She knew the makeup didn't fool him as she averted her eyes.

"Lyla, what happened?" he asked gently enough, but she sensed danger in the air.

"N-nothing," she said and tried to draw back.

Manny clutched her arms to hold her in place. She wasn't able to stifle her painful cry, which she bit back immediately. She tried to draw away, but Manny manacled her wrist, and she froze, forcefully reminded that she didn't really know the Pyres. Manny patted her down as efficiently as a TSA agent. Lyla couldn't contain her flinch when he located the bruises on her other arm and the ones on her neck. Manny smoothed her sleeves up and examined the black and blue marks before he tugged on the stretchy material of the high neck of her dress. Manny's hands fell away. Lyla took a step back, unsure what to expect from him.

"Who did it?" Manny hissed.

Lyla's mouth opened and closed soundlessly. "Manny, I—"

"Don't lie to me, Lyla."

For a moment, she wondered if she should fib despite the warning, but Manny possessed the same soul-searing gaze as his son. He was a human lie detector. Manny knew her better than her own parents. Surely, Manny knew she wasn't here by choice... "Gavin."

Manny jerked as if she shot him. His incredulous expression made her flush with icy fear. Did he not believe her? Fuck, she should have lied. Lyla reached out with placating hands as she tried to think of a way to fix it.

"I-It was nothing. It doesn't hurt. I'm fine. I bumped into —" she babbled.

Manny slashed a hand through the air, and she stopped. His face took on an ugly cast, and she began to shake. When Manny was pissed, heads rolled. Literally. She wasn't sure if his anger was aimed at her for daring to tell him such a thing or at Gavin. Either way, this wouldn't end well. If there was a choice between believing her or his son, she had no doubt who Manny would choose. She was on the precipice again, her life on the line. Lyla was lightheaded with terror.

"Why are you here?" Manny asked, voice devoid of emotion.

Lyla's heart shattered. She wrapped her arms around herself to ward off the sudden chill. Eyeing her painted toes, she whispered, "My dad embezzled. I'm here to pay his debt."

"How?" Manny bit out.

Lyla shook uncontrollably. "I-I don't know."

"He beats you?"

"N-no."

"Don't you dare lie to me."

Lyla took another step back. Manny had never used that tone of voice with her before. How could so much change in so little time? How could she have thought of Gavin and

Manny as family? They were capable of killing her without a second thought. She was a lamb in the lion's den. Once she walked into their lair, they would never set her free. She knew too much.

Voices echoed through the open doors that led to the backyard. Out of the corner of her eye, she saw Gavin, Carmen, and Vinny walk out of the house and come to a stop at the sight of her and Manny facing one another with her face covered in tears.

"Uncle Manny, what—?" Carmen began and would have run toward Lyla, but her husband pulled her back.

Lyla had never felt so alone. Surrounded by people she once considered family, there was a possibility she would be beaten or killed by one of them. She huddled in on herself and wished she could disappear. When would this hell end?

"Dad?" Gavin asked.

"I see Lyla's back," Manny said tonelessly.

Gavin didn't answer. Manny closed the distance between himself and Lyla. Memories of the guard's brutal beating flashed in her mind, and she bit back a moan of fear. When Manny withdrew a gun from his suit and pointed it at her, Lyla stared at the man she considered a father in shock and then numb defeat. Her biological father despised her. Her mother's loyalty was to her father despite his gambling addiction. She was no one's first choice. She was disposable, replaceable, a pawn. Lyla closed her eyes. She couldn't watch Manny pull the trigger. She hoped it would be quick. Her ears were ringing so she didn't hear the commotion around her, but she heard a gun blast and dropped to her knees with a scream. She hit the ground hard and waited for the pain, but it didn't come. Was she dead?

Lyla opened her eyes. Gavin was several feet away, shouting at his father who had the gun trained on him.

Vinny had Carmen locked in his arms as she fought him to get to Lyla.

"What the fuck? Are you insane?" Gavin shouted.

"Isn't this what you want?" Manny asked. "You want her frightened and down on her knees, right? You want to punish her for leaving you?"

Manny turned the gun back on Lyla who wrapped her arms around her middle and bowed her head. Why prolong this? Was Manny toying with her for his own sick enjoyment?

"This is how you treat someone you hate," Manny instructed as if he were showing Gavin how to balance his checkbook.

"I don't hate her."

"Really?"

Manny knelt with effort and jerked Lyla's face up. He roughly wiped off her lipstick with his sleeve and ripped Carmen's dress to show Lyla's bruised arms and neck. Lyla tried to get away from him, but his hand tightened on her in warning.

"Why is Lyla here?" Manny hissed.

"She's here to pay her father's debt."

"How?"

"I haven't decided yet."

"You disappoint me, son."

There was a stark silence.

"This is how you treat my daughter?" Manny asked softly.

Gavin looked as if he'd been struck. He paled, and his eyes flicked back and forth between Lyla and his father.

"This is how you treat someone *I* love?" Manny roared.

Lyla whimpered, overloaded with terror. Manny

dropped the gun and ignored Lyla's startled cry. He drew her into his arms and brushed gentle kisses over her face.

"I'm sorry, baby girl. I'm so sorry. I won't hurt you," Manny said and rose.

She stared at Manny, wondering what the fuck was going on. She was close to passing out. Her heart beat a rapid tempo in her chest. Manny gently helped her up. She sagged into him, and he wrapped an arm around her waist.

"I gave you something precious, and you broke it," Manny said to his son. "What you don't care for and cherish, you lose. I would die for your mother, give everything I own for one more day with her, and you treat Lyla like *this*?"

"Dad—" Gavin began and reached for Lyla.

Manny knocked his hand away as if Gavin was a child and not a man capable of killing with his bare hands. Carmen sucked in an audible breath.

Manny glared at his son. "You still have much to learn. I trusted you with Lyla, and she ran from you. Now that you have her back, you put bruises on her. The way to make a woman stay isn't by abusing her. It's by loving her so much that she can't imagine being without you." The silence stretched, and then Manny bellowed, "Ricardo!"

A Hispanic version of The Hulk appeared. Manny's body-guard took in the scene and went straight to Lyla. He acknowl-edged her with a gentle smile and picked up her quaking body.

"We're taking her home," Manny said.

Lyla was too shaken to say a thing as Ricardo carried her out of Carmen's home and deposited her into a Rolls Royce. Manny got into the back with her, but Lyla turned away from him and plastered herself against the car door, wondering if her status went from bad to horrific. Manny tugged her toward him and tipped her against his chest. She

trembled uncontrollably and moaned when he stroked back
her sweat soaked hair.

"I'm sorry I scared you. I promise I won't hurt you. I had
to show him, to make him realize... Well, it doesn't matter
now. It's over," Manny cooed.

"Y-you almost sh-shot ..." Lyla couldn't finish.

The car pulled out of Carmen's driveway. She
wanted to leap out and make a mad dash, but her
nerves were shot. She was wrecked. Too much
happened in too little time. Everywhere she turned,
doors shut in her face and fear yipped at her heels.
Since her arrival in Las Vegas, it had been a roller
coaster of uncertainty, dread, and terror. Gavin had
changed beyond recognition, and it seemed, so had
Manny. She loved these men, enough to look past the
way they did business. She would have died for them,
did anything they asked, and now she was being
bandied between them like a stray puppy. She wished
for Maine, the anonymity of the city, and Jonathan. She
felt as if she were tumbling headlong down the rabbit
hole with no exit in sight.

She must have dozed. When she came to, she was
cradled in Ricardo's arms, and she caught a glimpse of
Manny's mansion. Although he wasn't in her line of sight,
she heard Manny snapping out orders to the staff who were
running in every direction. Ricardo set her on the edge of a
heavenly bed, and a young woman wearing an old-fash-
ioned maid's uniform bowed.

"My name is Juanita. The master wants you to bathe."

Lyla stared at her blankly. She was having a hard time
concentrating.

"He says you might be a bit... upset. He thinks you're in
shock," Juanita said gently and helped Lyla walk into the

bathroom where she settled Lyla on the edge of the tub and began to fill it.

"I like tubs," Lyla said. For some reason, this seemed important enough to say out loud.

Juanita gave her an encouraging look. "That's good. You should soak and relax."

Lyla snorted. Relax when her life was spinning around so fast she couldn't get a hold of it? Juanita kept up a steady stream of mindless chatter as she helped Lyla shrug off the ruined dress and expensive diamond bracelet she forgot she was wearing. She didn't have the energy to be self-conscious or worried. In the past two days, she had been blackmailed, fucked by her psycho ex, bit, threatened, pampered at a salon, and looked down the barrel of her adopted father's gun. She was so fucking *done*.

Voices sounded from the bedroom, and Juanita discreetly left to deal with it. She came back a minute later with a chagrined look on her face. "Master is very anxious."

Manny was anxious? He didn't seem anxious when he pulled a gun on her. Seriously, how the hell had she ever felt safe with the Pyres? She must have been brainwashed. The Pyre family was dangerous, unpredictable, and had their own set of rules. Manny held her at gunpoint and threatened to kill her. Why? She tried to figure out his motive but couldn't process anything right now. She didn't even have the energy to wash, much less figure out how the Pyre mind worked. Juanita took over while Lyla's mind went on vacation. It took a lot of effort to scrub Carmen's makeup off, but they managed. Juanita had a prim nightgown ready for her. Whose nightgown was this? Did Manny have a girlfriend? This question seemed important for some reason.

Juanita asked if she was hungry, and Lyla shook her head. Having her life threatened took care of her appetite

for the foreseeable future. Juanita led her into Manny's
guest room, a room she had occupied with Gavin a million
years ago. The room was decorated in tasteful cream and
gold. Lyla sat on the edge of the bed after Juanita left.

Not even a minute later, the door opened, and Manny
stood there, dressed in plaid pajamas and house slippers. He
closed the door and approached her slowly. Lyla watched
him with detached wariness. Now what? After taking care of
her and making her feel safe, would he do something
dastardly and turn on her again? That seemed to be the
Pyre's MO so far.

Manny sat beside her and took her hand in his. Lyla's
skin prickled, but she didn't pull away. She waited.

"I'm so sorry," Manny said, and his voice sounded
strained. "I was very angry."

No shit, she thought. People with anger problems
shouldn't carry guns for obvious reasons. Manny stroked his
thumb over the back of her knuckles in a gesture that would
have been comforting if she trusted him.

"I love my wife," he said.

It didn't matter that she had died over twenty years ago.
Lyla heard the ache in his voice. She had no doubt he
mourned her every day. Manny squeezed Lyla's hand with
surprising strength.

"Even though we had so little time together, she gave me
Gavin and a lifetime of memories. No one can ever measure
up to her, and I'm okay with that. I would rather have the
real deal than a lukewarm imitation. Love is the most
complex and rewarding emotion we can feel. I feel sorry for
the poor bastards who never experience love or have it
returned."

Manny brushed her hair back from her face. She knew
he wanted her to look at him, so she mentally braced herself

and turned her head. Manny's eyes weren't filled with incandescent rage any longer. They were grief-stricken and imploring. It made her heart clench painfully because she loved him and hated to see that expression on his face.

"Lyla." He said her name like a prayer and kissed her hand. "I'm so sorry. I want you to know I would never hurt you. I love you as much as my own son, and I want both of you to be happy. I just wish you could be happy with each other. That's always been my dream for both of you."

A tear trickled down her cheek. She shook her head but said nothing. Manny kissed her hand once more and clasped it between his own. She felt him tremble ever so slightly.

"You came into my life at a time when I wasn't sure I could go on without her."

That penetrated through her numb fog. She frowned.

"I felt that Gavin knew enough about the business to take over. He was reckless, but I figured he would learn from his mistakes. I went into the office on the weekend to take care of some odds and ends, and you peeked into my office." Manny's mouth quirked. "You were waiting for your dad to finish work, and you asked if I needed help with something. No one dared to disturb me, and here you were, a slip of a girl, coming into my office and plopping down in a chair as if I was Santa Claus instead of the big bad wolf."

It was strange to think that that moment changed the course of her life. If she had kept to herself, she never would have gotten involved with the Pyres, and she wouldn't be here right now.

"I knew as soon as I met you that you were special."

Manny's words were an echo of what Carmen said earlier in the day. What the fuck was so special about her? No one, including herself, wanted to be where she was right now. If she was special, why did she have bruises on her body? If she was special, why were other people dictating her life? If she was special, why was she so afraid?

Almost as if Manny sensed her distress, he turned her hand over and pressed a kiss on her palm.

"You're special," he said again and searched her eyes. "Your father did a number on you, that worthless asshole. The only good thing he did in his life was bring you into this world. If he weren't so selfish, he would realize that. Your mother isn't much better, that airhead."

He shook his head. She saw a flicker of anger, which he instantly controlled.

"The day you came into my office, you changed my life," he said solemnly. "I couldn't believe you were Pat's daughter, that he managed to create something so beautiful and pure. You have so much of my wife in you; originally, I suspected you were a reincarnation of her."

Lyla stared at him. She wasn't sure how she felt about reincarnation, but she remembered being drawn to Manny, compelled even. As soon as they met, it felt as if they'd known each other all their lives. Manny felt like the safe haven she never had with her parents.

As she stared at Manny, she saw hope, loneliness, and a plea for understanding. Something inside her shifted. Lyla leaned forward and rested her forehead against Manny's. His tears fell silently. She wrapped her arms around him and tried to offer him a moment of respite from his grief.

"I wanted to tell you so many times, but I didn't know what you'd think. Now, I have to tell you or lose you like Gavin, and I can't allow that. I love you, baby girl," he whispered.

His words reverberated with truth and emotion. Lyla's heart split in two. She mourned with him—for what he lost and what she had never experienced. She wasn't sure how long they stayed that way, embracing and comforting one another before he moved. He sat with his back against the pillows and pulled her down, so her head rested on his thigh. His hand sifted through her hair. She had never felt more loved and cherished than she did at that moment. Nothing was sexual in his touch; it was pure human need for contact.

"Meeting you, it gave me life again and hope, not only for myself but for Gavin as well." When she stiffened, he made a cooing sound and stroked her hair and face until she relaxed again. "Since Gavin and I are so similar, I knew he would recognize in you what I did, and I was right. He's never committed to anyone the way he did to you. I knew he had other women on the side. I knew he would get rid of them once he made you his wife, but he kept putting it off and then it was too late. I saw you once after you found out he cheated. Your light, it was gone. It had a profound effect on Gavin. I thought he would be able to change your mind, but before he could, you left."

Silent tears ran from the corners of her eyes, absorbed by his pajamas. It hadn't been an easy decision to leave.

"I knew within two weeks where you were."

Lyla jerked and stared at him with wide eyes. He sniffed and wagged his pointer finger at her.

"Gavin still has a lot to learn, but I have my contacts."

"You knew and didn't tell Gavin?"

"Gavin fucked up. I thought you deserved time to do what you wanted. I had a man check on you at least once a week in the beginning, and then once you got established, once a month. One time, Gavin's investigator got close to discovering where you were, so I derailed him with false information. That was kind of fun."

Lyla laughed weakly. How could she be laughing after the hell she'd been put through? But, miracle of miracles, she was. She also felt calm and safe, two things she shouldn't feel unless she was away from the Pyres. "Why did you do that?"

"Because you deserve to live your own life. You were content, and Gavin had fucked up. Sometimes you only get one chance, and I wanted him to learn that lesson."

Lyla hesitated and then asked as gently as she could, "So are you going to let me leave?"

"No."

Lyla closed her eyes as disappointment flared. She made a movement to get away from him, but his hand, gentle but firm, kept her in place.

"Let me tell you why."

Lyla gave a curt nod and waited.

"Gavin changed when you left. He's relentless and merciless. That's why, when the investigator located you this time, I didn't interfere. Gavin needs you."

"Manny, I can't—" she began brokenly.

"The longer you've been away, the more remote he's become. I thought he might find someone else, but he never did, and he never stopped searching for you. I know he's using your father to keep you in line. I would do the same thing."

Manny smiled when Lyla clucked her tongue in disgust.

"What I didn't expect was for him to take his frustration and anger out on you. I assumed he would woo you gently so he could persuade you to stay." Manny's smile faded. "If I'd known what he would do, I never would have let him find you."

"What happens now?"

"Now we see how stupid Gavin is. I threatened you." He

paused to stroke her hair and pressed a kiss on her forehead to comfort her before he continued. "I wanted him to see how quickly you could be taken from him. You've been gone for three years. He should be kissing the ground you walk on, not scaring or hurting you. I gave you into his keeping, knowing that he needs light in his life to beat back the darkness. You humanize him, but if he's too far gone, I won't put you in his care. I'll get you out."

Lyla felt giddy with relief. "You promise?"

Manny had a pained expression on his face, but he said, "Yes. As much as I'd like you to stay for myself because you make me happy, I know you deserve freedom."

"But not yet," she said sardonically.

He tapped her on the nose. "No. We're going to give Gavin one last chance."

"And if he fails?"

"Then I might have to kill my own son."

6

THE FOLLOWING DAY, Lyla felt almost normal. She walked downstairs and was directed outside to the pool where Manny was eating lunch. He kept up a steady stream of chatter that reminded her why she enjoyed his company so much. He held her hands as he spoke to her. He treated her with care to erase last night's horror. No trace remained of the ruthless man she encountered. At times, she had flash-backs of Manny with the gun in his hand and then remembered his admission that he had been contemplating suicide when she walked into his office all those years ago. Destiny. Lyla pushed that to the back of her mind and enjoyed the moment.

Manny teased her about her not-so-delicate probing into the criminal side of the business before she left. Lyla gave him a mock glare before they laughed. She saw movement out of the corner of her eye and saw Gavin standing nearby, watching them. Her smile disappeared. She would have pulled away from Manny if he didn't tighten his hold.

"Son," Manny acknowledged with a chill in his tone.

Gavin walked forward and stopped several feet away. "I want to talk to you."

Even as her hands clutched Manny's, he kissed her knuckles and rose. Father and son disappeared inside the house. She paced around the pool, twisting her hands together. She believed Manny. He wouldn't let her be around Gavin if he suspected his son wouldn't treat her right, but Gavin was a master manipulator and must be furious at his father for his interference. Or maybe Gavin wanted to wash his hands of her, and she would be free earlier than expected.

"Lyla."

She stiffened and turned to find Gavin less than three feet from her. She couldn't stop herself from taking a reflexive step back or her instinctive glance around for help. She was not happy to see that they were alone. Where was Manny?

"Lyla."

She took another step back when Gavin took one forward. His hands twitched at his sides. Did he want to strangle her? Her heart began to race.

"I'm sorry," Gavin said.

Lyla blinked, sure she hadn't heard him right. "Excuse me?"

A muscle clenched in his jaw. "I'm sorry for putting my hands on you."

"Oh," she said, not sure how she was supposed to respond. "I'm okay."

He ran a hand through his hair, which was mussed and untidy. She scanned him and noticed his eyes were blood-shot and he looked exhausted. The fury and hatred he displayed toward her yesterday were absent, and he seemed more human.

"What Dad did last night..." Gavin shook his head and then fixed her with an intense stare. "He knows how to make a statement."

"Yes, he does," she agreed.

"Do you want to be here?"

"Yes," she said hastily.

Gavin didn't look pleased with her answer, but he didn't push. He clasped his hands behind his back and took a deep breath. "I know I haven't given you any reason to trust me, but the reason I brought you back was to re-establish our relationship."

So he blackmailed her to force her into a relationship that ended three years ago. Seriously, who could understand Gavin Pyre? "And if I don't want to go back to our old relationship?"

Gavin's face hardened, and she saw him bite back whatever he wanted to say. His body was rigid with tension. "I want you to give me a chance."

"Why?"

"Why?" he echoed in a dangerous voice.

"Yes. Why?" She threw her hands up, confident in the knowledge that he couldn't touch her and wasn't able to kidnap her from Manny's house. Gavin was the only obstacle stopping her from going back to a normal life. She wanted to get to the bottom of why he fixated on her. There was no reason he couldn't find someone more compatible for him. Gavin was good-looking, rich, and could be charming when he chose. Surely, a woman in Las Vegas existed who could give him what he needed. "I'm nobody. There must be someone you've met since I've been gone... or even before?"

He'd been with a crapload of women. Although he tried to conceal it, she could feel his anger rising. Why?

"You're not a nobody. My father loves you like the daughter he never had. You make him happy," Gavin said.

"Is that why you think you need to be in a relationship with me? Because of him?"

"No."

He didn't elaborate, and she raised her brows. "Just, *no*?"

"Yeah."

She shook her head. "I don't understand you."

"Likewise." He stared at her as if she were a jigsaw puzzle. "I want to spend time with you. Come to dinner with me."

"No."

His eyes narrowed. "No?"

"Yes. My answer is no," she said firmly and prepared to run when he tensed.

"What if Carmen comes?"

Lyla hesitated when she saw Manny watching from a lawn chair. She didn't want to go, but she wanted her life back, which meant spending time with Gavin and showing Manny they weren't meant for each other. Gavin wouldn't change for her. He was too far gone to be kind or considerate, and the sooner Manny saw that Gavin was a grenade waiting to self-destruct, the sooner he would send her on her way.

"Where?" she asked.

"My club, Lux."

"And Carmen will come?" she asked, needing to know she had a witness.

"And Vinny. Dad tells me he'll send Ricardo as well."

Lyla relaxed, knowing that Ricardo would report everything to Manny. "Okay."

Gavin looked a tad suspicious, but he didn't push. He didn't know about her deal with Manny. If he knew that his lack of control would help her leave a second time, maybe he wouldn't be so keen to face her when she roused him to such anger. Lyla knew that stonewalling someone like Gavin was dangerous. He had been raised to take what he wanted, and her resistance went against everything he'd been taught. Lyla was sure that tonight would put her one step closer to leaving Vegas behind.

"I'll see you tonight, then," he said.

"Yes."

"Can I send you something to wear?"

Lyla hesitated and then shrugged since she didn't have anything at Manny's and Carmen's dress had been destroyed. "Okay."

He nodded and took a step forward, but stopped when she stiffened. His amber eyes flickered with some emotion before they became unreadable.

"I honestly regret that I hurt you. That was never my intention. I want this to work. It was never about the debt; it was just a means to get you here without fighting. You may not admit it, but this is your home, Lyla. It always will be."

She didn't deny it because it was partly true.

"I won't hurt you again; you have my word."

She wanted to believe him, but the kitchen incident was too fresh in her mind. And she knew what he was capable of.

"I hurt you by having other women. You hurt me by leaving. We're even."

They were *not* even, but she wasn't going to argue with him. She just wanted him to leave.

"I'll see you tonight, baby girl."

With that, Gavin left. Lyla watched him go before she walked over to Manny who acted as if he was sleeping on the lawn chair. Lyla decided to do the same.

At four o'clock, Carmen arrived. She looked great, as usual, but even her excellent makeup job couldn't mask her worry. Lyla rushed to her and hugged her tight.

"I'm fine," she said immediately.

"Are you really?" Carmen asked.

"Really," Lyla assured her.

"Holy shit, I hardly slept at all last night." Carmen waved at Manny who was talking on the phone at his desk.

Lyla led Carmen upstairs and closed the bedroom door. "Gavin sent a dress." She gestured to the white sheath dress, which had a high neck and sleeves that ended at her elbow. The dress had an open back that packed the sensual punch all club clothes required. The dress looked demure in the front and scandalous from the back. It fit just right, which didn't surprise her. It arrived an hour ago with silver stilettos and a diamond necklace. Lyla couldn't deny that she felt a pang of nostalgia, but she wasn't an idiot. Making sure Gavin failed to win her back was her goal. The sooner he failed, the sooner she could go back to a normal life where death didn't lurk around every corner.

Carmen started on her makeup as Lyla told her bits and pieces of what happened with Manny. She didn't tell Carmen about Manny's wife or the reincarnation part because it was too personal and Carmen may not understand. But she explained Manny's agreement to let her go if she and Gavin couldn't reconcile.

"And Gavin doesn't know about this pact you have with Manny?" Carmen asked, aghast.

"He doesn't need to."

Carmen pursed her lips. "Girl, you should have seen him last night. He was a wreck."

Lyla snorted. "You know who was a wreck? *Me!*"

Carmen waved a hand. "I know, but when Manny turned the gun on you, Gavin ran forward. Manny fired off a warning shot at Gavin. I've never seen him like that. He panicked. He may not show it, but he has deep feelings for—"

"Let's just finish up. I'm hungry," Lyla said. Now that she had some measure of control over her life, she felt more like herself. She had an objective and wouldn't stop until it was completed. Gavin wasn't a part of her future.

Carmen gave her a judgmental look but let the subject drop. It almost felt like old times as they got ready and strutted downstairs. Manny was there to admire and kiss their hands gallantly. They rode in the Rolls Royce with Ricardo at the wheel. Lyla tried to calm her nerves as they approached The Strip in all its colored glory. It had changed in the short amount of years she was gone. New hotels replaced old ones, but the hyper, manic energy of those on the streets hadn't changed. People could be whoever they wanted here. They could pretend to be players, single, high rollers, or daredevils. As the slogan said, "What happens in Vegas, stays in Vegas." If only people didn't take it so literally...

They pulled up to a Pyre Casino. Lyla took the hand that reached into the car to help her out and didn't realize who it belonged to until she was pulled against a hard body. Lyla went rigid as she stared up at Gavin.

"You look great," Gavin said and gave her a quick kiss before he twined their hands together.

Lyla gave an experimental yank and got nowhere.

"Lyla!"

Lyla received a kiss on both cheeks from Vinny who she thought of as a brother. He was even-tempered, which made him a good partner for both Gavin and Carmen. He was tall, dark, and handsome like Gavin, but his easy smile was genuine. Lyla tried to get away from Gavin to give Vinny a hug, but Gavin didn't let her go. A large group of employees milled around nervously, probably confused about the president and vice president appearing to help someone out of a car.

"I've missed you," Lyla said with genuine regret and felt Gavin tense beside her. What the hell was his problem? He always had a quick temper, but now it was on a hair trigger. She looked around to make sure that Ricardo was watching and found that he was.

"Let's eat," Vinny said and kissed Carmen before they went inside.

The casino was bustling with people. The familiar smells and sounds reminded Lyla of a simpler time. When Manny hired her as his assistant, she walked through the casino with such pride, knowing she was a part of this. She took in the crowd and picked out the high rollers, gold diggers, tourists, and underage teens. As they neared the club, Lyla heard the pump of music and saw the crowd waiting to get in. Gold ropes were cast aside as they approached, and they slipped into madness.

Lux was a new club with a massive dance floor and multiple bars to accommodate the crowds. Built like an amphitheater, it had five levels so everyone could see everything going on in the club. Strategically placed platforms highlighted professional dancers writhing in gold spotlights.

Gavin cut a path through the swarm. Despite the chaos, workers appeared to lead them to a large booth on the second tier. Lyla scooted in and was disconcerted when Gavin sat beside her, so close that she was pressed against him. Ricardo slipped into the booth while Vinny sat on the end with Carmen on his lap. Workers in small leather skirts, tops, and hooker heels that lit up with each step brought trays of elegantly crafted appetizers and crazy-looking drinks that smoked.

Lyla wanted to ask Gavin what she was drinking or eating, but she didn't want to engage him in conversation. She scooted farther into the booth so they weren't touching. The sheer number of people was staggering. It was like New Year's Eve in a club. After four drinks and clearing two plates of food, Lyla felt flushed and restless. A steady parade of workers and VIPs stopped by to talk to Gavin. There was a wealth of respect there. He answered several phone calls and even responded to emails. He was a busy man, always had been. So why was he sitting with them in the middle of a club when he should be in an office?

As Lyla looked over the dance floor, she focused on a man who walked on the fringes of the crowd. He wasn't dressed to impress. He wore jeans, a white shirt, and sneakers. He ignored the women who tried to get his attention. Even across the distance, she could see that he was hot. *Really* hot. He was tall, had a great body, and something about the way he moved reminded her of Gavin. As he approached, she saw that his eyes were a turquoise shade that stood out against his olive-toned skin. He had short-cropped hair and was clean shaven. Lyla straightened as he made his way toward them. Gavin's security stopped him before he could reach their booth.

Vinny glanced at Gavin nervously a moment before the stranger lashed out. Two guards dropped to their knees. Ricardo and Vinny withdrew guns, and more security rushed forward, but everyone halted when Gavin raised his hand. The man approached with an aggression that would have scared Lyla if she cared for Gavin's well-being. When he stopped in front of Gavin, Lyla saw that the collar of his shirt was soaked with sweat as if he had jogged here. He was wound so tightly that Lyla scooted backward in the booth.

"I want names," the man said, eyes trained on Gavin.

"What are you doing here, Eli?"

There was no deference in his attitude for the power Gavin wielded. Eli leaned toward Gavin, a muscle clenching in his jaw.

"You *know*."

Eli's eyes flicked to Lyla, and her heart skipped a beat. Eli was hanging on by a thread. There was disdain in his eyes, but also a rage so potent that if Gavin weren't in front of her, she would have run like hell. Gavin shifted, and Eli's attention flipped back to him.

"You should have set up a meeting, not approached me in public like this," Gavin said.

"My mom's in the hospital in a coma. You think I'm going to wait for you to set up a *meeting*?" The tendons on his neck stood out as he tried to rein in rampant emotions. "I want names, Gavin. I want them now."

"And you think I know who did this to your mother?" Gavin asked in a cool voice that put Lyla on edge.

Eli's tension increased. "Are you telling me you don't know who did this to her?"

"I didn't call the hit."

"But you know who did," Eli said, chest heaving as he tried to control his breathing. "Give me their names. Now."

"I'll take care of it, Eli."

Eli cocked his head to the side. "Did you not hear me, Pyre? They tried to kill my mother. She's not a part of this. This wasn't supposed to touch her."

Lyla's skin rippled with goose bumps.

"I'll deal with it."

"No, *I* will."

"You can't. You're a cop," Gavin said.

"And you think I'm going to leave it up to you when this happened on your watch?" Eli hissed.

Gavin rose. Lyla's heart nearly beat out of her chest. She knew Gavin was armed, dangerous, and fully capable of blowing someone's head off without a second thought. Vinny slipped Carmen into the booth and got between them. Vinny put a hand on Eli's chest with a sympathetic expression.

"Eli, let Gavin take care of it," Vinny said.

Eli ignored Vinny and didn't move his eyes from Gavin. "Nothing happens without your say so."

"I don't handle low level thugs," Gavin said.

"As crime lord, every fucking crime should be on your radar. This is unacceptable, Pyre," Eli hissed.

"Don't tell me how to run my business," Gavin said, voice thick with threats. "We've been associates for many years. You know how I work; I know how you work. If anyone sees you here tonight, your testimony in court may not hold up. You're putting everything on the line."

"I don't give a fuck," Eli said through gritted teeth. "Give me the names, Gavin."

"Grand, Frak," Gavin said.

Eli relaxed fractionally. He eased back from Gavin and glanced at Lyla again. She couldn't read his expression.

"We're done," Eli said and walked away.

Gavin's security moved out of Eli's way. Gavin sat and took a drink of water as calmly as if nothing out of the ordinary had happened. The look in Eli's eyes disturbed her. He would kill those men, cop or not. What other deals was Eli involved in? Lyla glanced at Carmen who was unperturbed by the incident. She downed the last of her drink and beamed at Lyla.

"Let's dance!" Carmen shouted over the beat of music.

Lyla nodded. She didn't want to sit here and listen to Gavin's business. She looked at Gavin, who was blocking her way and completely unaware of Carmen's suggestion... or her. Did he ask her to come tonight to ease his father's mind and make up for putting bruises on her? It only reinforced her suspicion that bringing her back to Las Vegas had everything to do with his pride and Manny's affection for her. Gavin didn't want *her*. He saw her as a possession that slipped through his fingers. Gavin respected and loved his father more than anyone in the world. He even dated her to please his father. How far would he go to make Manny happy? Lyla glanced at Ricardo who wore a deceptively uninterested expression. It was time to prove her point.

"Let me out," Lyla said, and when Gavin ignored her, she placed a hand on his arm to get his attention.

His head snapped toward her. The intensity of his gaze startled her.

"I'm going to dance," she said. When he gave her a puzzled look, she was forced to lean toward him. "I want to dance with Carmen!"

Gavin didn't move immediately. He scanned the dance floor and the surrounding tables before he stood. He held out a hand to help her out. Lyla heard women at a nearby table grumble, jealous of Gavin's display of old world charm. Of course, the dress covered her bruises. If only these women knew that beneath the gorgeous exterior, a killer lay in wait. When she and Carmen linked arms, Gavin gripped her hip to stop her.

"Stay in my sight," he said, lips brushing her ear.

Lyla slipped away without saying a word, pushing

thoughts of him away as she and Carmen walked onto the
dance floor. Of course, Carmen didn't stop until they were in
the middle of the crush. Lyla was seized with panic when
people pressed in around her, but Carmen wrapped her
close and squeezed.

"Feel it, Lyla!" she shouted. "Stop thinking and *dance*! We
used to do this all the time, remember?"

Lyla closed her eyes and forced herself to move. She and
Carmen used to go to parties and clubs every night, but it
felt like a lifetime ago. She didn't know how to move with
the reckless abandon she once had.

Carmen hugged her from behind and moved to the beat.
Lyla smiled as Carmen's hips did ridiculous things that
probably made Vinny wild. She loved Carmen and missed
her craziness. Carmen had her best interests at heart and
risked her life to get Lyla out of Las Vegas and had given her
a huge chunk of money to make her way in the world.

Lyla opened her eyes. It took a minute for her to
pinpoint Gavin through the blinking lights and sea of
people. He was on his feet, leaning casually against the
booth, talking on his phone. He looked good enough to be
on the cover of a magazine. He was effortlessly masculine
and gorgeous. No woman would pass him without a second
glance. On impulse, Lyla glanced around. She grabbed the
arm of a woman two men were fighting over. The woman
came willingly enough, and Lyla found herself in a hot girl
sandwich that made the men brush their hands over their
crotches.

"You straight?" Lyla asked her.

The gorgeous brunette tossed her hair and rubbed
herself against Lyla's front. Carmen, never one to miss an
opportunity, copped a feel of the woman's fake breasts and
gave her a thumbs-up.

"Who's your doctor?" Carmen shouted.

Lyla elbowed her cousin aside and leaned toward the brunette. "You see that guy?" Lyla pointed at Gavin who paced while he talked on the phone.

"Holy shit," the woman breathed.

"He's working too much," Lyla said with a pout. "You think you can get his attention, distract him?"

The brunette licked her lips before she turned to Lyla with a frown. "You his wife?"

"No. Trying to prove that he's still a cheater."

"Don't have to ask me twice," the brunette said and kissed Lyla on the lips before she made her way off the dance floor.

Some of the men chased after her, but the bombshell didn't give them a second glance. She was focused on her target.

"What the hell are you doing, Lyla?" Carmen demanded.

"He's still a cheater," Lyla said and switched places with her cousin so she could watch the show over Carmen's shoulder. "He always will be. I need Ricardo to tell Manny we aren't meant for each other."

She and Carmen moved together in the middle of the bumping and grinding bodies and watched the brunette slowly make her way toward Gavin. Damn, the brunette was good. She leaned on the railing in front of the booth next to Gavin's, just far enough that if he were interested, he would have to turn his head.

"Get off the damn phone!" Lyla shouted, frustrated.

"He's not interested, Lyla!" Carmen shouted back gleefully.

"She's being too subtle... oh!"

Gavin finally caught sight of the brunette and looked her up and down. He hung up the phone and looked over the dance floor. Lyla whirled Carmen in the opposite direction. When Lyla looked back, Gavin and the brunette were talking. Even while something sharp sliced through her stomach, Lyla was grimly satisfied. Ricardo would report back to Manny. That was easy.

Lyla danced until her feet ached and her dress was soaked with sweat from the press of bodies.

"Drink?" she shouted at Carmen who nodded.

Lyla made her way through the crowd to the bar and found herself face to pecs with a shirtless bartender. He grinned at her and made the muscles in his chest dance.

"What can I get for you, gorgeous?" he asked with a very white smile.

Lyla pointed at some interesting looking drinks. "We'll try those!"

It wasn't until he was making the drinks that she realized she didn't have any money. She turned to see if she could get Carmen's attention, but that would be an impossible feat.

"I can get this for you."

Lyla glanced at the man beside her. He had strange, angular features. He was the same height as she was and had extremely narrow shoulders. The shirt tucked into his slacks brought attention to his tiny waist.

"Um, no, that's okay," Lyla said uneasily.

"I insist."

Before she could say anything, he held out a fifty-dollar bill to the bartender. The bartender ignored him and took drink orders from two scantily clad women. The man beside her flushed, and Lyla felt a flicker of sympathy for him.

"Thanks," she said. "What's your name?"

There was a flicker of surprise in his eyes before he lowered his arm and said quietly, "Steven."

She held out a hand. "I'm Lyla."

She tried to hide her grimace since his palms were damp with sweat. He quickly withdrew his hand, wiped it on his trousers, and then grasped her hand again to give it a vigorous, awkward shake. Lyla stared at him for a moment before she burst into laughter. She put a hand on his arm when he tried to slink away.

"It's okay," she said, taking pity on him.

"I don't know how to talk to women," he muttered.

"I don't either," she said, deadpan.

Steven's thin lips twitched as if he wanted to smile, but he didn't have much practice. He opened his mouth to speak but was rudely elbowed out of the way by another man who gave her a cocky grin. The newcomer was lean, muscled, and well put together in a button up shirt instead of thin cotton like most of the men in the club. He was attractive and stared straight into her eyes.

"Here you go," the bartender said, setting two smoking drinks on the bar.

Before Steven could extend his money, the newcomer handed a one-hundred-dollar bill to the bartender without moving his gaze from her.

Lyla raised a brow. "I know the club is called Lux, but I think you're paying too much for my drinks."

He shrugged. "Money is no object, and I expect to be buying you drinks all night long. I'm Rafael."

Lyla gave him a wide-eyed look. "Oh, really?" The alcohol and environment were giving her confidence.

Rafael winked at her. "Yes. You're gorgeous. Is my brother bothering you?"

"Your brother?" Lyla asked without comprehension before Steven stepped sideways to stand beside the much larger man.

There was no resemblance between them in looks or build.

"Steven makes people uneasy," the brother said with a careless wave at Steven who wore a blank expression. "He isn't wearing heels or his shoulder pads, so you might have mistaken him for a child."

"Um, no," Lyla said and shot a look at Steven who didn't react to his brother's barbs. Was he transgender?

"Your name?" the attractive brother asked.

"Lyla," she said without extending her hand.

"Lyla, you're beautiful."

"You're not so bad yourself," she said.

Rafael grinned roguishly. "I try. You here with someone?"

That brought her back to reality with an unpleasant jolt. "Yes."

"Pity," he said and finally let his eyes roam over her. "You'll give me a call when you're free?"

When he reached into his pocket for his phone, she shook her head. "I don't have a phone, and I have to get going."

"You don't have a phone?"

She shrugged as she grabbed the drinks. "That's the honest truth." She spotted Carmen making her way to the restroom and smiled at Rafael. "Thank you for the drinks."

"Anytime," Rafael said.

In the bathroom, Lyla was mortified to find that her white dress was nearly see through. A moment later, she shrugged. She was more covered up than most of these women, and this *was* Vegas. Innumerable people touched her ass on the dance floor, so who cared if they got an eyeful of her body? Lyla was sipping her drink when the brunette she sent to Gavin bustled into the bathroom and squealed.

"He's so *nice!*" she said as she rushed toward Lyla. "He offered me a job."

Lyla choked on her drink. "What?"

"He said I have a good face and body. He wanted to know if I had a job, and if I wanted to be a hostess at one of his restaurants. You didn't tell me he's Gavin *Pyre*. Oh. My. God."

"Wait, so he didn't hit on you?" Lyla demanded.

The brunette gave a one shoulder shrug. "He said I was beautiful, but it was more like he was sizing me up. He asked if I had references and gave me the number of a restaurant manager. I have an interview tomorrow!" At Lyla's dumbfounded expression, the brunette said, "Maybe he's not a cheater anymore. Why would you want him to be? He seems like a great guy."

No, no, *no!* Lyla glared at Carmen who was laughing her head off. Lyla downed her drink and wished the brunette luck before she made her way back to the bar to order two more frothy drinks. Rafael and Steven were nowhere to be found.

"You trying to get drunk?" Carmen asked without judgment as she knocked back identical drinks to Lyla. She believed that whatever pain Lyla went through tomorrow that it was her job to go through it with her.

"Hunting for more women for Gavin," Lyla said distractedly as she scanned the crowd. "Maybe he doesn't want a brunette. Maybe he wants an Asian chick. I saw him with a black girl that day..." Lyla shook her head to banish the images. "She was pretty before I broke her nose. *Anyway...*"

Carmen mumbled under her breath as she followed Lyla onto the dance floor. Lyla chose a handful of women who Gavin wouldn't be able to turn down, and each woman was more than willing to test his control. Some were aggressive while others played hard to get. One thing was certain. Each of them gained Gavin's attention for a time, but none of them stayed by his side. Some came back to her to report that he offered them a job or asked if they were trying to get back at an ex.

"What the hell? Is he the Santa Claus of jobs in Vegas?" Lyla growled.

Carmen laughed hysterically. Lyla was talking to an exotic woman of Indian descent when a hand wrapped around her waist. She didn't need to look to know who it was.

"You have excellent taste in women," Gavin said in her ear, "but your parade is interrupting me from doing business."

Lyla turned from the Indian woman who tugged down the neckline of her gown to give Gavin a better look at her cleavage. Lyla turned in Gavin's arms in time to see him wink at the woman before he led Lyla off the dance floor. He didn't go back to their booth; he led her behind the bar, into a small hallway off the kitchen. He backed her against the wall and stared down at her.

"What are you playing at?"

"Playing at?" She was drunk enough to give him a mystified expression even though she'd been caught red-handed.

"Are you interested in threesomes now?"

His question sobered her instantly. She dropped the act. "I don't do threesomes."

"Then why are you sending me all these women?"

"So you can pick one."

"For what?"

"For *yourself*!"

"I have you."

She stared at him, astounded by his bone headedness. "You *don't* have me, jackass!"

The predator in him rose and reflected in his eyes. "I will have you again, Lyla."

"You will never have me," Lyla said, the drinks in her system making her reckless and not giving a crap about the consequences of pitting herself against Gavin Pyre. "You hurt me!" She slammed her hand against her racing heart and then over the bruises on her neck. "I don't trust you, and I never will."

Gavin said nothing. His face was expressionless.

"I want a normal life with a sweet guy," she said forlornly, her anger fading as suddenly as it swept through her. She stared up at him, imploring. "There must be someone else for you. These women want you, would do anything for you—"

"I don't want them."

She thumped his chest with her fist. "You're mad that I left you, that I was happy without you—"

He cupped her face and leaned down so their lips were centimeters apart. "You weren't happy without me."

"What?"

"You weren't happy without me," he stated with complete certainty. "You can't be happy without me."

"I was!" she insisted and shoved at him.

He lifted her, so they were at eye level. Servers rushed in and out of the revolving kitchen door, but no one paid them any mind, and they were too locked on one another to notice the pandemonium behind the scenes that made the club such a success. Gavin's finger traced the curve of her cheek and then her throat. When her breath hitched, his eyes glinted with triumph.

"If you were in love with that boring fuck you were living

with, you wouldn't respond to me." He pressed against her core, letting her know he was fully aroused. "You've been living a safe, boring life, baby girl. You missed this, missed me."

"No, I—" Lyla bit back a moan as he rocked against her. "Stop it!"

"You're soaked for me, aren't you? Just like in your sleep. You want me, need *me*, Lyla. The moment I touch you, your body responds. It's still mine."

Lyla was stunned. How had this backfired so badly? Her plan to incriminate Gavin crumbled as he turned the tables on her and showed her how susceptible she was. What the fuck? "Let me go."

"No."

Gavin seemed content to keep her pinned against the wall with his cock nestled between her legs. Lyla wriggled and froze when the bulge in his pants pressed against her clit. She hissed through her teeth and thumped his shoulder.

"Back *off*, Gavin!"

"So you can send more women to me? I'm content right here," Gavin said and squeezed her ass.

Lyla bucked, and they both groaned. It took more effort than she wanted to admit to remember why she was holding him off and why she didn't indulge in the lust roiling through her. "You're doing this for Manny!"

"I'm giving myself a hard-on for my dad?"

"Don't get smart with me, Gavin! You're oversexed. We both know it. You don't know how to commit to one woman. You cheated on me the whole time we were together. One of those women," she jabbed her finger toward the club, "won't care that you fuck around. They won't say a thing. Just give them an unlimited credit card, and they'll do whatever you want. I'm not that girl, not anymore. The sooner we find you a girl, the sooner you get over your ego trip, and I can go back to—"

"You're not going anywhere," Gavin interrupted and rocked himself against her core.

Her mouth fell open with a gasp.

"I've been looking for you for three years. You think now that I have you back, I'm going to fuck around again?"

"Why not? You did the first time. By the way," she prodded his rock-hard chest, "you didn't use a condom the other night."

Gavin stilled. "You aren't on anything?"

"I have an IUD. I'm more worried about an STD," Lyla said without tact.

Gavin looked murderous. "You think I'm that careless?"

"I don't know what you use when you fuck your whores," she said.

"I'm not fucking anyone."

Lyla didn't believe him. They'd had sex almost every day when they were together, and he still had women on the side. Thinking of an abstinent Gavin was ludicrous. "So you've been tested recently?"

"You're really trying to piss me off, aren't you?"

"By asking you justified questions?" Lyla sighed and shook her head, feeling weary all of a sudden. "If Manny hadn't thrown me at you, you wouldn't have looked twice at me. How many women did you have at that time?" He didn't answer, and her stomach twisted. She shoved against him. "I'm not interested in replaying our history, Gavin. Manny's not going to disown you if you let me go. He knows we're not meant for each other."

"Do you want to go home?" Ricardo appeared beside them. He didn't look surprised by their intimate position.

"Yes." Lyla pushed at Gavin, but he didn't move. She met his glittering eyes. "Let me go, Gavin."

"For now," he said and released her, deliberately sliding her down his frame.

Lyla grimaced against her body's reaction. She was ashamed that her legs quaked as her feet touched the ground.

Gavin stepped back and then scowled. "Your dress is see-through!"

Lyla shrugged. "You picked it. I thought that was the point. No one cares. It's Vegas."

"I fucking care," Gavin snapped and slid out of his suit jacket and draped it over her.

She didn't want to be encased in his scent or heat. "I'm hot," she said as she tried to shrug off the jacket.

"You'll wear it to the car," Gavin decreed.

She couldn't spend another second with him. He was such a bullheaded ass. Nothing she said made an impression on him. He was intent on replaying their history. On top of the fact that their relationship had been based on Manny's approval and Gavin's infidelity, she had to remind herself about the guard who lost his life in the basement. Gavin was dangerous. She was determined to get away from him and his propensity for violence. She wanted a simple life. She wanted a man who loved her more than anything in the world. Once upon a time, she thought Gavin was that man. What a fucking reality check it had been to realize she was living a lie.

They made their way through the club. Gavin tucked her under his arm and ignored her attempts to get away from him.

"What about Carmen?" she shouted.

"She'll go home with Vinny," he said and walked her out of the club.

He took her hand as they walked through the casino with Ricardo several paces behind them.

"Did you like the club?" Gavin asked.

Surprised by his attempt at civil conversation, she said, "Yes. The music is great, the bartenders are fast, and the people who get in look like they should be in a magazine."

His mouth curved. "Well said. It's the most successful nightclub on The Strip. You sent me a good array of girls tonight. I hope they work for me."

Lyla rolled her eyes. "What positions did you offer them?"

"Front desk, dancers, bartender. Doesn't matter to me."

Lyla was relieved to reach the hotel entrance. While Ricardo went to talk to the valet, Gavin turned her toward him with a grip on the jacket.

"You still want to be at my father's house?" he asked.

"Yes," she said emphatically.

"I'll send some of your clothes over."

"How gracious of you," she drawled, "since you threw away what I brought with me."

"It's an insult to your body to wear such shoddy clothes."

Lyla glared at him. "Bank tellers don't have the budget to wear Armani or Prada."

"If you stayed with me, you wouldn't have to work at all."

"I don't mind working."

Gavin surveyed her for a moment. "You could always work for me."

"No thanks," she said quickly.

"Come, Lyla," Ricardo called as the car pulled up.

Ricardo got into the driver's seat. Gavin walked her to the

car. Before she could slip out of his jacket, he gripped the lapels and jerked her against him. His mouth covered hers before she had time to defend herself. His tongue stroked hers while his hands splayed on her bare back and caressed. She staggered back, breaking the kiss. He grinned and gave her one last chaste kiss before he tucked her into the back of the car.

"Me wanting you has nothing to do with my father," Gavin said as he buckled her in and deliberately brushed his hand over her breasts. "And if you think I've waited three years to let you leave me again, you're dead wrong."

With that threat hanging in the air, he stepped back and slammed the door. He strode into the hotel without looking back. Lyla tried to steady her breathing and saw Ricardo watching her in the rearview mirror.

"He's an ass," she said.

"Yes, ma'am," Ricardo said with a grin.

7

THE FOLLOWING MORNING, Lyla descended the stairs wearing a fitted jersey dress that flirted around her ankles. Gavin had made good on his promise to deliver part of her old wardrobe.

Manny sat at the large dining table, surrounded by an assortment of breakfast foods. He set the newspaper aside; his face lighting up as if his day didn't start until she joined him. A streak of pain darted through her chest. She recognized the feeling. Love. Even as she tried to reassert common sense, she rounded the table and went to Manny. He held his arms open as if she really was his daughter, and her eyes stung with tears as she fell into his embrace. Manny's love washed away the fact she was being held here against her will.

"You slept well?" Manny asked when she drew away.

"Yes," she said and sat beside him. "What are you up to today?"

"I thought I would go antique shopping. Interested?"

"Yes." Anything to distract her from her bizarre circumstances. She was a captive of the Pyre men who had different wants from her. Although she missed Jonathan and felt guilty for whatever pain her leaving caused, she couldn't deny she enjoyed spending time with Manny. Her own parents were too self-involved with each other to care what happened to her, so being around Manny was the closest thing she had to a parent. It just sucked that Manny was connected to Gavin.

"How did you like Lux?" Manny asked.

Lyla gave him a similar answer to what she told Gavin the night before. Like Gavin, Manny seemed pleased.

"Ricardo tells me that you tried to find Gavin a replacement."

Lyla paused in the middle of nibbling on a piece of bacon. While Manny's voice was mild, his eyes sparkled with mischief.

She lifted her chin defensively. "What of it?"

He smacked the table, making her jump. "That's great!"

"It is?"

"The woman he wants doesn't want him and offers to help him find another. That's rich!" Manny howled with laughter.

Lyla forked up some hash browns. "I don't think it's funny."

"I do." Manny shook his head. "I know my son. What you did last night will only make him more determined to have you."

Lyla's fork clattered to the table. "What? *Why?*"

"Lyla, you need to know something about men," he drawled, spreading his bejeweled hand over his chest. "We don't like being told no."

"I didn't tell him no. I'm letting him do whatever he wants. I want him to follow his natural instinct and leave me alone—" Lyla stopped because Manny was laughing hysteri-cally. "Seriously, Manny, what's so funny?"

"Baby girl," he said, wiping tears from his eyes, "Gavin has been looking for you for three years."

"I know that."

"And why do you think he's done so?" he asked curiously.

"He's doing it for you," she said accusingly.

He blinked. "Me?"

"He craves your approval. You practically demanded he marry me on our first date."

Manny cocked his head to the side. "And you think that Gavin would date a woman he didn't like because I told him to?"

"Yes," she said without hesitation.

"I told him to marry you many times."

"I know," she said.

"If he wanted my approval, why didn't he marry you to please me?"

"Because he doesn't want to tie himself to me *perma-nently*. He was just... indulging you."

"Gavin wants my approval, and he loves me," Manny conceded, "but Gavin wouldn't fuck one woman for four years to please me."

"He didn't fuck one woman; he fucked many," Lyla said crisply.

Manny's face softened. He reached out and ran a hand down her hair, which hung loosely around her shoulders. "That wrecked you, didn't it?"

Lyla wasn't sure where the tears came from, but she valiantly shoved them back into the darkness where they belonged. "Finding out that it wasn't a one-time thing, that he'd been cheating from the beginning destroyed me. The only thing that makes sense is that he kept me for your sake. He had no intentions of marriage or really committing himself to me." Lyla blew out a breath and was relieved to feel the tears recede. "I want a man who loves me more than anything, especially other women. Gavin made me feel like nothing." And he wouldn't get the chance to make her feel like that again.

Manny shook his head. "Boy screwed up."

"No, it was meant to be. It woke me up. I got to see the world a bit, and I found a great guy." She ignored Manny's derisive look. "Jonathan's really sweet."

"I'm biased, mi amor."

"Of course, you are," she grumbled. "I just want normal, Manny."

"But you aren't normal."

She straightened in her chair. "Yes, I am."

"If you were normal, you wouldn't be here."

She didn't know how to challenge that statement and didn't have the chance to since he rose.

"Eat, and we'll go shopping," he said and left her at the table, staring after him.

Of course, she was normal. If she hadn't gained Manny's attention as a teenager, her life would have been extremely ordinary. Maybe she would have followed her father into accounting or gotten married to some Joe Schmo and been a stay-at-home mom. She wasn't Carmen—adventurous and sexy with a personality that electrified the room. Lyla was definitely normal. Everyone *around* her wasn't normal, which was why she clung to Jonathan. He was safe and ordinary. Gavin's words came back to haunt her. *If you were in love with that boring fuck you were living with, you wouldn't respond to me.* Of course, she loved Jonathan. The fact that she responded to Gavin was... It was...

"You ready, Lyla?" Manny asked.

He was dressed in jeans with a gold chain around his neck, a gold cane, and gold-framed sunglasses.

She got to her feet and grinned at him. "You look like a pimp."

"This is Vegas, baby girl; you have to dress with flair."

Ricardo had a Mercedes waiting for them in the driveway. When they got into the back seat, she wasn't surprised when Manny clasped their hands together.

"Why did you retire?" Lyla asked.

"I was too old for the bullshit." At her inquiring look, he shrugged. "I was losing my touch. They needed someone tougher at the helm. That wasn't me."

"And Gavin is tougher than you are?" she asked carefully.

He squeezed her hand. "I made sure he's tougher than I am. He needs to see the business through to the next generation."

Next generation? Lyla ignored that and asked, "You're completely out of the business?"

"Yes, I don't know a thing," he said and waved a dismissive hand. "It's fantastic. True freedom."

That was what she wanted. She didn't want to wonder how many Gavin murdered or if the man holding her hand with such care taught him to kill.

"Gavin is the CEO, Vinny the COO. They work well together. While they slave away all day, I do what I like."

"Which is?" Lyla asked with arched brows.

"Sometimes, I gamble for the hell of it. I went on a Mediterranean cruise and a safari. Whatever whim I have, I do."

"Do you have any trips planned?"

He kissed her knuckles. "Not right now. If Gavin is a fool, you can choose a place you wish to visit."

If Gavin let her go, she would leave, not go on a vacation... But she didn't want Manny to go alone. Lyla had to remind herself that she wanted away from Vegas and the Pyres. When had she begun to accept that being a captive was acceptable?

Ricardo pulled up to a sketchy building where the man behind the counter greeted Manny by name and assumed that Lyla was his young mistress. Of course, the man wasn't stupid enough to say it out loud, but he didn't need to. The shopkeeper's poorly concealed jealousy made Lyla edge closer to Manny. They browsed aimlessly, poring over knick-knacks or laughing over offensive paintings and statues they stumbled across. The day passed by pleasantly.

When they stopped for lunch on The Strip, Lyla was relieved to see they weren't at a Pyre establishment. Manny led her into a dimly lit, quiet, and beautiful restaurant with nice views of the city. Despite the fact this wasn't one of their restaurants, the staff still fawned over Manny and called him by name. The Pyres were Las Vegas kingpins, and everyone knew them. Once they ordered drinks, Lyla excused herself to go to the bathroom. She felt underdressed, but that couldn't be helped. She was on her way back to the table when someone called her name.

Lyla paused and saw Rafael and his brother, Steven, rise from a table. Rafael sauntered toward her while Steven ambled behind with his strange eyes fixed on her face.

"Fancy meeting you here," she said.

"Yes." Rafael raised a brow. "You have no phone, but you seem to have no problem getting into exclusive places. It must be that pretty face."

"I have good friends," she said.

"I could be an even better friend," he said, spreading his arms wide and giving her a devilish grin. "And a more generous one."

He obviously thought she was someone's arm candy and could be bought. "Thanks for the offer," she said carelessly, "but I like my friends."

Rafael was about to say more when he looked past her and reached for something in his jacket. Lyla took a step back and collided with an unyielding body. A hand gripped her waist. She had no doubt who was holding her so possessively. What surprised her was the way Rafael's face morphed into cold fury. What the fuck?

"Stay away from Lyla," Gavin hissed.

Rafael's eyes flicked from Gavin back to her. "You've been holding out on me, beautiful. You didn't tell me who your *friend* is."

Gavin's grip tightened. "Keep your distance. She's mine."

Rafael's face turned calculating as he looked at her. He went from friendly stranger to dangerous in a millisecond.

"What if she doesn't want to stay away from me?" Rafael asked.

"She will," Gavin said. "I'll make sure of it."

Rafael inclined his head. "We shall see, Pyre."

The men at Rafael's table watched Gavin as if he were a ticking bomb. Maybe he was. Gavin ushered her past Rafael to their table in the back where Manny waited.

"We're leaving," Gavin said shortly. "Rafael is here."

Manny rose without a word, and they left the restaurant. Gavin took Lyla's hand and squeezed a bit too tightly. She slapped his wrist, and when he looked down at her, she felt a chill. He looked murderous.

"What the—?" she began, but he shook his head and walked even faster.

He led her out of one casino and into the next, which he owned. He pointed at a restaurant.

"Dad, get us a table. I need to talk to Lyla," Gavin said with a savage bite.

Manny eyed Lyla before he ambled into the restaurant. The servers screamed and rushed to hug and kiss him in welcome while Gavin walked her in the opposite direction. It took her only a minute to figure out where they were going. She tugged to get away from him, which resulted in him picking her up without breaking his stride.

"Let me go," she hissed and tried to smile reassuringly at the employees who goggled at the sight of their CEO toting a woman around. "You're making a scene."

"I'm trying *not* to make a scene," Gavin hissed. "Shut up, Lyla."

She wanted to push it but decided getting into a public knockdown, drag out fight in front of his employees wasn't the best place to confront him. When he slammed into his office, he locked the door. Lyla knew from her time working for Manny that the executive offices in every casino were soundproof. That realization penetrated a moment too late.

"How do you know Rafael?" Gavin asked, body vibrating with tension.

"Who is he?"

"Lyla." Gavin's hands balled into fists at his sides, and she took a step back. "Tell me how you know him."

"I met him last night."

Gavin blinked. "What?"

"I met him at Lux."

"How the *fuck* did Rafael Vega get into my club?" Gavin shouted, veins in his neck popping.

The explosion propelled Lyla backward. The back of her

legs hit the couch, and she sat with a plop. She shrank into the cushions as Gavin approached.

"So you met him at Lux," Gavin said, voice calm but everything else about him pulsed with rage. "Where in Lux? What did he say?"

"He didn't say much. He bought me drinks." When he gaped at her, she said defensively, "I don't have money!"

Gavin leaned down, fists depressing the cushions on either side of her. "Lyla, you don't let *anyone* buy you a drink, least of all Rafael Vega."

"Who is he, and why are you so pissed?"

"He's a sadistic fuck. He runs the prostitution ring in Las Vegas."

Lyla's stomach churned. The charming, cocky guy who bought her a drink last night ran a prostitution ring? Seriously, how the fuck did she attract men like that?

Gavin caught her chin in his hand. "You don't *ever* talk to him."

"I don't want to," she said honestly.

That didn't seem to make any impact on Gavin's simmering rage.

"I can't leave you alone for a minute," he hissed. "Did he say anything else?"

"He asked for my number but—"

"He what?"

Gavin grabbed a paperweight and hurled it. Glass exploded, leaving a fist-sized hole in the wall. Lyla got to her feet as he swept everything off his desk and onto the floor. Papers flew, his lamp shattered and pens flew like daggers.

"Gavin, stop!" When he reached for his computer, she rushed forward and grabbed his arms. "Gavin!"

At her touch, he froze. She could feel him vibrating

beneath her fingertips. The force of his emotions was nearly physical. She felt battered by it but didn't back away.

"Nothing happened," she said, hoping to get through to him. "He didn't even touch me."

For a moment, she wasn't sure he heard her, and then his mouth was on hers. He clasped her head still for his assault. Fear collided with lust and exploded inside her, sweeping away all rational thought.

"You're mine," Gavin said when he drew back, gazing down at her with a hunger that should have made her run. "No one else's."

Gavin gripped her hips and set her on the edge of his desk. Before she could figure what he was doing, he brushed her dress up, spread her thighs, and ripped her thong.

"Gavin, what—?"

His tongue slipped into her vagina, and her mind went blank with shock. Gavin dragged her to the edge of the desk and ate her as if his life depended on it. One hand pinned her thigh open for his assault while the other cupped her ass, drawing her tight to his intimate kiss. Lyla couldn't think as pleasure ricocheted through her. Gavin's talented mouth suckled her clit. Before she could counteract the pleasure or get a hold on it, her climax, violent and unstoppable, blasted through her. Lyla wrapped her legs around his head, body bowing as he slammed his fingers into her, eliciting mind-numbing pleasure so great, her mind shut down and her body took over. When it became too much, Lyla yanked on his hair, trying to get his mouth away from her. Gavin moaned but didn't move. She could hear him swallow as he lapped up her juices.

"G-Gavin, please stop," she said hoarsely, shuddering.

Without moving his head, he pushed her, so she sprawled on her back in a boneless heap on the slick surface of his desk. He used his fingers this time, curling and stroking. The heat began to build again. She tried to kick him, but his hands pinned her wide, and she had no defense as he teased oversensitive nerves.

"I-I can't," she panted even as another climax punched through her.

Lyla erupted, body jerking as Gavin pulled the strings like the master he was. When rational thought returned, she found him standing over her, fingers still buried between her legs. His eyes were ablaze with lust.

"I didn't ask the first time. You say I raped you. Will you let me have you?"

It would feel damn good, but... "No."

Gavin's finger gave her clit a last swirl that made her gasp. He took his hand from between her legs and licked it. Lyla's stomach clenched.

"This will tide me over until you ask me."

She forced herself to sit up as she trembled uncontrollably. "Ask you?"

"You will," Gavin said as he walked into the bathroom, washed his hands, and fixed his hair. He came back with a washcloth and efficiently cleaned her before he dragged her off the desk and gave her a deep kiss. "Dad's waiting."

Lyla's mouth fell open. Before she could get her wits together, Gavin ushered her to the door and past his secretary.

"Have someone clean up my office. I made a mess," Gavin said.

The hand on her waist tightened when she hissed at the double entendre. Lyla's feet moved, but she didn't remember the trip through the casino back to the restaurant. Manny was in the middle of his meal when they walked in. He took one look at them and clapped his hands together.

"You are back together?" Manny shouted, drawing the attention of the other patrons and half the staff.

Lyla wanted to disappear. "No, Manny."

Manny looked crestfallen.

"Soon," Gavin predicted as he guided Lyla into a chair, kissed her cheek, and took the seat beside her.

"Progress is good," Manny said as he cut into his steak. "I ordered for you both. Eat up. I'm sure you're both starved."

Lyla choked and ignored Gavin's chuckle. Gavin went from The Hulk to a gentleman in the blink of an eye. What the fuck? He made her orgasm. Again. Multiple times. No dream to blame this time. His expertise was undeniable, but if it had been any man between her legs, would she have responded the way she had?

"Eat," Gavin said firmly.

When she glanced at him, he gestured to her pasta.

"It's our specialty. You'll like it."

He was acting as if the tantrum in his office never happened... as if the *three years* she was gone never happened.

"You're insane," she whispered.

Gavin shrugged. "Where you're concerned, I don't act rationally."

That was the understatement of the century. Nothing was rational about Gavin. He blackmailed her into coming back to Las Vegas and wanted to resume a nonexistent relationship. He made no sense. He wasn't a homeless psycho or ugly bastard who had to pay for a mail-order bride. He could have *anyone*. Why fixate on her? And why oh, why did she go off like a geyser every time he touched her? This couldn't be happening.

"I can feed you," Gavin said and reached for her fork.

She slapped his hand away. "I can feed myself."

"You need to keep your strength up," Gavin said with a straight face.

"Fuck you, Gavin," she hissed.

"I can't wait."

Manny nearly choked on his steak from laughing so hard.

8

"No!" Lyla shouted.

Carmen put a hand on her hip. "What the hell is wrong with you?"

"I am *not* going to another club with Gavin!"

"I'm going too," Carmen said.

"Big help you were last night when he had me pinned against a wall!"

Carmen licked her lips. "You fucked in a hallway?"

Lyla wanted to pull her hair out. "No!"

Carmen lost interest immediately. "Vinny will be there too. I haven't been to The Room yet. It's not crazy like Lux. It's a classier club."

"I'm not going."

"Don't be such a baby. I brought you a hot dress."

Lyla gave the cute dress a cursory glance. "I'm not leaving this room."

"You wanna bet?" Carmen asked, tapping her heel.

Lyla's heart sank. Carmen could be a bulldog when she wanted something. If she told her cousin that Gavin ate her out as if she were the elixir of life and gave her a mind-blowing orgasm, Carmen would be even more ruthless.

Lyla had barely survived lunch. Gavin talked to his father as if the incident with Rafael and interlude in his office had never happened. He was so calm and collected; she would've thought she imagined everything if her body didn't have aftershocks still coursing through her. Manny was gleeful and wouldn't listen when she told him not to get his hopes up. While she considered nailing her bedroom door shut, Carmen barged in and announced that they were going out again. Her life was seriously fucked.

Carmen forced her into a shower and made her look presentable while Lyla tried to fortify her defenses. She had no idea where she stood with Gavin, and she lost major ground with Manny today. He thought they had sex. Well, *she* had. Manny nearly danced into the house this afternoon. Her escape route was closing, and she needed it to reopen. Gavin was wise to her tricks and wouldn't respond to her attempts to find him a distraction. So what tactic could she adopt to keep him at bay?

Even as they pulled up to another Pyre Casino and Gavin and Vinny appeared, Lyla still wasn't sure how to handle him. Gavin helped Lyla out of the car and gave her a thorough kiss.

"I can still taste you," Gavin said when he drew away.

Appalled, she elbowed him in the stomach and tried to walk into the casino without him. He laughed and caught up with her, dragging her beneath his arm.

"No one tastes like you, baby," Gavin said.

"You'd know," she snapped.

"You really think I still want other women?"

"Nothing's changed."

He opened his mouth to respond, but the club bouncers inclining their heads respectfully distracted him.

"Mr. Pyre," they said, tones nearly reverent.

The Room was a high-end club with modern lounging furniture and blue lighting. A live band played bluesy, melancholy music that set the mood. Gavin guided her up the stairs where behemoth-sized security manned the second floor. It looked out over the club with private alcoves and white pod chairs that two people could comfortably sleep in. Frosted white glass separated the top floor into private sections. Lyla could see the silhouettes of the people next to them. Did people come here to fuck or watch other people fuck? Who wanted to fuck in a club? Gavin, of course. It turned her stomach, and when he tried to pull her down to share his pod chair, she resisted, but Gavin wasn't going to take no for an answer. He gave her a firm yank, and when she plopped down beside him, he wrapped her close. Carmen and Vinny took another pod chair while Ricardo took the last.

Scantily clad women swarmed around them, dropping artfully arranged appetizers on a tiny table in front of each pod. Even though she knew Carmen, Vinny, and Ricardo were nearby, they weren't able to talk to one another over the music. The pods were designed to encase each couple in a dome of privacy. This was too intimate for her peace of mind.

"Eat," Gavin said.

Because she wanted to calm her jittery stomach, she complied. The food was excellent, and the champagne washed it all down, mellowing her out. Lyla watched the singer on stage perform, face rapt with emotion. Was that Ariel, Jonathan's favorite female singer and celebrity crush? Lyla downed the rest of the champagne but couldn't drown out the guilt and pain. How was he? She wished she could call him to apologize, to explain, but she couldn't. Her eyes burned.

"What are you thinking about?" Gavin asked, his warm breath brushing over her cheek.

Lyla reached for another champagne glass and glanced sideways at Gavin who looked devilishly handsome. She tried to put the events of this afternoon out of her mind, but it was impossible. How much of what Jonathan said during the dream had actually been Gavin? Lyla licked her lip, which was nearly healed. Her mind moved over the way Gavin took care of her that first night, bathing and tending to her with soft kisses and gentle hands. The next morning, he'd morphed into a monster. Then he exploded over Rafael asking for her number and gave her orgasms? Who was he? *You humanize him*, Manny claimed. Gavin and Manny straddled the line between legal and illegal business and had no qualms about it. Gavin lived an unconventional, no-holds-barred life. It was no wonder he was part civilized, part barbarian.

"What do you want, Gavin?" The question popped out of her mouth before she could stop it. The champagne loosened up her tongue and body, which leaned against him.

"I want many things," Gavin said.

"And you always get what you want?" Lyla asked.

"Until you, yes."

"What do you want from me? You can get what you want from anyone."

Gavin's hand splayed on her spine, branding her. She tried to twist away from him.

"Gavin—"

"I cheated on you because I hate the power you have over me."

Lyla froze. The hand on her back increased its pressure ever so slightly before it relaxed again. She could feel his internal struggle. Lyla shook her head, absolutely sure she didn't want to hear what he had to say.

"No, Gavin—" she said and tried to push away.

"When Dad introduced us, I knew you were it for me. I didn't like it. I was too young to commit to one woman, so I fucked around because I could."

Lyla let out an angry, disgusted sound and shoved against his chest. Man logic. Ego. She had no patience or interest in either.

"I thought no matter what I did, you would forgive me. I took your love for granted. When you found out, you changed. The way you looked at me... You wouldn't let me touch you, and no matter what I promised, you didn't believe me. You wouldn't let me fix it. I could feel you slipping through my fingers. I was going to propose, but you took off." He brushed a soft kiss on the corner of her mouth. "I know I drove you away. I was so fucking scared that someone had you and would..." He shook his head. "I figured that if you weren't being held against your will, you'd come back to me eventually." His eyes hardened. "Then I found out no one took you, and you weren't just okay, you were doing fucking fine without me. I hated that. That you could live without me, that you had moved on. I hate it because I can't be without you."

Panic spread through her, a cold wave that made her skin erupt in goose bumps as he stared at her, resolve and something dangerous clear in his yes.

"I'm going to do whatever it takes to make you love me again," Gavin vowed.

Lyla didn't want to be here. She didn't want to be won over or seduced. She wanted a man who didn't have a dark side, a hair-trigger temper, and a basement where he tortured and killed. She wanted a man who wouldn't hurt her—emotionally or physically. She didn't want a man people feared, including herself. She wanted a man she could depend on. When would Gavin realize she wasn't a love-struck fool? That she couldn't give him what he wanted? He wanted the girl she'd been.

"We're over, Gavin," Lyla said, willing herself to believe it.

"We've never been over."

"Three years, Gavin. *Three.*"

"That wasn't my choice. I don't care how much time passes. We're meant for each other."

Lyla shook her head wildly, willing him to see, to understand. "We're not. I can't. I'm not what you want."

"You're exactly what I want."

"You don't know what you want!"

"Of course, I do."

Lyla *hated* feeling like this—desperate, afraid, and fucking needy. When her eyes filled with tears, Gavin groaned.

"Fuck, don't cry."

"I can't do this."

"You can. You can take it, Lyla."

"I have a life, Gavin. I was happy—"

"You weren't," he said in a near feral snarl.

"Stop saying that!"

Gavin's hands sank into her hair as he pulled her close. "Just as I know you were meant for me, you know it too. You feel it."

"No," she whispered and tried to shake her head, but his grip wouldn't allow it.

"No matter what you believe about me, Lyla, I care. I

never stopped looking, never stopped wishing you were here with me. Does that sound like a man who doesn't know what he wants?"

"It sounds like an obsession. That means nothing."

"Obsession." He tasted the word and apparently approved of it because he nodded. "Yes."

Lyla couldn't stop the flare in her belly. There was a war taking place inside her. Heart and mind clashed. Was it better to live a safe life or live dangerously, straddling the line between love and hate and life and death?

"Whatever you need to be mine again, I'll do," Gavin said.

"I don't trust you."

"I'll work on it. What else?"

Having Gavin's entire focus unnerved her. He looked at her as if she mattered, as if his life depended on the words that fell from her lips. Lyla couldn't take it. She averted her eyes and tried to regulate her breathing.

"What else, Lyla?" Gavin insisted. "What do I have to do to get you back?"

Was she in an alternative universe? Was she actually contemplating giving him a chance? He wanted a list of rules? She would give him one. "Don't threaten me; don't threaten people I love," she said.

Gavin's face hardened, but he nodded.

"You don't hurt me *ever*."

"I won't."

She didn't believe him. His temper had gotten worse over the years, not better. "If this doesn't work out, you have to let me go. You can't expect anything I feel to be genuine if I'm a captive."

His fingers twitched. She could see that this last one went against his need to control, to dominate. Before, his alpha personality excited her. Now, she saw the damage it wrought, and it scared her. She wasn't a child who needed to be monitored. She was a full-grown woman who had been on her own for years and was fully capable of accomplishing what she set her mind to.

"How long?" Gavin asked.

"Three months?"

"Give me three years."

"You have to be joking."

"I'm not," he said through clenched teeth. "You took away three years; you give me back three."

She shook her head at his logic. Psycho Pyres. "Six months."

"Two years."

"Eight months."

"One year."

Their negotiating was pointless since she already had a deal with Manny, but if that backfired, she needed another out. Could she last a year? She could hibernate in Manny's house when Gavin became too much to handle. A year in Vegas for real freedom where she didn't have to look over her shoulder? A year in Las Vegas with Carmen, her parents, Manny, and Gavin. Before she discovered Gavin's infidelity, she'd been happy here. She could spin this to her benefit and spend time with Manny and Carmen. She was giving Gavin a year, but that didn't mean she was spending a year with *him*. She was committing to staying *in Vegas* for a year.

"Final offer?" she asked, and he nodded. "Fine. One year."

He closed his eyes. When he opened them, they were unguarded and filled with joy. When was the last time she saw Gavin like this? When she first met him? When Manny began to step back from the company, Gavin had changed. With more responsibility came less free time. It wasn't just the legitimate side of the business he had to tend to, either. At the thought of the man in the basement, Lyla's stomach clenched. It was a good thing she was staying with Manny. She didn't want to witness any more beatings or become Gavin's punching bag if he lost it. Distance was key when dealing with him.

Lyla leaned forward to see into the other pod where Carmen and Vinny were making out. "I want to dance!" she shouted.

Carmen heard her because she broke her lip lock with her irritated husband and bustled over. She took Lyla's hand and led her downstairs. The music picked up when they stepped on the dance floor. Lyla gave herself up to the beat. Life was too complicated to plan, and it would do whatever it felt like anyway. She had no control over anything. She was so fucking tired of being on the run, of trying to antici-pate bad shit. She let it all go and danced her troubles away.

Large hands splayed on her abdomen and pulled her back against a solid body. Lyla kept her eyes closed as they moved. Songs changed, but the hands didn't leave her. At some point, she turned to face him and realized what a big mistake that was. His cock pressed against her belly and she saw that his face looked carnal in the blue lights from above. She hated that she responded to the desire on his face. How could she want him even after all the things he'd done? Ashamed, she turned to Carmen who was dry humping Vinny.

"I'm done. I want to go home," Lyla said.

"I'll take you," Gavin said.

"I rode with—" Lyla began.

"I know."

Gavin pulled her off the dance floor and jerked his head at Ricardo. They walked out of the club and past the line of people still waiting to get in. They were both soaked with sweat. Lyla was tired. She wanted to take a shower and crash in Manny's guest bedroom, away from Gavin. His energy buzzed around her. People felt the force of his personality and got out of the way. Gavin had been groomed to lead, protect, and succeed. A woman who belonged to a man like Gavin had to stand toe to toe with him and be able to take the heat. She wasn't that woman.

The Rolls Royce was waiting for them. Ricardo got behind the wheel, and when Gavin helped her into the car, she let out a long breath until Gavin rounded the car and got in on the other side.

She gaped at him. "What the hell are you doing?"

"Seeing you home. That's what you do after a date."

A date? Oh, fuck no. "And how are you going to get home?"

"Blade can pick me up from Dad's house."

She relaxed fractionally and belted herself in. She wanted away from him, but of course, he wouldn't go until he was ready.

"Tell me about the life you built without me."

Lyla's head whipped around. "What?"

"Tell me why you want to return to that life." His eyes flashed in warning. "Don't bring up that fuck. We both know you don't have feelings for him."

"I love—"

Gavin clamped a hand over her mouth. "What did I say?"

She glared mutinously at him. She loved Jonathan, didn't she? Then why had the ache of leaving him gone from relentless pain to a distant pang?

"Don't test my control where he's concerned. He should never have touched what was mine. Be grateful I've had you since you arrived and that allows him to continue living his pathetic life."

Gavin dropped his hand, and she stared at him.

"You really are obsessed."

"I claimed you at eighteen."

"You claimed me when I was too young and stupid to know any different!"

Gavin snorted. "You're an old soul, Lyla, and wise beyond your years. You knew what you were getting into with me."

Lyla hated that he was right. She'd suspected a dark side to Gavin and his business, but she chose not to focus on that and put her head in the sand.

"I didn't know everything," she mumbled.

"I can protect you from that shit. It's not an issue."

"Not an issue?" she repeated incredulously and thought of Eli and his mother who was now in the hospital.

"There are safeguards in place to make sure the Pyre Casinos continue even if the other side of the business is questioned."

"You have enough money from the casinos. Why bother with the illegal stuff?"

"If we don't run the underworld, someone else will, and there would be another asshole to deal with. It's easier to run it all."

"I don't want to be a part of that, Gavin."

"You aren't," he said, his voice clipped and impatient.

"I am."

"How so? You don't know what I do."

"I do." The words were out of her mouth before she could stop them.

"Explain."

Lyla stared at him, mouth dry. She couldn't retract her words and didn't have a hope in hell of distracting him. Gavin's eyes pierced her through the dim light. Something dark unfurled between them. She saw suspicion and then comprehension in his eyes a moment before they went expressionless.

"I always wondered why you left when you did. You didn't run because of the girls, did you?" Gavin murmured.

Lyla reached behind her for the door handle. Lyla could taste violence in the air. The taut silence and the way he watched her made her heart skip with fear. This was the man capable of strangling her, the one who terrified her. This was the man she fled from.

"You saw what happened in the basement, didn't you?" Gavin's flat voice scared the crap out of her.

"Gavin—"

"Answer me."

The car stopped, and Lyla bolted. She ran into the mansion and heard Manny call her name as she streaked past the living room, but she didn't stop. She couldn't. Fear had her by the throat. Lyla ran into the guest bedroom and bolted the door. She wrung her hands before her eyes fell on a dresser. She pushed and heaved with all her might until it was in front of the door as an extra barricade. When that was done, Lyla escaped into the bathroom and locked that door too. Nothing would stop Gavin. She knew that, but she wouldn't make it easy on him. What would he do now that she knew his secret? She was a liability. Oh, fuck. Oh, *fuck*. How could she be so fucking stupid to let that slip? He was too sharp not to figure out that her timing was suspicious.

Lyla searched the bathroom for a weapon, but nothing

would protect her from a gun or fists trained by UFC fighters. Lyla sat on the lip of the tub and waited for pounding fists on the door or a chainsaw, but there was nothing. Lyla paced, and when she couldn't stand the suspense, she got down on her stomach and looked beneath the door into the bedroom. The dresser was still in place.

Lyla waited for what felt like hours. Her anxiety didn't wane. She decided to take a shower, wrapped herself in a robe, and waited. No sound. No entreaty from Manny to open the door and no forceful entry. What did that mean? Lyla didn't have the energy to figure it out. She made a nest of towels on the ground, curled into a ball, and waited for whatever came next.

Lyla woke slowly, warm and content. She stretched beneath the covers and yawned as she opened her eyes. Morning light filtered through the window of Manny's guest bedroom. Something niggled at the back of her mind, but she was too tired to concentrate. She sat up in bed and froze when she saw Gavin sitting on a chair.

Lyla stilled as memories of last night flooded back. Her eyes went to the door. The dresser was back in place against the wall. She was in bed instead of on the bathroom floor where she fell asleep. What the fuck? How—?

"How much did you see?" Gavin asked.

His voice was rough and raspy. He wore the same suit from last night, which meant he never left. He looked dangerous with a five o'clock shadow and bright amber eyes.

Lyla opened and closed her mouth but couldn't find her voice.

"Lyla, how much did you see?"

Lyla swallowed hard and gripped handfuls of the bed sheet before she admitted, "Everything."

The air in the room thickened. She didn't notice Gavin make any movement, but she sensed his body tighten in preparation. Her flight instinct urged her to run, but she knew it was useless. Nothing would stop him from getting to her.

"Why did you go to the basement?" Gavin asked.

There was no use in trying to cover up the truth now. "I didn't trust you after the orgy. I thought you might be..."

"You thought I would cheat on you in our own home? Even after I said I wouldn't?"

Lyla didn't have to answer. A muscle jumped in his jaw. He leaned forward, bracing his elbows on his knees.

"You heard why he was there?"

Lyla was glad her stomach was empty so she wouldn't embarrass herself and vomit. She could see the guard's face in her mind, clear as day. He haunted her. Could she have stopped Gavin or would she be dead and buried along with that man three years ago?

"I did what I had to," Gavin said.

Lyla couldn't look at him. Before she witnessed the brutality in the basement, she ignored what the Pyres did in the dark because she could. When she saw what Gavin was capable of, his infidelity seemed trifling. She didn't want to be around someone who could do that to another human being. She left, disillusioned and chilled to the core.

"So you left because of what you saw in the basement, not the women," Gavin said.

"I left because of both. I don't want to be a part of this life, Gavin." Her voice broke, and she looked down at her trembling hands.

"You shouldn't have seen what you did."

Lyla lifted her head. "But I did. Now what?"

Gavin's silence made her heart race. In a sudden burst of anger that startled them both, she erupted from the bed. She rearranged the robe to cover her adequately and fisted her hands at her sides as she faced Gavin.

"I know what you do for work, Gavin, and I can't stand it," she said, voice shaking. "His face haunts me. I can hear his pleas in my sleep. You didn't stop. You *tortured* him." She had to stop as bile rose in her throat.

"I needed to know if he was telling the truth."

Lyla slashed her hand through the air. "Slicing his throat would have been better than what you did."

"You don't understand—"

"And I don't want to!" she screeched.

Gavin flinched but showed no other outward reaction to her outburst. She could feel herself splintering into pieces. Watching the man she loved torture someone to death destroyed her. When she left Las Vegas, she was a shadow of her former self.

Her emotions were a tangled mess. This man incited so much in her—fear, lust, confusion, and love. She hated that even after all this time, she cared for him. She loved Gavin with every particle of her being and had never been the same since. Gavin stole her innocence in more ways than one. He branded her soul. No matter what she did, she couldn't exorcise him. She clung to Jonathan because he was Gavin's polar opposite. Did she really love Jonathan? She was grateful he took her in, but what she felt for him paled in comparison to what she felt for Gavin.

"You don't have to do this," she said, voice shaking.

Gavin said nothing.

"You have more money than you could possibly spend in

your lifetime. Why risk the Pyre Empire over another revenue with so much risk?" Lyla's eyes filled with tears. "How do you think I feel, knowing that the food I eat and the clothes I wear were bought through blood and murder? Why do you think I left everything behind? I would rather work forty hours a week to earn just enough to survive and have a clear conscience than—"

"Don't, Lyla. That blood's on my hands, not yours."

"And that makes it better?" she challenged.

He looked so remote. She hated it. Lyla took her life in her hands and walked toward him. His eyes tracked her every move and went heavy-lidded when she knelt in front of him. Moving slowly, she reached out and grabbed his hands. She cradled them in hers and looked up.

"You don't have to have blood on your hands, Gavin."

"You have no idea what's at stake."

"*Your life* is at stake. What if they catch you? You could go to prison for murder!"

"That won't happen."

Lyla dropped his hands and rose. There was no reasoning with him. "So arrogant and pigheaded." She paced away and then turned back. "I don't understand you, Gavin. I loved you. I gave you everything only to find out you cheated the whole time. Not only that, but you have this other life you don't tell me about that forces you to do things you shouldn't have to do. You can't tell me it doesn't haunt you. Is that where the other women come in? Is that where *I* come in?" She paused, but there was no answer. "What else aren't you telling me? What else am I too stupid or young or naïve to know about? What we had, Gavin, it wasn't a relationship. It was a role, one you can have any woman fill."

Lyla wrapped her arms around herself. His eyes were trained on her, monitoring every nuance.

"I want out," she whispered.

"No."

"I never told a soul, and I won't!"

Gavin ran his hands through his hair. "God, you're a piece of work."

"And you aren't? You're hot, cold, hot..." Her voice faded away when their eyes locked. A shaft of heat burst in her belly and spread low. "Fuck! I hate you!"

"Is that why you don't want my hands on you? Because of what you saw me do?"

"You were so cold." She shivered and tried to shake away the awful memories. "You can turn your emotions on and off. That's why you were able to cheat on me and come home with a clear conscience. It's why you're good at doing the illegal side of the business." She tapped her chest, trying to get him to understand her. "That's not me."

No response, no flicker of emotion in his eyes.

"I told you, this isn't going to work," she said, voice low

"It will if you let me take care of it."

"By controlling what I do, where I go?"

"It's the only way I know to keep you safe."

"If you weren't doing whatever the fuck you're doing on the side, you wouldn't need to keep me safe! Don't you see that?"

"This is what my family has always done."

"And traditions are meant to be broken," she spat.

"I never let that shit touch you, not then and not now."

"The thing with Rafael... You can't stop it from touching me."

"You won't see him ever again."

She shook her head. "You can't control that."

"Yes, I can."

"By keeping me imprisoned?"

"By putting a man on you for your own safety."

"Now we're back to square one. If you weren't in the business, I wouldn't need a bodyguard. I can't live this way. It doesn't matter how long I'm here. I know what I can and can't live with." Lyla shook her head. "I *won't*."

Gavin got to his feet. Lyla couldn't stop her quick retreat and noticed his jaw lock.

"You think I'm a monster."

His voice was completely devoid of emotion.

"It doesn't matter what I think," she whispered.

Gavin stared at her for a long minute before he walked out the door. Lyla stared after him, not sure what just happened. She felt as if she had just avoided an execution. She was breathing hard, and her palms were damp with sweat. Her cell phone rang on the nightstand. She glanced at the screen and picked it up with a sigh of relief.

"Carmen."

"Hey, girl. I'm heading to the mall. Want to keep me company?" Carmen asked.

Lyla could tell from the whooshing sound in the background that Carmen probably had the top down on her convertible. "Yes!"

"Be there in five."

Lyla dashed into the bathroom and made herself look decent before she rushed downstairs where she found Manny pacing.

"Baby girl, we need to talk." Manny's eyes were troubled. "Gavin just left. What did you say to him?"

Too much, too little. Lyla shrugged. "We're not meant to be, Manny. I think he's beginning to see it."

"I'm sorry you saw what happened in Gavin's basement." Manny ran a hand through his hair. "It was business."

Lyla had no doubt that Manny did atrocious things

during his time as ruler of the underworld. How was she supposed to feel about these men she cared for? How did she reconcile the men she knew with the ruthless dictators that did what had to be done in the crime world? "I know it's business, Manny; I just don't want to be around it."

"He can shield you from it—"

"Manny," she said and squeezed his hand, "this type of stuff isn't for me."

"We're not asking you to deal with it. You were never supposed to see... Gavin, the look on his face when he left..." He stared at her imploringly. "You have to fix it."

Lyla ignored the stab in her belly. She was well on her way to making Gavin realize that they weren't meant for each other. Letting him believe she thought he was a monster got her a gigantic step closer to freedom. She averted her eyes from Manny because she couldn't stand to see him in distress.

She squeezed his hand as a car horn honked. "I love you, Manny, but I'm not the one for Gavin."

"But you are," Manny insisted. "I know it!"

The honk came again. "I'm going out with Carmen. I'll be back," she said and kissed him on the cheek. How could she explain that she couldn't condone the things they did? She didn't see things in shades of gray like them. They justified murders by putting it under the label of business. She wasn't that open minded and didn't want to be. Her time away from Las Vegas had solidified her beliefs. It was better to live a clean, uneventful, possibly boring life than to live on the edge.

Lyla rushed out the front door, desperate for fresh air and time away from the Pyre men. Sure enough, Carmen's convertible top was down. She would have been windblown, but her hair was done in a slick, kickass braid. Lyla slid into the passenger seat, and they were off.

"Anything exciting happen last night?" Carmen hollered.

"No!" Lyla shouted back. She wasn't in the mood to discuss Gavin. "What are we shopping for?"

"Don't know yet."

Carmen sped toward the city and kicked on the radio, which spat out old school tunes. Lyla sang along in an effort to forget Gavin's expression as he walked away from her. Why the hell did she feel so guilty? She was being honest. She didn't want to live that way. It would kill her slowly but surely. The people of Las Vegas had questionable morals. When you grew up in a city of illusions and sin, it was easy to justify almost everything. But murder? No. Gavin was too volatile. She couldn't handle him and honestly, never had. He wasn't meant for her. She just had to convince Manny of that.

She and Carmen shopped hand in hand. Lyla was distinctly aware of the fact that she had no money and wondered how she could access her bank accounts but then shrugged that off. It wasn't worth looking into, not when her life was so out of sorts. Plus, she had a sneaking suspicion that Gavin took care of it.

Carmen loved beautiful and well-made things. She took pictures of what she wanted and sent them to Vinny in a not so subtle hint even though she could whip out a credit card and pay for it herself. Carmen loved presents.

"You're happy," Lyla commented, examining her cousin who modeled lingerie in a mirror.

"Of course," Carmen said without hesitation. "Vinny loves me, I get to do what I want, and you're back."

"I'm back temporarily."

Carmen snorted. "Girl, don't think I didn't see the way

Gavin looked at you last night. Stop fooling yourself. The man is gone over you. You could ask him for anything and get it in a snap."

"He's in temporary lust with me," Lyla corrected.

Carmen turned to face her, and Lyla had to admit her body looked amazing.

"Lyla Dalton, you need to get your head out of your ass."

Lyla blinked. "Excuse me?"

"Gavin Pyre can have anyone he wants. Capisce?"

"Yes," she agreed.

"Then why would he look for you for three years and take time away from work to dance with you last night? He's been taking you to *his* clubs, so everyone will know your face and give you whatever you want. I'm gonna tell you something, cousin, and I don't care if you believe me or not. I haven't seen Gavin with anyone since you left. I know that doesn't mean a lot to you, but he could have replaced you, and he didn't. You are the only woman he claimed, the only one he lived with. That's huge. I know you don't trust him, but if you talk to him, like *really* talk to him, you might be surprised what he's willing to do to get you to stay."

Lyla didn't tell her cousin she already committed herself to a year. There was no sense in getting her hopes up. If she had done as much damage this morning as Manny implied, her one-year commitment might be void.

"I'll wait outside," Lyla said, rising.

Carmen gave her an impatient huff, which she ignored. Lyla made her way out of the shop bustling with Playboy bunny type women, strippers, and male oglers. The mall was teeming with people. She narrowly avoided a collision with a reckless senior in a wheelchair and ambled over to the restrooms, texting Carmen as she went.

Lyla used the facilities and was in the middle of wiping

her hands with a paper towel when the door burst open. She looked up and caught a fleeting glimpse of two Hispanic men before they were on her. Lyla tried to scream, but one of them covered her mouth with a cloth soaked in something. She couldn't breathe. She fought against her attacker, but her head was spinning, and then everything went black.

9

LYLA'S HEAD THROBBED, and her body ached as if she had
the flu. She tried to sit up and discovered that her hands and
feet were bound, and she had a strip of duct tape over her
mouth. A sheer red cloth covered her eyes, and she lay on a
dirty, lumpy mattress in a concrete room with one window.
Unadulterated panic filled her as she remembered the
attack in the mall bathroom. Who were these men and why
had they taken her? She held up her bound hands up and
saw a plastic tie cutting into her skin. There would be no
getting out of this. She looked around the barren room and
focused on a small window high up on the wall. Even if she
managed to get to her feet, she wasn't tall enough to see
outside.

Lyla heard the echo of voices a moment before the door
slammed open. The Hispanic men who attacked her in the
bathroom stood there. One of them swaggered in with a
cocky grin while the other hung back, expressionless. They
were dressed in basketball jerseys and low riding shorts that
showed off their underwear. They couldn't be older than
twenty-five. Punks. Wannabe gangsters. The fact that they

didn't bother to conceal their faces made her stomach curdle with anxiety.

"Had a nice nap?" the one who entered the room asked. "I was hoping you were still asleep so I could wake you up the way I wanted."

He gave her a lecherous smile that made her shuffle backward until she hit the wall. Her useless hands twitched in front of her as she waited for him to make a move.

"You don't look like Pyre's type," he said.

Even though she suspected that Gavin had something to do with this, the confirmation made her body go icy with fear. Oh, fuck.

The cocky bastard sat on the edge of the bed. Without hesitation, he reached out and squeezed her breast through the thin material of her dress. Lyla screamed through the tape and tried to knock his hand away with her bound hands. He lay beside her and dragged her on top of him. His hands went under her dress, clutched her bare ass and mashed their crotches together. He moaned and bucked, bouncing her on top of him like a depraved animal, his hot breath fanning her face.

Lyla struggled, but she couldn't do anything with her hands being held over her head and her legs bound together. This couldn't be happening. He dry humped her while his partner watched from the doorway. Lyla screamed into the tape as the man beneath her thrust faster. The thin material of his pants stopping him from full penetration.

"Hurry the fuck up," the other man said, leaning against the doorjamb.

"You like that, bitch?" the man beneath her panted.

Lyla screamed profanities as he went faster, pumping his hips so hard she knew her thighs would bruise. Lyla looked away as the man came in his pants, grunting and then going

completely lax beneath her. Afraid of puking with tape over
her mouth, Lyla rolled and landed on the dirty concrete.
She used her elbows to push herself into a sitting position
and looked at the remote man standing by the doorway,
watching her with blank eyes. Beyond him, she saw they
were in what looked like an abandoned warehouse. Where
the fuck were they? Were they still in Vegas? It was easier to
focus on that rather than the man panting on the bed
behind her. She felt as if there were spiders crawling over
her skin. She shuddered and fought the plastic tie around
her wrists even though she knew it was pointless.

"Fuck, I needed that," the man on the bed said and
pulled a phone out of his pocket and dialed.

They all listened to the phone ring as he put it on
speaker. Lyla closed her eyes and tried to control the urge
to hurl.

"Who the fuck is this?"

Gavin's voice on the other end of the phone made her
head snap up. Painful relief burst in her chest.

"You don't need to know who it is. All you need to know
is I have your girl," the man on the bed said and winked
at Lyla.

"Let me talk to her," Gavin ordered.

The man on the bed rolled with a squeak of rusty
springs. He gripped her face and ripped the strip of tape off
her mouth. Lyla's face burned, but she didn't make a sound.
Did she still have lips?

"Lyla?" Gavin snarled.

"Gavin—" she said through throbbing lips.

The man shoved her carelessly. Her back hit the wall
hard, and she moaned. She looked up as he stood over her,
the wet spot on his pants obvious.

"Got your attention, Pyre? Your chick is a great lay."

"You touch her, even one finger, and I'll murder you with my bare hands," Gavin said, voice so chilling that her captor stared at the phone for a second before he walked over to his partner and handed the phone over.

"We want ten million. Cash," the calm captor said.

"Drop off?" Gavin asked without missing a beat.

"Reno. Ten o'clock. I'll text the address."

"Who's your boss?"

Gavin sounded calm, but Lyla knew that when his voice went icy like that, heads rolled.

"We don't have a boss," the hotheaded pervert snapped, taking the phone back from his emotionless counterpart. "We're our *own* boss."

"You made a mistake, taking something of mine," Gavin said quietly. "You're walking dead men."

"You have many enemies," the quiet man said. "What did you think would happen once you revealed a weakness?"

"I want to speak to her again," Gavin ordered.

"She can hear you," the stupid captor said in a singsong voice.

"Lyla, I'm coming for you."

The line went dead before she could respond. Lyla couldn't stop shaking. Gavin would come for her; she had no doubt about it. These men, these despicable, perverted, and cold men were walking corpses, and for the first time in her life, she understood that some people shouldn't live. The captor, the one who used her like an inanimate object with no feelings, caught her attention when he brushed his hand over his crotch again. Lyla forced herself to look at him. She poured all the loathing she could into her eyes. She should stay as compliant as possible, but fury pumped through her veins.

"Fuck."

Lyla's heart skipped when she saw that the pervert had another hard on.

"One more time," he said and started forward.

"No." His partner pulled him back. "I shouldn't have let you do it even once. If Pyre thinks you fucked her, he might give us less money."

These men didn't know who they were dealing with. They had no idea how possessive Gavin was. Touching her with one finger was too much. What these men did— kidnapping and using her as a sex doll—bought them a first class ticket to a slow and painful death.

The disgusting captor slipped his hands into his pants and pumped his cock, eyes focused on Lyla's face. "I won't touch her. I'll just come on her face."

"No."

"Come on. I know you want her too."

Lyla gagged as he ran a hand over his partner's crotch, obviously trying to arouse him. The quiet man didn't push his partner's hand away. He stood there, letting the other man stroke his dick through his pants. When the horny pervert dropped to his knees and pulled the man's pants down, Lyla pressed against the wall, wishing it would absorb her. She tried to block out the sounds of what was happening behind her. Oh, God. She heard quickening breaths, moans, and then a grunt of relief.

"Can I have her now?" the eager one asked.

"No."

"*What?* I just sucked you off."

"I'll give you a twenty later."

The door slammed on the pervert's whines. Lyla vomited and then scooted into the opposite corner of the room. This *couldn't* be happening. She jumped at every little sound, praying they wouldn't come back. These men were animals. They didn't look at her as a human being, but something to be used and tossed away like trash. They would fuck her and slit her throat without blinking an eye. There were too young to be so cruel and inhumane.

Lyla closed her eyes and willed Gavin to find her. If she was in Vegas and they were sending him to Reno... Gavin was smart, ruthless, and had countless resources at his fingertips. He would find her. She had to believe that or go mad.

Lyla woke when a hand clamped over her mouth. It was dark. The only light in the room came from a cell phone propped against the wall, which blinded her. As her eyes adjusted, her heart nearly leapt out of her chest when she saw a pair of desperate, depraved eyes staring back at her. The pervert was back. Even as her mind snapped into full wakefulness, he slapped a fresh strip of duct tape over her mouth.

"He stepped out for some cigarettes. We don't have much time," he panted and ripped her dress from neck to belly button.

Lyla bucked and slammed her bound wrists against his chest. The force of it knocked him on his ass. She tried to get to her feet, but with her ankles bound, she toppled back to the floor.

"Stupid bitch. You think you're too good for me, huh?"

He rolled her onto her back and finished ripping her dress in half. Lyla went cold with terror as he grabbed his phone and raised the light so he could see her body, clad only in underwear.

"Fuck, your skin is so pretty. If I had my knife, I'd mark you so every man who fucked you would know I was the first to brand you."

Tears leaked out of the corner of her eyes. Her body trembled in revulsion. He appeared even younger in the harsh light, yet the expression in his eyes was an ancient evil that had no place in a human.

"The world is divided into two types of men," the pervert said as he slid a grubby, dirty hand over her breasts, down her quivering stomach, and then beneath her thong. "Men who ask, and men who *take*." On the last word, he shoved his fingers into her dry core.

Lyla's head kicked back at the pain. Her head hit the concrete so hard she saw stars. The pervert jammed his fingers into her body unmercifully, completely immune to her cries and body's rejection of the intrusion.

"Come on, get wet for me, slut," he said and picked up the pace. "We don't have time."

Lyla cried out as his dirty fingernails jabbed into the wall of her vagina. What the fuck was he doing? Apparently, he only fucked sex dolls because he didn't seem to know that no woman would respond to this. If she wasn't gagged, she would have told him this while she ripped his balls off. Lyla had never been so furious and terrified in her life. Despite her throbbing head and the hopeless situation, she struck out with her bound hands and managed to claw his face. He screeched and dropped the phone, throwing the room into complete darkness.

"You *bitch!*"

The blow came out of nowhere. Lyla's head collided with the floor, and everything went black.

Someone was screaming, and the sound of agony pierced through her pain. Lyla's eyes opened. Dim orange light filtered through the small window high up on the wall. Something warm and sticky covered her. A flurry of movement to her left caught her attention. Even as she tried to remember where she was, she heard an awful gurgling sound, and the screams abruptly stopped. She saw a faint light nearby. Pervert's phone. The light was smothered by the floor and something else...

As memory returned, she reached for the phone. The darkness and awful silence made panic dig into her belly. She raised the phone, which was wet and sticky and aimed the light in the direction of where that awful screaming had been coming from.

A large man crouched over a mangled thing Lyla didn't realize was a body until she registered that the floor was covered in red. Lyla let out a choked sound, and the man turned his head and looked straight at her. At first, she didn't recognize the murderous savage as Gavin since his face was covered in blood. The image of his face bared in a snarl, of his eyes, feral and eclipsed by hatred, made her fingers contract with fear. The phone fell from her hands and lay face down in its owner's blood. The prism of light exposed a gory room out of a horror movie.

"Lyla."

She didn't recognize Gavin's voice. It sounded hoarse as if he'd gargled with glass.

"Lyla, are you—?"

She ripped the tape off her mouth and retched. Even after she emptied everything out of her stomach, she continued to dry heave. Hands skimmed down her back, and then a soaked jacket fell around her. She didn't realize how cold she was until his animal heat engulfed her. When

Gavin lifted her into his arms, she buried her face against his slick chest. Voices echoed around them.

"Holy fuck! Lyla?"

She recognized Vinny's voice but couldn't look up and tell him she was all right because she wasn't sure. Gavin spoke, and she recognized Blade's voice as well. There was a flurry of activity around her, but she blocked it out. Gavin ducked, and then a car door slammed. He cut the ties on her wrists and ankles. Her limbs were numb from being in one position for so long. She wasn't aware she was crying until Gavin spoke.

"Shh, Lyla, you're safe," he said gruffly.

Lyla grabbed fistfuls of his ruined suit and shook her head. She couldn't begin to tell him what happened. He didn't ask. Her body hurt, but what scared her the most was the throbbing between her legs. How far did pervert go before Gavin arrived? How many times did he fuck her? What did he do to her? A sob escaped and then another until she was crying, as she'd never cried before in her life. She pounded Gavin's chest with her fists until she was exhausted. He didn't say a word.

When the car stopped, he carried her outside. The cold night air made her very aware of the fact that Gavin's jacket concealed her nakedness. The tattered strips of her dress were melded to her bloody legs. She hiccupped against Gavin's chest and fought the need to vomit again. She felt so dirty, so violated. Gavin hurried somewhere, never easing his hold on her, never letting her feel for one moment that she was alone.

More voices, hushed and concerned and then the sound of running water. Lyla heard a hollow echo as he stepped into a shower stall. He let her feet touch the tiles. She hissed as feeling returned to her arms and legs with a vengeance.

Her limbs quaked, unable to handle her weight. When Gavin tried to tug the jacket off, she yelled unintelligibly, desperate to hold onto anything that would cover her. With an arm around her waist to hold her up, Gavin stripped off his clothes.

The spray bounced off them and tinged the glass stall with red droplets. Lyla gagged. Gavin turned her sideways so she could puke, but he didn't let her go. He shampooed her hair. Lyla couldn't look at him, her mind locking in a blank state she didn't try to fight. She slumped against Gavin and watched the water wash him clean. He carried her from the shower to the bathtub, which was filled with steaming water and climbed in with her. He wrapped her close and rested his forehead against the back of her head. The heat didn't penetrate, and the bright lights in the bathroom made her feel exposed after the darkness in that hellhole. She couldn't stop shaking.

"I'm sorry. I'm sorry, Lyla. Can you forgive me?" he whispered.

Tears slid down her face. She hugged the jacket to her and pushed at the hands around her waist. She needed to be alone. His arms tightened for a moment before they fell away. They sat like that until she scooted forward so they weren't touching. Gavin left the tub. The water level dropped, and she sank deeper into the water. She heard the rustle of clothes and then dropped her head forward when the bathroom door closed.

She wasn't sure how long she sat there when the door opened again. A woman Lyla had never seen before knelt beside the tub. She had long white hair twisted into a French twist and smiled kindly at her.

"Lyla, I'm a doctor. I want to have a look at you," she said.

"I-I'm fine," Lyla replied through chattering teeth.

"I was told you went through something traumatic. I know you're cold. Mr. Pyre gave me pajamas for you." She held up a pair of sweatpants and an oversized sweater. "You can have these."

Lyla wanted the clothes but didn't want to leave the safety of the tub.

"That jacket is stained. You want to wear something clean, don't you?"

Lyla shuddered and then nodded.

"Are you in pain?" the doctor continued.

Lyla nodded, staring straight ahead. Her head throbbed, and she felt seasick, stomach pitching and roiling even though she was sitting completely still.

"I can give you something for the pain, but I want to examine you first."

Silent tears slipped down Lyla's cheeks. A gentle, cool hand brushed over her hair.

"I can help you, Lyla."

She swallowed hard and slowly released her death grip on the jacket. She parted it and began to sob. The doctor spoke soothingly as she allowed the jacket sink to the bottom of the tub. She slipped the tiny strips of her dress off her shoulder and that too pooled around her.

"Can you stand?" the doctor asked.

Lyla gripped the side of the tub and pushed. It took a moment for her legs to steady, for her head to stop spinning. The doctor immediately engulfed her in a robe, which she buried her face in. The doctor helped her out of the tub and sat her on the seat in front of the vanity.

"I'm going to give you a quick exam, okay? Then we can get you into your clothes," the doctor said.

Lyla nodded and got a glimpse of herself in the mirror.

Her face was bloodless, and her eyes shone with glassy horror. Lyla looked away and felt faint when the doctor brushed her hand over her head.

"You have several bumps on your head."

The doctor's calm, clinical tone kept Lyla from losing her mind. The doctor knelt in front of her and slowly opened the robe.

"I just want to make sure you're okay. We don't want any scratches or cuts to get infected."

Remembering the pervert's dirty hands in her, Lyla jolted. The doctor spoke quickly and firmly, stroking her rigid back.

"We want to make sure there are no repercussions, yes?"

Lyla nodded and closed her eyes. She opened the robe and felt the doctor's hands move quickly and efficiently over her body. A steady stream of tears slipped down her face.

"Are you on birth control?"

"IUD." Thank God.

"I want to check you down there. Can you handle that?"

Lyla nodded. The doctor positioned her on the bench seat and with her eyes still closed, felt the doctor prod, pause.

"You're bleeding. Are you on your period right now?"

Lyla shook her head wildly.

"Your IUD isn't in the right place. I'm going to take it out and examine you more thoroughly, okay? Tell me if I'm hurting you."

Lyla trembled like a plucked bow. "I can't... I can't get pregnant, right?" Her whole body hurt. Her mind was a dizzy whirlwind of fear and pain. She didn't feel anything as the doctor examined her and reported that there was a tear in her vagina. That fucker's fingernails. "H-He was dirty. He was rough. I-I—"

"Let me clean you up and swab you to see if anything was transmitted."

Transmitted? Lyla wanted to scream and fight. Instead, she lay there and let the doctor finish her examination. The doctor cleaned the cuts on her wrists and ankles and wrapped them with bandages before she helped Lyla into her pajamas.

"You have a concussion, vaginal lacerations, and bruises. I'm prescribing painkillers. You need a lot of bed rest. I'll let you know the results of the test."

"C-can you tell how many times he—?" Lyla asked, stumbling over her words.

"You're bruised, bleeding and tender, but I don't see semen. I'll let you know the results. But just in case, I've brought you a morning after pill to take."

Lyla held out a hand and downed it even though her mouth was dry as dust.

"I'll be back in a few days. I'm only a phone call away." The doctor hesitated and then said, "If you need to speak to someone, I know a lot of great counselors."

The doctor helped her into the bedroom, and she realized for the first time that she was at Gavin's house, not Manny's. The doctor helped her to bed and handed her painkillers. She took those too, but this time drank from a water bottle on the nightstand. She pulled the covers up to her chin and tried to get warm. The doctor left, dimming the lights as she left. Lyla lay there, tossing and turning. Her body hurt, her insides hurt, and every time she closed her eyes, she saw that fucker's face. She needed someone beside her, someone who would beat back the memories battering her. She needed her monster. He came for her and destroyed that twisted human being. Suddenly pissed, Lyla staggered to the bedroom door and flung it open.

Blade stood in the hallway. His eyes flicked over her, but his expression was unreadable.

"Lyla?" he asked cautiously.

"Where's Gavin? I want Gavin," she said through chattering teeth.

"He's—"

"Get him for me." He hesitated, and she screamed, *"Now!"*

Blade backed away with his hands up and ran. If she weren't so shaken, his turnabout in attitude would have amused her. Instead, she tried to keep herself in one piece as she stood there, waiting. Male voices echoed down the hallway and then she heard the sound of running footsteps. Gavin stopped in front of her, hollow-eyed and wary. Lyla hesitated only a second before she launched herself at him. Gavin caught her as she wrapped her arms and legs around him.

"You can't leave me," she babbled.

"Lyla—"

"You can't!" she shouted and buried her face against his neck, trying to absorb his heat, his scent. "You can't leave me like this."

A tremor passed through Gavin as he walked to the bed and got in with her clinging to him. He lay on his back and pulled the covers over them. She tucked her head under his chin and lay over his big, strong body. *I'm safe, I'm safe,* she chanted in her head and willed herself to believe it.

"You stay with me," she ordered.

"I won't go anywhere," he promised.

Lyla closed her eyes and let his presence wash away the horror. Her shaky breaths filled the room. Gavin's hands moved over her gently as if she were made of glass. Her tears soaked his shirt. Neither of them said a thing.

Lyla woke with a scream.

"Shh, baby girl, I'm here."

Lyla shoved at the man until she focused on his face. She wept into Gavin's chest as he held her. She wasn't sure if hours or minutes passed. She dozed fitfully and took turns demanding he not touch her and then plastering herself against him. Gavin didn't say a word and obeyed whatever dictate she issued. He didn't leave the bed. He fed her bland foods so she could take more painkillers and forced her to drink water. He held her hair when she barfed it all up and filled the bathtub when she couldn't stop shaking. He carried her back to bed, blocked out the sunlight, and slid in beside her. No one disturbed them and neither spoke.

10

Lyla woke on her side, facing Gavin. She wasn't sure how many days had passed since she and Gavin locked themselves in his master bedroom. He was asleep with his hand gripping hers, their only skin contact. It was the first time she woke without lashing out or trying to defend herself from a dead man. Her body was still sore, but she felt better. Although she had been in bed for days, she was exhausted. Her mind and body weighted down with the knowledge of what lurked outside these walls. She had been touched by pure evil. Her mind desperately tried to punch through to fresh air, but her heart cowered in darkness, trying to piece itself together.

Lyla slipped her hand from Gavin's. He shifted and reached for her, brow furrowing. She hesitated a moment before she ran a hand down his face. He relaxed instantly as if he recognized her touch and settled into deeper sleep. He had dark circles under his eyes and hadn't shaved in days. He looked dark and dangerous even in sleep. A layer of tension existed around him, a coiled readiness to strike out. Instead of making her back away, it made her want to burrow against him. Gavin kept his word. He killed the pervert with his bare hands.

Lyla went into the bathroom and filled the tub. She'd taken more baths in the past couple of days than she would normally in two weeks. She tossed in salts and oils before she slipped in. She sat with her arms wrapped around her legs and let the heat penetrate her aching body. It was hard to think of anything but what happened in the warehouse. She couldn't get her captors' faces out of her mind, couldn't think past pervert's attack. She was grateful that she didn't remember... but what did Gavin see? Lyla moaned and buried her face against her knees. It felt like a lifetime that she had been back in Las Vegas. In less than two weeks, she had changed irrevocably. There was no way to backtrack or deviate from the path laid out in front of her. She was on a bullet train, and there was no getting off.

Lyla heard the door open, and Gavin appeared. He sat beside the tub, watching her. Lyla didn't meet his eyes. She couldn't. There were things she wanted to say, things she wanted to know... and not know.

"The doctor will be here in an hour," he said.

With the test results. Lyla clenched her teeth and nodded. It was better to know what pervert did to her.

"Do you want to see Carmen?"

She shook her head. Carmen was over the top, and she couldn't handle that right now. She could barely handle her own emotions, much less someone else's.

"Do you want me here when the doctor comes?"

Lyla turned her head. He still looked tired, but his eyes were clear and lethal. He was still on edge. So was she.

"Do you want to be?" she asked.

"Yes."

"That's fine with me." After rescuing and caring for her,

his presence was a welcome buffer between the horror of what happened and reality.

They sat in silence until there was a knock on the bedroom door. When Gavin went to answer it, she got out of the tub and slipped into a robe. The same doctor from the night of the assault was in the bedroom and wasted no time.

"There was no trace of STD, semen, or anything else," the doctor said.

Something within her loosened. For the first time in days, she felt as if she could take a full breath.

"You're looking better. Let's look at your tear." The doctor gave Gavin a long, direct look, but when he didn't move, and Lyla didn't object, she snapped on her gloves and got to work. "It looks good. You're not spotting?"

"No."

"Great."

The doctor checked the wounds on her wrists and ankles and approved of Gavin's dressings before she prodded Lyla's concussion. Lyla still felt like she might pass out, so the doctor prescribed more rest and painkillers. The doctor asked if she wanted to speak to a counselor, and when Lyla declined, she handed her a business card in case she changed her mind. When the doctor left, Lyla changed into yoga pants and Gavin's sweater that stopped at mid-thigh.

"I want to go outside," she said.

Gavin didn't say a word. He opened the bedroom door, and they came face to face with Blade. Knowing he witnessed her being carried out of the warehouse and her breakdown and outbursts over the past couple of days, Lyla didn't meet his gaze. She passed him and walked down-stairs, through the kitchen and thrust open the door that led into the backyard. Lyla stepped onto heated tiles and tipped her face up to the sun. She didn't have to look around to accustom herself to her surroundings. An Olympic-sized pool occupied most of the yard. In the middle of the pool was a sunken cabana with oversized pillows and cushions.

Lyla stood there until she felt uncomfortably warm. She crossed the oversized stones that led to the sitting area in the middle of the pool. The sound of the waterfall cascading into the other end of the pool soothed her. Gavin settled nearby, never taking his eyes from her.

"What did you see?" she asked.

Gavin jerked as if she slapped him. "Don't ask me that."

"I am," she said, their beautiful surrounding at odds with the hell they were dancing around.

"You're recovering. You don't need to—"

"Gavin, tell me."

He rose and turned his back to her but not before she saw his murderous expression.

"He was on top of you, dick out. I didn't know if he was finishing, beginning..." Gavin let out a growl and ran his hands through his hair. "You weren't moving. I fucking lost it. I didn't even look at you; I just wanted to kill."

"Gavin."

She held her hands out to him and saw that he was shaking. He turned, movements stiff as he walked to her. When she tugged on his wrist, he fell to his knees in front of her. His eyes focused on a target over her shoulder that no one could see. Lyla could taste the violence and rage bottled up inside him. She clasped his face between her hands and kissed the corner of his mouth. He didn't relax, didn't look at her.

"I'm fine, Gavin."

"Are you?" he asked, voice gritty and rough.

Lyla wrapped her arms around his neck and leaned into him, needing and giving comfort.

"I don't know," she whispered. In less than a day, being held in a hellhole changed her. How long would it take to feel normal again? To feel safe? When would she feel clean or close her eyes and dream of something other than the monsters who kidnapped her?

She rested her chin on his shoulder, but his hands stayed fisted on the cushions on either side of her. She thought back to that night and tightened her hold on him, needing reassurance even though she saw what he was capable of.

"Maybe he didn't have a chance to fuck me," she whispered.

"That's what I have to believe," Gavin bit out.

Lyla bit her bottom lip. She wanted to believe that pervert didn't rape her, that Gavin interrupted before he had the chance. Lyla nuzzled Gavin even though he felt like a block of stone. "Thank you."

"For what?"

"For coming for me, for taking care of me." She cursed the tears that rose. At least their position meant she could talk freely without being pinned by his soul-searching eyes. "I've been difficult, and I kept you from work—"

Gavin jerked back, forcing her to loosen her hold on him.

"I promised that it wouldn't touch you ..." he said harshly.

For a moment, he looked crazed. Then he dropped his head to hide his expression. The cushions shifted beneath her as he strangled them. He was a bomb waiting to detonate. He wouldn't lash out at her, Lyla knew, but the waves of violence emanating from him turned her stomach.

"He's dead," she reminded him.

He raised his head. The intensity of his gaze made her uneasy.

"You saw what I did," he said.

"Yes." Even while the savagery of Gavin's rage terrified her, she would sleep better knowing that the pervert was dead. He didn't deserve to live.

"You think I'm a monster?" he asked gruffly.

Lyla clasped his face. "You're my monster."

Gavin shuddered and wrapped his arms around her waist, head on her breasts. "Can you forgive me?"

"Yes." She didn't need to think about it. He was swimming in guilt, tortured by the kidnapping. Her hands sifted through his hair in an effort to dim the awful energy engulfing him. "How did you find me?"

"Carmen called us when she couldn't find you. Stupid bastards didn't get rid of your phone until they were downtown. I had men searching the area when they called. I kept them on the phone to track them. It still took a couple of hours. Too long."

"You got the second guy?"

"Second guy?"

Lyla went rigid. "There were two men."

"He wasn't at the warehouse when we went through last night."

"He went to get cigarettes. He's still out there." Her voice was hoarse with fear.

"I'll get him."

Lyla heard the bloodthirsty eagerness in his voice, and it distracted her from the memory of the dead eyes of the captor who hadn't touched her but scared her just as much. "You're going after him?"

"Him and everyone associated with them."

The flat tone of his voice sent chills down her spine. He wasn't really with her; he was planning murder and revenge. She splayed her hand over his heart. "So they kidnap me, you kill them, and then what? When does it end?"

"It ends when they're all dead."

He still wouldn't look at her, wouldn't let her touch penetrate. Her hands dropped from him. It always came back to this part of his life. Even while she was glad that the pervert was dead, Gavin had paid a price. They both had. Interacting with people like her captors chipped away at Gavin's soul and pulled him deeper into their world. She saw him in action, face dripping with blood and no trace of humanity in his eyes—just blind rage. Knowing the filth he dealt with, she couldn't stomach it.

She beat back the pain and asked, "When am I going back to your dad's house?"

Gavin's eyes snapped to her. "What?"

"I agreed to stay for a year, but I can't be around you, not when you're involved in this."

Silence. She pushed against his chest, but he didn't move.

"I told you I couldn't live like this. They went for me because they think I mean something to you. They'll come after me again. They'll kill me next time. I can't—"

"Baby—"

She shoved his hand away. "No, Gavin. I want out."

Gavin's hands moved to her hips and gripped tight. "Out?"

Lyla ignored the bite in his words. She had to put as much distance between herself and Gavin as possible. The bond between them was incredibly tight, especially after being kidnapped. She needed to break it off now while she could. She couldn't reach him. No one could. He would go on a killing spree, and she couldn't talk him out of it.

"I think we both know I can't..." She waved a hand at herself and then the house where she forced him to hibernate with her. "I can't," she repeated. "I'm better. Y-You helped, staying with me. I'm grateful—"

"Lyla—"

She shook her head and hated she still had a store of tears in her. "I can't be around you when you're doing this shit. I can't go through this again." Her throat tightened. They left the warehouse covered in another person's blood, and she still hadn't washed it all away in her mind. Gavin wouldn't be satisfied with the death of the other captor. How many would he kill before the rage dissipated? Before he felt that justice had been served? How many would die, and what toll would it take on his soul? Every kill pushed him further into the dark, further from emotion and anything normal. "You won't give it up, and I—"

"I give it up, you stay with me."

Lyla wasn't sure she heard him right. "What?"

His eyes bored into hers. "I let go of that side of the business, you stay with me. Permanently."

Lyla was stunned speechless.

"That's why you left me the first time; why you want to leave me now?"

She shook her head to clear the buzzing in her ears. "You'd give it up?" She couldn't keep the skepticism out of her tone.

"Yes."

The man before her was a dangerous predator. The businessman was the civilized part of him. The savage side surfaced when he dealt with people like the pervert. There were two sides to Gavin's nature—both lethal and both a part of him. How could he get rid of the darkness that was so inherently a part of him? Where would the aggression go? How could he let go of the need for revenge and let others handle it? Giving up control wasn't part of his DNA.

"Tell me what you're thinking," he ordered.

"*Can* you give it up?"

"I need to find someone to take my place, but it's possible."

"Who?"

"Lyla," he said impatiently, "answer my question."

"Why can't you quit that shit for yourself?"

"Because I don't care about myself."

Her head snapped back. "What do you mean, you don't care about yourself?"

He tightened his hold on her. "Yes or no, Lyla."

"If I say no, you continue doing this on the side?"

"Yes."

The force of his personality battered at her. He was too much for her to handle. "Gavin, you're so angry—"

"Yes, I'm fucking angry!" He wrapped his arms around her when she tried to back away. "No, you don't run when I'm pissed. You go toe to toe with me as you did in my office and when you took my hands in yours. You've seen the worst in me, and you wanted me to hold you after that fucker—" He cupped her face between rough, shaking palms. "I did you wrong. I made you cry and showed you parts of my world you should have never seen. I can't take it back, but I can try to make it right this time. You have to give me a chance, a real one. No holding back, no hiding in my dad's house. Before, you were handed to me on a fucking platter. I didn't have to work for your love; you took me whole. You were tailor made for me, fucking spoiled me. Then you left. I won't take you for granted, ever."

Lyla's hands twisted in his shirt as her mind whirled.

"What little I feel revolves around you. Haven't felt a fucking thing since you left. I brought you back, and I keep fucking it up. I feel too much for you." Brooding eyes traced her features. "I learned to control my emotions at a young age. I learned what to let in and what to keep out. I saw what Mom's death did to my dad. I didn't want to be at someone's mercy like that, so I held you at arm's length on purpose. I thought I had you under control, that I hadn't let you in. It wasn't until you left that I realized you were already in. The woman meant for me, gone without a trace." His eyes burned with a fevered light. "You can't leave me, Lyla."

"Gavin," she whispered.

His kissed her tears away and ran his hands down her sides as if reassuring himself that she was here with him.

"When I held you in the tub, you pulled away. Fucking killed me. I thought after what you saw, you wouldn't let me touch you ever again. Then you demanded I stay with you, hold you."

He rested his forehead on hers, amber eyes staring into hers with a desperation that made her heart ache.

"I won't let you go this time. Whatever you want, I'll give. You want me to quit; I'll do it. But I quit the business, you stay with me."

"W-what if—?"

"No ifs. Yes or no." When she hesitated, his face hardened. "I have you for a year. If you think I'm going to let you hide in my dad's house, think again. I'm not letting you out of my sight. I'll do everything in my power to make sure you want to stay another year and then another. You try to leave; I'm coming with you. I won't leave you alone. I can't."

They were both surprised by her watery chuckle. She framed his face with her hands. Gavin Pyre was a scary bastard. He was fire and ice in a gorgeous package she wasn't sure she could handle, but it looked like she had no choice.

"You're so romantic," she said and kissed him.

Gavin drew her closer, so she was at the edge of her seat. She could taste his need and the sharp edge of danger that was so much a part of him. When she drew back, his hungry eyes searched hers.

"When you say permanently, you mean ...?" she asked.

"No running, no time limit. You stay here, not with my dad."

Lyla chewed her bottom lip and then said, "I don't know if I can give you what you want."

He laughed and wrapped himself around her. There was a dark edge to it, but it was still a sound of humor.

"Baby, you make me happy just by being."

A warm ray of hope lit her soul, and she hugged him to her. "I'll stay."

He didn't move or speak for a long minute. Locked in their own world, it was just the two of them. When he pulled back, he smiled at her. The joy made him look ten years younger, stunning her. He pressed a gentle kiss to her lips and unwrapped himself from her.

"Are you good?" he asked.

"Yes."

"I have work to do," he said and rose.

"What?"

"The sooner I get rid of the title, the sooner we can move on."

"Oh. Who are you going to pass it off to?"

"Don't worry about it. We'll get that other fucker. He isn't allowed to live."

Lyla didn't bother to contest that. She would feel better

knowing that demon in human flesh was dead. "But you won't ...?"

"No. I'll get someone else to make the hit. You okay if I go to the office?"

She didn't want to be alone but knew he had to work and get this other shit tied up. She nodded.

He cupped her chin in his hand and brushed his thumb over her bottom lip as he considered her. "You want to see my dad?"

Her eyes filled with tears, and she nodded.

"Come, I'll drop you off before I go to work."

Twenty minutes later, Gavin donned a tailored suit while she opted to stay as she was in her oversized sweater and yoga pants. Gavin drove his own car while Blade and another group of men followed.

"I won't stay past eight," he said as he grabbed her hand and placed it on his thigh.

Lyla glanced at his intimidating face as his fingers threaded through hers.

"Blade and several others will stay with you. My dad will be insulted if I leave more than five of my men on his turf. He has his own security."

She nodded.

"You want me to come and get you, you call me. You have your new phone?"

"Yes." She had a small bag with a change of clothes, painkillers, and a new phone he gave on their way out the door.

"It'll take me some time to put things in order."

"I know, Gavin."

The Pyres had been running the underworld for generations. There was a niggle of doubt in her mind that he could get out, but she pushed it away. He didn't make false promises.

Gavin drove as his thumb stroked her absently. She stared at his possessive hold and thought of the deal she had made. Permanent. No future of independence, no Jonathan. Lyla closed her eyes and said goodbye to the man who had been there for her when she needed him. Jonathan deserved more than what she could give him. She had given her love to Gavin Pyre before she was old enough to understand the consequences. She committed willingly this time, knowing what he was capable of and witnessing the stain on his soul. She sensed a yearning in him and something else... Need? He was capable of unspeakable cruelty and incredible gentleness. He was complicated, possessive, calculating, and *hers*. He was her monster, and she loved the hell out of him— always had, always would. The experience with her captors knocked down all barriers between them. On impulse, she raised his hand. Lyla kissed his raw and bruised knuckles.

"What are you doing?" he asked hoarsely.

"Loving you."

His fingers flexed around hers. The look he shot her made her stomach jitter. She cradled his hand in both of hers and placed it on her lap.

"You won't regret it," he said gruffly.

Lyla relaxed in her seat and closed her eyes. When Gavin pulled up to Manny's house, they saw him standing on the steps. He rushed to her door and shouted in Spanish as he pulled her into his arms. Manny pulled back to look at her, crushed her against him, and then pulled back once more to make sure she was whole. Gavin replied in Spanish, the words spoken too rapidly for her to catch. Manny stiffened. She looked up and saw his dumbfounded expression.

Gavin pulled her away from his father and into the house. Manny came after them, spewing angry Spanish. Father and son faced off. When Gavin took a threatening step toward his father, Lyla stepped between them.

"What's going on?" she asked.

"Nothing," Gavin said shortly and tipped her face up for a kiss. "You call me if you need me."

She nodded, and he walked out of the house without another word to his father. Lyla stared at Manny who looked flustered and disturbed.

"What is it? What's wrong?" she asked.

Manny shook himself and hugged her again. "You want him to give it up."

Lyla could tell from his tone of voice that he didn't approve. She stiffened and drew back. "Yes, I do."

Manny sighed and ran a hand through his hair. "I understand. I do, but..."

"But what?" Lyla demanded. "He could be killed. Don't you care how doing that side of the business affects him... and me?"

"Of course, I care, baby girl, of course, but... we have contracts and deals."

Lyla crossed her arms, seeing Manny in a new light. Gavin agreed to give it up for her, but apparently, Manny wasn't so eager. Her belly clenched. "What happened to me isn't more important than your deals and contracts?"

Manny drew back as if she struck him.

"I was almost raped, Manny," she said, voice thin and jagged. "He touched me. That doesn't matter to you?"

"Lyla."

He reached for her, but she stepped back.

"I love you," she stated, "and I love Gavin, but I don't like what you do for a living. I don't like that you take chances with your lives, your souls. You think I can heal Gavin, but you have to stop sending him into the dark where the other monsters are. You don't know what—" She wrapped her arms around herself and fought the urge to vomit as she remembered Gavin covered in blood. "The price is too high. It's not worth it."

Manny stared at her for a long minute before he said, "I've done many things. Things I'll never tell a living soul. At the time, they were necessary measures that had to be taken. Somebody needs to rule the underworld, and I groomed Gavin to take that position. He's damn good at it." When she opened her mouth, he held up a hand and allowed, "Maybe *too* good. Gavin has built himself a reputation that keeps everyone in line. If he steps back, no matter who replaces him, they'll have problems."

"Yet his reputation didn't protect me," Lyla said quietly.

"A strike like this has never happened before. It was suicide. Someone who was testing the waters contracted those men. We need to send a message back, a bloody one that will send ripples through the underworld."

Manny didn't look like a seventy-year-old man; he looked like a ruthless general, which reminded her of Gavin. That intensity in his personality would never fade, never yield to anyone. It was still thriving in his father who went antique shopping and had retired from the business.

"So Gavin won't be able to get out of it?" Lyla asked, stomach rocking.

Manny's face softened. "He'll find a way."

"But you think it's a mistake?"

"He's the best man for the job, but I see why he's stepping down. You have a profound effect on him, and this is your requirement to move forward." He nodded. "If this is what you want, I wouldn't hesitate to tell him to step down either. It was just the shock. I wasn't prepared for it." He gave her a small smile. "I hear you're moving out?"

She tried to smile but was still troubled. "Yes, but Manny—"

He waved his hands. "Don't worry. I shouldn't have said anything. Don't be upset with me."

"I'm not," she said even though she was.

"Come, we'll watch movies," he declared and led her into his ostentatious living room.

"Manny—"

He clasped her face. "Everything will be okay. Gavin will make sure of it."

WHEN MANNY ASKED what she wanted to watch, Lyla asked for *Die Hard*. The choice surprised Manny but he didn't question it. Juanita brought a steady stream of food until Lyla pleaded for her to stop.

It took her a long time to relax, but eventually, Manny coaxed her to stretch out on the couch. After a slew of action movies, Manny popped in *The Godfather*. With her head on Manny's lap, she watched the movie unfold. It was Manny's favorite, no surprise there. Even while she saw parallels between the movie and the Pyre men, she found it amusing that Manny could imitate Vito Corleone perfectly. He could quote the entire movie word for word. Manny cussed people out while he played with her hair.

She dozed and woke when she felt herself being lifted. Lyla tensed and then relaxed when she realized that she was in Gavin's arms. He spoke to Manny in Spanish. Manny's tone was a lot softer than it had been earlier in the day. Gavin carried her to his car and deposited her in the passenger seat. She belted herself in and turned toward him as he got in.

"Okay?" he asked.

Sleepy and relaxed, Lyla nodded. "Get a lot done?"

"Yes, but I have to go in tomorrow." A pause. "You okay with that?"

"Yes." He had an empire to run, and she had to learn how to live, knowing what type of evil was out there.

"I'll ask Carmen to keep you company. You up for that?"

"Yeah." She felt steadier. She deliberately brought up the image of the pervert. Her heart began to race, and her hands felt clammy. She reached out for Gavin. He took her hand, laced their fingers together, and she could breathe again. She would fight this. It would be okay. She wouldn't let psychos, perverts, and murderers stop her from living her life.

"You okay?" he asked.

"Trying to be."

He squeezed her hand. "You will be. Just give it time."

"Is everything okay with you and Manny?"

"Just a difference of opinion. We're fine. You had a good time with him?"

"Yes. I love your dad."

His hand tightened on hers, but he said nothing else. They drove home in silence. One of the guards opened her door when the car stopped. She nodded to him and went inside.

"I'll meet you in our room. I need to take care of some things," he said.

She nodded as he went into his office and closed the door. She went upstairs and checked the closet, bathroom, and under the bed before she stripped and got into the shower. It was the longest she'd gone without bathing herself. She saw that as a small victory. The feeling of being filthy was all in her mind, but that didn't stop her from scrubbing her skin so hard that she was bright red when she stepped out of the shower. She claimed another oversized sweater and had just finished slathering on lotion when Gavin walked into the bathroom. He kissed her cheek and stripped. Lyla watched him in the mirror and saw his cock standing at attention. Gavin ignored his body and stepped into the shower, washing briskly. Although Lyla felt a tingle of response between her legs, she walked away. She couldn't. She wasn't ready.

Lyla got into bed and curled on her side, staring out of the window at the stars. Gavin came out of the bathroom in a pair of boxers and nothing else. His shower was too quick to get himself off. He tossed his cell phone on the nightstand and brought his laptop to bed. Lyla relaxed as she listened to him type. She buried her face in her pillow, drew in Gavin's scent, and slowly let sleep take her.

"Lyla."

She moaned into her pillow.

"Lyla, come on, baby. Wake up."

Large hands flipped her over. She hung onto the pillow so it covered her face. Gavin chuckled and with one swift jerk, sent the pillow flying. She glared balefully at him.

"What?"

"There's my girl," he crooned and brushed kisses over her face. "You slept through the night."

Lyla blinked. Another victory. She didn't dream at all. Dressed for the office, Gavin smelled delicious.

"I have to go. Carmen should be here any minute. I thought I'd give you a warning," he said.

"Thanks."

"You're okay?" he asked, brushing a gentle hand over her body.

She rested her hands on his chest and remembered his hard-on last night. He usually woke up hard. Did he get off this morning? She was annoyed with herself for obsessing about Gavin's dick. Didn't she have more pressing things to worry about besides his masturbating schedule? *He wouldn't cheat on you after what happened*, she told herself. But what if she couldn't... Gavin had needs, and she might not be able to—

"Lyla?"

"What?"

"You're okay?" he repeated.

"Uh-huh."

He gave her an odd look before he kissed her forehead. "I'll have my phone on me at all times. Do you need anything?"

"No."

"I'll see you tonight."

Gavin grabbed his phone and laptop and walked out of the room. Lyla lay there for several minutes, letting her mind drift before she showered. This time, she didn't scrub herself hard enough to bleed. Another victory. Lyla took the time to braid her hair and put on a little makeup. For some reason, it was painful to look at her reflection. She settled for jeans, and because she felt too exposed, pulled on a slouchy jacket.

When she walked downstairs, she saw Blade standing guard. She averted her eyes until he called her name. When she looked up, he came forward.

"I-I want you to feel safe," he said awkwardly.

Lyla considered this and muttered, "Thanks."

"What happened the other day, no one else will ever touch you. Not on my watch."

"I'm okay, Blade."

He clasped his hands behind him and spread his legs in a military stance. "I want you to know I'll protect you with my life."

This was a far cry from the man who laughed at her fear when he picked her up in Maine. "Thanks, Blade."

He gave a curt nod and then said, "You make the boss happy."

The front door burst open, saving Lyla from having to respond. Blade drew his gun before he turned. Carmen stood in the doorway, tears streaming down her face. She didn't notice Blade or the gun in his hand. She let out a scream that could have shattered glass and hurled herself at Lyla. She cried as if her heart were breaking.

"Carmen?"

"It's all my fault!" Carmen wailed. "If I hadn't tried on those crotchless panties, I would have been there!"

Blade hastily holstered his gun and walked away while Lyla ran a hand down Carmen's back.

"We would have both been kidnapped," Lyla said, holding her cousin tightly.

"At least you wouldn't have been alone, and I could have helped kill those bastards!" Carmen howled.

Because her body was still sore, Lyla led Carmen to the sofa. Carmen went willingly enough, but she didn't release her. Carmen babbled about all the ways she would have defended her.

"Carmen, I'm fine," Lyla said.

Carmen drew away, makeup streaming down her face. *"Are you?"*

Her eyes burned with tears, but she took a deep, forti-
fying breath and gave a small nod. "Yes."

Carmen clasped their hands together. "Tell me
everything."

Lyla stared at her. She hadn't told anyone what
happened. No one asked and even a day ago, she wouldn't
have been able to. But she had to discuss it, get it off
her chest.

"Tell me," Carmen insisted.

She took a deep breath and told Carmen about her
hours in hell. She faltered when she talked about what the
pervert did. Seeing the horror on Carmen's face made her
feel guilty and relieved at the same time.

"Go on," Carmen said, squeezing her trembling hands.

Lyla brushed away the tears and continued. She told
Carmen about Gavin's rescue, how he stayed by her side all
these days, and about the test results from the doctor.
Carmen hugged Lyla and bawled her eyes out. She felt
better now that it wasn't festering in her chest. Carmen
raged enough for them both. They went through half a box
of Kleenex before Lyla felt a very basic urge.

"I'm hungry."

Carmen snapped to attention. "Yes. You need to eat.
I'll cook."

"You cook?" Lyla asked as Carmen led her to the kitchen.

"Is pouring milk in cereal cooking?"

Lyla cracked a smile as she sat at the dining table.
Carmen rummaged through the fridge.

"We're in luck. Breakfast burritos are already made that
we just have to heat. Thank God."

Carmen set the oven and then made coffee. She sat,
grabbed Lyla's hand, and teared up again.

"God, I'm so sorry—"

"Carmen, I'm okay."

"How can you be? You were kidnapped, nearly raped... or raped. We don't know." Carmen's eyes flamed. "I'm glad that fucking pervert is dead. Gavin should have shoved a rusty spike through his asshole and let him suffer for days until the Devil came to drag him down to hell where he belongs."

Lyla blinked. "Wow. Gross."

"What about the other fucker?"

"Gavin's looking for him."

"Good. I want to know when he's dead."

Carmen fetched her purse and pulled out a hand mirror with her name spelled on the rim in rhinestones. She repaired her makeup and squirted a fresh wave of perfume on her chest. When the bell dinged, Carmen jumped up to put the burritos in the oven. Lyla drank her coffee and tried to recover from the draining talk.

"So you're here instead of at Manny's," Carmen commented.

"Yes. Gavin stayed in bed with me for days. Whatever I needed, he was there."

Carmen clasped her hands over her heart. "I'm glad."

"Yes." Lyla turned the cup between her hands. "You know why I left the first time, and now this... I can't live like this, knowing what he does at night, risking himself. You don't know what he looked like that night. He's so distant. Nothing can reach him. He goes cold and shuts off. It scares me."

"That's what he needs to do, Lyla."

"I don't want him to do it so... he said he would give it up if I stay with him permanently."

Carmen goggled. "What?"

"So he's giving it up."

Carmen held both hands up like a traffic cop. "So you're *staying*?"

"If he gives it up."

"Which he will since he's in love with you." Carmen erupted from her seat and did an energetic twerk, interrupted by the oven buzzer. Still shaking her ass, Carmen pulled the burritos out of the oven and made them both a plate. She slapped the plate in front of Lyla, kissed her on the mouth, and did a shimmy. "Yaaaaaasss! Go, Gavin, go Gavin. You can do it; you can do it. You're a badass, yes, yes! Get yo' girl! Woohoo!" Carmen plopped down in her seat and forked up a mouthful of burrito, eyes shining. "I am so happy!"

"No kidding," Lyla said with a smile.

"This is amazing. Who knew this kidnapping business would have a good outcome?"

"Not me."

"So you forgave him for... before?"

"Yes." They ate in silence and then she said, "Manny's worried."

"Why?"

"He says Gavin's reputation keeps everyone in line, and if he leaves, it ..."

Carmen shrugged. "Don't worry about it. That's Gavin's business."

Lyla tried to put it out of her mind. Carmen noticed her preoccupation and smacked her arm.

"Lyla, stop worrying."

"Easy for you to say."

"Yes, it is, because I trust Vinny to take care of me. Maybe after Gavin gives it up, you'll feel the same, and you guys can go back to the way you were before."

"The way we were?"

"Yes. We do whatever we want and love the hell out of our men when they come home to us."

No job? She couldn't deny that not having to worry about bills would be nice, but would staying at home make her stir-crazy?

"Girl, I can hear your wheels turning. You're a worrier, always have been. You're always thinking ten steps ahead and biting your nails about things that haven't happened. I think it comes from your parents. You got a job while you were in high school to help with the bills when things with your dad went sour."

"You taking psychology classes?" Lyla asked with raised brows.

Carmen rearranged her nipples in her top. "Just because I'm hot doesn't mean I can't be smart too."

"I guess. What are you doing today?"

"We aren't going anywhere. You and I are going to talk, eat, cry, and laugh. Nothing else."

Carmen was as good as her word. The day passed in a blur of emotion. They migrated from the house to the pool cabana where Carmen persuaded her to get rid of the jacket. Lyla wasn't sure why she was so self-conscious of her body, but Carmen distracted her too quickly for her to ponder it. Carmen was exhausting, entertaining, and supportive. When Lyla took a nap, Carmen cuddled with her in bed, arms holding her tight. It wasn't as comforting as Gavin's hold, but Lyla was grateful nonetheless.

They ordered pizza for themselves and the guards and watched chick flicks while they French braided one another's hair. Gavin's cook arrived and asked if Lyla had any food preferences and explained that she prepared and delivered meals once a week. She showed Lyla the instructions on the meatloaf for dinner and left.

When Vinny arrived at sunset, Carmen launched herself at him as if she hadn't seen him in years. They shared a deep kiss before he set her down. His eyes were cautious when they shifted to Lyla. Thanks to Carmen, she felt almost normal. She smiled and allowed him to give her a long, tight hug.

"Lyla," Vinny began and said nothing else.

"I'm okay."

He drew back. "Anything you need, you let us know."

"Thanks, Vinny."

"Gavin said maybe another hour, and he'll come home."

"Is everything okay at the office?"

He rubbed a hand down her arm. "Yes. He's just catching up. Gavin's never spent more than a day away from the office. He needs to learn how to delegate."

"Oh." And she kept him away from the office for days.

"This is a good thing, Lyla," Vinny said. "Work was his life. Now he has a reason to change."

"So you have more responsibility?" Lyla asked.

Vinny laughed. "Oh, yeah, but I'm looking forward to it. Gavin's changing a lot of things. Promoting, firing, and putting people through their paces."

"Why's he doing that?"

"I think he wants more time away from the office." Vinny wagged his brows suggestively, and she laughed.

Lyla put the meatloaf in, and they chatted around the dining table, drinking wine while it cooked. Lyla was disappointed that Gavin didn't arrive in time, but she had fun with Carmen and Vinny. They were so meant for one another. They finished each other's sentences, and even though they'd been together since their teens, their love hadn't waned. Lyla felt a pang watching them. They were so open and in sync with one another. She and Gavin were...

She wasn't sure. They had a volatile relationship that was still a work in progress.

Gavin arrived as Carmen and Vinny were on their way out. It was past nine o'clock, and Lyla saw the hard look Gavin and Vinny exchanged before he made his way to her.

"Sorry I'm late," he said and gave her a long, deep kiss. "You taste good."

"It's meatloaf."

"Damn, that sounds good." Gavin kissed Carmen on the cheek. "Thanks for keeping Lyla company."

"No problem, and thanks for keeping her here permanently." Carmen winked and dashed to Vinny's car as he revved it.

"Had a good day?" Gavin asked as they walked inside.

"Yes. I'm glad she came." She hadn't known that she needed girl time. "How was work?"

"Busy."

She made him a plate of meatloaf and a glass of wine and sat with him as he ate. Something was wrong. She sensed it but didn't press. Instead, she told him about her day and then waited until he finished eating.

"What's wrong?" she asked.

"The other guy who kidnapped you is dead," he said without inflection and drained his wine.

Lyla let out a sharp breath. "How?"

"Gunshot to the temple."

"You?"

He gave her a very direct look. "No. Eli."

"Eli? The angry cop from the club?"

Gavin drained his wine. "Your captor was present the night Eli's mother was attacked. Eli got to him before one of my men could."

Lyla waited for him to continue. He drank another glass

of wine and held the delicate stem between his fingers. She sensed his attempt to smother his emotions, but they filled the room. Lyla could taste his rage although nothing showed on his face.

"Someone's testing me," he said quietly.

A chill ran up her spine. He turned the glass slowly between his fingers, not looking at her.

"I've made some progress with shifting things over to another caretaker, but it'll take time."

"Okay."

"I'm rearranging things so I can spend time away from the office." He focused on her. "I thought we could go on a trip somewhere. Get away."

The last time they were together, they never traveled. Their lives revolved around The Strip. He was always working, even then. *He's trying to change*, she thought and smiled. "That sounds nice."

"Good. I'm trying to make my schedule more flexible and normal."

"That's great."

He surveyed her. "You look good."

"I feel better."

He nodded and rose. "I'm exhausted."

Lyla put everything in the sink, and they went upstairs. She hesitated when he stripped. Gavin turned to her and gently slipped her out of her clothes before he shuffled her into the shower. She allowed him to wash her hair since he liked to do it. He was hard again. She turned from him to wash the suds out of her hair. Because he was with her, she didn't scrub her skin. She rinsed and stepped out before him. She donned another sexless garment and slipped into bed before he emerged. Lyla's teeth clenched as he got in on his side. This time he didn't bring his laptop to bed. He settled her against him and sighed. Within minutes, she heard his breathing even out. It took a long time for her to go to sleep.

The next day, Carmen arrived with junk food and a stripper workout video. They danced on the dining room chairs. Lyla lost her inhibitions when she saw Carmen dancing as if her life depended on it. They celebrated the workout by eating brownies and then taking a dip in the pool. She wondered if Carmen noticed her awkwardness with her body yesterday and was urging her to take back her sexuality. If that was her intention, it was working.

Gavin came home at a more reasonable hour, but he seemed preoccupied and excused himself during dinner to take a call. He never came back to the table. Carmen kissed her goodbye when Vinny swung by to pick her up.

Lyla paused by Gavin's closed office doors and couldn't hear anything since it was soundproofed. She wondered if something was going wrong with Gavin turning the under-world over to someone else and worried about it as she went upstairs to shower. She took her time, but Gavin didn't appear. She got into bed and waited, but he still didn't show. She closed her eyes as she snuggled under the covers. She needed to sleep alone eventually. Gavin wouldn't always be there to tuck her in. She wasn't a child. Lyla forced herself to take deep breaths and eventually yawned. Using the deep breathing method, she lulled herself into an uneasy doze.

Lyla dreamed of the pervert. He held her down and laughed

as she did everything in her power to get him off her. She breathed through her nose since there was a strip of tape over her mouth and tried not to panic. He grabbed her face between his hands and squeezed cruelly.

"I'm going to ruin you so Pyre won't want you anymore." He kissed her lips over the tape. "He can have anyone he wants. Why would he want you? Women beg to be with him. You've been nothing but trouble. He'll tire of you and give you back to me."

There was the sound of clothes tearing. His hand quested down her stomach, between her legs, and shoved in.

Lyla woke with a scream, sitting up and clawing at someone who wasn't there. Gavin ran out of the bathroom, a towel in his hands, body dripping.

"You okay? Bad dream?" he asked, coming toward her.

Lyla wrapped her arms around him, forcing him to sit on the bed. She rested her forehead, covered in cold sweat, against his chest. She was trembling and could still feel that hand moving down her body, into her.

"Touch me," she said.

Gavin stiffened. "What?"

Lyla grabbed his hand and slipped it beneath the sweater and placed it on her stomach where the pervert's hand had been in the dream. She relaxed instantly. She wouldn't mistake Gavin's large hand with the pervert's grubby, clammy paws. She shuddered. Gavin tried to pull his hand away.

"No, I need—" she began and stopped, realizing how crazy she was acting. "I'm sorry, I—"

"Don't apologize," he said and kissed her. "What else do you need?"

Lyla searched the hard planes of his face. He still had water droplets on his eyelashes, and he was naked. His body was strong and unapologetically masculine. As she stared into his amber eyes, she had a vivid memory of what happened in his office. Her body tingled. She held the memory of Gavin going down on her rather than the recent dream, which chilled her.

"I need *you*," she said and moved his hand from her stomach to the apex of her thighs.

Gavin's eyes didn't waver from hers. "You really want this?"

She nodded emphatically. She needed to exorcise the pervert from her mind and body.

Gavin's hand moved, and she forced herself to spread her thighs. When his fingers stroked her, she clenched her teeth, and he stopped.

"You're not okay," he said and withdrew his hand.

Lyla wrapped her arms around herself. "You don't want...?" She couldn't finish the sentence. Maybe he didn't want her after the pervert—

Gavin lunged forward and kissed her. His tongue swept in and claimed her. Lyla shuddered and clutched him as relief swept through her in a heady wave. She could taste his hunger, his need. It called forth her own. She pressed against him, desperate to feel. His hands moved over her, rough and seeking. His mouth fused with hers, demanding everything she had to give.

When she was aching for him, he broke away. She let out an irritated sound and saw his brilliant smile. He dragged her to the edge of the bed so her legs dangled over the side. He knelt beside the bed. Her breathing turned heavy with trepidation and excitement.

"Eating you out in my office was a mistake," he said.

Lyla paused as she lifted her hips so he could pull off her sweat pants. "Mistake?"

He tossed her pants and draped her thighs over his shoulders. "*Big* mistake."

She was confused by the way he stared at her vagina as if it was gold and his contradictory words. "What are you talking about?"

"At work, all I think about is your pussy. I've been hard and aching at my desk for two days," he growled and leaned down to lick her.

Lyla hissed, and he moaned.

"Fuck, watching you come for me, having you give in to me that day made me so fucking happy." He spread her lips and stabbed his tongue into her. "You're about to do it again."

Her back arched, and she grabbed his hair and tugged. "Oh, my God."

"Say my name," he mumbled.

"Gavin."

"Louder."

His tongue hit her clit, and she clamped her thighs around his head. "Fuck!"

"*My name,*" he insisted. "Let everyone know who you belong to."

"G-Gavin?"

"I'm not a question, baby. I'm the answer to everything."

How could he make her laugh at a time like this? Lyla moaned and then screeched when he sucked on her clit, toying with her and making her crazy. She was close to an orgasm when his mouth disappeared. She opened her mouth on a protest and sucked in a breath as he thrust inside her. Gavin leaned down to kiss her, sharing her taste.

"You taste that? That's ambrosia. My ambrosia," he said against her lips and planted himself deep. "My Lyla. Mine."

"Yes," she whispered.

Gavin moved slowly, letting her body adjust to him and watched her face closely.

"Okay?" he asked with a pained expression.

"Mmm," she said and felt him twitch inside her.

"Can you take it hard? Do I need to go slow?"

His words tumbled over one another. She smiled and wrapped her thighs around him, in no doubt what he wanted.

"Ride me hard."

She saw his eyes glaze a moment before he gripped her hips and fucked her. It was hard and glorious. The light from the bathroom shone over them. She watched his hunger for her erupt. She climaxed first, legs convulsing. Gavin came a minute later, hands dragging her as close as possible before pouring himself into her. His top half collapsed on top of her while his legs stayed solidly planted on the ground.

"Thank you," he whispered into her hair.

"For what?"

He raised his head. "For trusting me that much."

Her eyes burned with tears. "I wouldn't have made it without you. You make me feel clean again."

"If that's the case, you're about to be the cleanest person on the planet."

In a show of effortless strength, he lifted her limp body in his arms, rounded the bed, and then lay on his back with her sprawled on him without once losing contact with her. His hands slid beneath her sweater and stroked her back.

"I needed that," he said and let out a long breath. "That first night I found you in our bed; I touched you, and you turned to me, wrapping your arms around me. I knew you were asleep, but I was starved and not about to turn you down." Hungry eyes scanned her face. "How can you be better than I remember?"

"It was good for you?" Lyla asked.

His brows shot up. "You have doubts?"

Fuck. Her insecurities were showing. It was hard to imagine satisfying a man like Gavin. She hadn't been able to before, and now she was a fucking mess. "Just checking."

He smiled as if she was funny and played with her hair. He didn't insist that she take off the sweater. She felt more comfortable with it on for some reason.

"Something went wrong at work?" she asked, stroking her hand over his chest.

"Nothing important."

That was a lie. If it weren't important, he wouldn't have left during dinner and locked himself in his office. Lyla glanced at the clock and saw that it was three in the morning. He'd been working for hours.

"It has to do with you letting go of the underworld, doesn't it?"

"Seriously, baby, don't worry about it."

"But you're still following through?"

Gavin tensed. "I said I would."

"But you're having trouble turning it over to someone else?"

He sighed. "Nothing in business is simple and dealing with something like this takes more time and care."

She accepted that explanation and relaxed on him, very aware of the fact that he was still penetrating her. "What do you want me to do?"

"What do you mean?"

"You're working all day, and I'm here. Maybe I can help."

He squeezed her ass. "Knowing you're at home waiting for me is helping. I need to know you're safe."

"I'm used to working. I can get a job—"

He kissed her and tipped them both to the side. He pulled her thigh over his hip and moved slowly in and out of her. She forgot what they were talking about as the chemistry between them rekindled. He moved leisurely while he savored her mouth. Time passed, and when she couldn't take the playful lovemaking anymore, she shoved him onto his back and straddled him. Gavin laughed and then groaned.

"Are you trying to make me crazy?" she snapped as she rocked on top of him.

"It's what you deserve for running from me," he said through gritted teeth.

"Is this a game to you?" she asked, enjoying the burn in her thighs as she raised and lowered herself on his thick cock.

Gavin's eyes glinted. "I don't play games when it comes to you."

"So what are you doing?" she panted.

He sat up and sank both hands in her hair. He took her mouth hungrily, tilting her head sideway for better access. Lyla lost her rhythm and sank her nails into his chest. When he pulled back, allowing her to breathe, they stared at one another.

"I want you desperate for me."

He flipped her onto her back and held one thigh high as he thrust in. Lyla screamed, and he gave her a feral smile.

"I want you bound so tight to me you can't imagine life without me."

He pounded her hard, demanding her compliance and need. Lyla reared up and bit his shoulder as she climaxed.

"Marking me, baby girl?" he asked, voice filled with amusement. "That's a good start."

Gavin waited until she calmed before he began to move again, holding off his own climax to make her mindless. Her skin was so fevered that she ripped off the sweater and cupped the back of Gavin's neck.

"Fucking finish me," she commanded.

"Who do you belong to?" he asked.

"You."

"Who?" he demanded, dropping the easygoing façade. "Who do you belong to?"

"Gavin."

"Say it. Say you belong to me."

"I belong to you."

"For how long?"

"Forever."

Gavin's eyes glinted a moment before he slammed into her. He bounced her on the bed, letting their momentum cause him to penetrate deeper than he ever had before. Lyla was breathless and delirious with lust. She kissed, bit, and sucked what she could reach of him. She came again, screaming his name, and he finally joined her, shouting her name and planting himself deep. He raised his head and looked down at her, golden eyes staring straight into her soul.

"Whatever it takes to have you with me, I'll do. Never doubt it."

12

Lyla woke alone. She moaned because she was definitely feeling the effects of her night with Gavin. It was nearly noon, and she was tangled in bed sheets. She hadn't felt him leave the bed or get ready for work. She must have been dead to the world. How much sleep did he get? She worried about him as she showered. He was dealing with the scum of the earth. He needed to be on his toes. She didn't want him out there half-cocked. Once she dressed, she searched the bedroom for her phone but couldn't find it. Annoyed, she went into the kitchen and made herself a bowl of cereal. She spied the phone on the counter and texted him. *Did you sleep at all?*

He replied a minute later. *Enough.*

She rolled her eyes and texted him back. *You need to sleep more.*

Worried about me, baby girl?

Stupid man. Of course, she did. *Yes.*

"That's good to know."

Lyla shrieked and whirled, milk and cereal splashing

over the floor. Gavin walked into the kitchen wearing sweat-pants and nothing else.

"I thought you went to work!" she snapped and grabbed the roll of paper towels.

"After you let me have you again?" He wrapped an arm around her, lifting her clear of the mess and plopped her on the marble island. "I'm not leaving here unless I have to."

"But what about—?" She lost her train of thought when he unbuttoned her blouse and licked her nipple through her sheer bra. "W-What are you doing?"

"Making up for lost time." He grinned when she gripped his hair. "You don't want me to go, do you, baby?"

"I..." She couldn't align her thoughts. They scattered in every direction.

"I have to take care of something tonight, but today, I'm spending my day in you."

Gavin was as good as his word. He ate her out and then fucked her on the marble island. When she tried to clean up the mess, he carried her into his office where he sat her on his lap and ordered her to ride him. Watching his eyes go blind with lust was something she quickly became addicted to. The first time they were together, they had sex daily, but it hadn't been so intense, consuming, and insatiable. He couldn't keep his hands off her and spent most of the day stroking every inch of her he could reach. She had never seen him like this. Before, there had always been a cool distance. Now, he looked at her as if she was his savior.

They shut out the outside world and spent the day making love, eating, and just being. Feelings Lyla thought were long gone rose up as she watched him nap with his head on her lap. It was like having a lion sprawled over you —strong, wild, and capable of anything. This man, this terrifying, unstable being was hers. Always had been, always would be. He claimed her heart the moment they clapped eyes on each other. Confident, mature, and powerful, he had her from the start and knew it. But Lyla had never been completely sure of him, and seeing him eating out one woman while another fucked him and two others licked and kissed his body destroyed her. The man he became in the intervening years was nothing she could prepare herself for. He was more forbidding, passionate, volatile, and more dangerous than she could have imagined.

Now, here they were. Gavin seemed perfectly content stretched out on the couch with her, but she knew better. He was a born leader and businessman. The craving to acquire spurred him on. He was naturally restless. Lyla had no idea what her life would be like tomorrow, in a week, or one year, but she committed herself to him. Permanently. Her hands twitched nervously as she touched his hair. Would this sudden need for her wane with time? Would he crave the dark violence she was asking him to give up? She shook away worries she couldn't control and forced herself to concentrate on what was playing on TV.

Gavin got up at seven and ate her out again before he showered. She warmed up the leftover meatloaf, and they ate together before he left.

"Are you going to be okay?" he asked.

"Yes."

"You can call me if you need me. If you have bad dreams, I want to know about it," he said.

She nodded and gave him a kiss before he headed out the door. This felt so domesticated, almost normal aside from the fact he was leaving at nearly ten o'clock at night. She didn't have to ask to know he was dealing with the illegal side of his business.

She showered and was in the middle of thoroughly

cleaning herself when a thought struck fear into her heart.
She wasn't on birth control. She always had an IUD so pregnancy wasn't a worry she ever contemplated, but because of
the pervert, it was gone.

Lyla stumbled out of the shower and found the doctor's
business card. She dialed while she tracked wet footprints
over the carpet. The doctor was alarmed at first, but Lyla
quickly reassured her that everything was fine. She wanted
another IUD, but the doctor was out of town and wouldn't
be back until next week. Lyla swallowed her disappointment
and made an appointment. She thought of going to another
doctor or Planned Parenthood, but she had no insurance, no
ID. Her only choice was to wait until Gavin's private doctor
returned. She didn't even have money to buy the morning
after pill.

She and Gavin had never discussed children. Ever. She
didn't even know if he liked children. They were together for
years, and he never spoke of marriage, so children were
completely out of the question. Did she want children?
Deep down, she did. She wanted the white picket fence, and
she wanted to be a stay-at-home mother. It was a dream that
had briefly seen the light of day with Jonathan, but *Gavin*?
She had extremely light periods to the point where she
barely noticed them. She had no way of knowing
where she was in her cycle. She sat on the edge of the bed
and put her head between her legs because she felt close to
passing out.

Gavin said he was going to propose after she discovered
his infidelity. Would she have said yes? She had no idea.
Even as she imagined a child, a son, that looked just like
Gavin, her stomach rocked with terror and elation. No. Her
life was unstable and her relationship with Gavin, even
more so. He wanted her now, but long term? She wanted to

believe he really did care for her, but she couldn't be sure. She had agreed to stay because her heart wouldn't let her say no. Gavin was an enigma. There was nothing special about her. She was ordinary in every way. The only difference between her and other women was her relationship with Manny. She still suspected his father was a factor Gavin wouldn't admit to.

When Lyla could think clearly, she realized that the bed sheets were soaked through. She stripped the bed and finished her shower. She found another set of sheets and remade the bed. She stomped on towels to absorb the water she had tracked around the room and went to the kitchen to do the dishes and sterilize the countertops and floor. When that was finished, she searched for a vacuum.

"What are you doing?"

She jumped and whirled to find Blade standing in the living room with his gun at his side. Lyla turned off the vacuum and gestured vaguely.

"I'm just ... cleaning."

"It's one in the morning."

"Oh." She searched for a plausible explanation and decided on, "I can't settle."

Blade holstered his weapon. "You want me to call Gavin?"

"No!" When his expression turned suspicious, she waved her hand. "I mean, I-I'm fine. Just keeping busy."

"He'd want to know."

"It's not an issue. I'll go to sleep now," she said and began to roll up the cord.

"You want a sleeping pill?"

She should have done that hours ago. "Yes, please."

Blade fetched her sleeping pills. She popped one in her mouth and was very aware of Blade watching her closely.

"I'm fine. Really. I don't want to bother him," she said quietly.

"Anything to do with you isn't bothering him," Blade returned.

Lyla gave him a strained smile and climbed the stairs. She slid between the fresh sheets and was glad the pills worked quickly.

———

Despite the pills, Lyla woke around six. The first thing on her mind was the risk of pregnancy. She felt like she had a hangover. She crept downstairs and peeked in Gavin's office, but he wasn't home. Lyla made herself a cup of coffee and paused during her first sip. Pregnant women weren't supposed to drink coffee, right? Fuck. She felt like pulling her hair. She rushed upstairs to get her phone. She paced the room as she dialed.

"Hello?" a cautious voice answered.

"Mom?"

"Lyla?"

Her mom was a notoriously early riser. She'd been counting on that. Some things never changed.

"Whatcha doing today?" she asked, trying to sound normal.

"Grocery shopping. Baking."

"Can I come with you?" She needed to get out of the house and didn't want to chance letting something slip to Carmen or Manny. They would be ecstatic. Logically, the chances of getting pregnant were slim. It would be a miracle if she got pregnant after two days of unprotected sex, but it was a possibility.

"Of course. How have you been, honey? Is this your new number?"

"Yeah. Let me get ready, and I'll be over."

A pause and then, "With Gavin?"

"No. Just me." She grimaced. "Maybe Blade."

"I don't know how your father's going to feel about that."

"Blade will stay outside," she said as she went into the closet and paired a dress with a jacket and gladiator style sandals.

"Okay. Well, I'll see you soon."

Lyla put on enough makeup to hide the dark circles under her eyes and hurried downstairs. When she opened the front door, she came face to chest with Blade. His eyes narrowed suspiciously.

"I'm going to see my mom," she said.

His brows arched. "Why?"

A valid question since she left her parents' house in a hurry last time. But her mother was her mother. "Because." When he didn't budge, she said, "You don't have to come with me. I can drive myself."

"Not likely. Does Gavin know?"

She'd been hoping to avoid that. "I don't want to bother him. He must be really busy if he hasn't come home yet."

"Call him."

It was part dare, part demand. She could see that he wouldn't budge without Gavin's consent. She clenched her teeth as she pulled the phone out of her pocket and found his name under contacts. She turned away from Blade and paced to the fountain as the phone rang.

"You're up early," Gavin said.

"Yes." She paused, mind going blank with nerves before she said in a rush, "I want to see my mom."

A short pause. "I'm going to be finished in a couple of

hours. I was hoping to be home before noon to spend time with you."

"I'll be back before then. I just need to talk to her."

"Okay."

She swallowed hard. "Thanks. See you later."

"Call me if you need anything."

"You're okay?" she asked belatedly.

He chuckled. "Of course."

"Okay. Just checking."

"Bye, baby girl."

When she turned, she saw Blade on his phone. She crossed her arms, wondering if Blade called Gavin to make sure she had been talking to him or whether Gavin was making arrangements. Honestly, it didn't matter. When Blade opened the back door of an SUV, she climbed in and was surprised when he climbed in beside her. Two guards sat up front. No one spoke, and the tension got on her nerves. She leaned against the window and watched them approach the city.

"I want a donut," she said absently.

"What kind?" Blade asked.

"Maple."

The driver pulled up to a Dunkin' Donuts. Lyla was mildly amused when Blade put in his donut preference as did the guard in the passenger seat. She felt marginally better when he came back with two dozen warm donuts. She snatched a chocolate and maple donut before anyone else could claim theirs and finished both before they pulled up to her parents' house. When she threw open the door to get out, Blade put a restraining hand on her arm.

"Let us check it out first," he said and jerked his head at the two guards who climbed out.

When the guards gave the all clear, she slipped out and

walked into the house, which had already been searched by the driver. Her mother appeared to be serene, but Lyla saw the unease and fear beneath the façade. Lyla shooed the guys outside before she hugged her mother.

"Hi, Mom."

"You look great! Gavin must be doing something right." She wore an overly bright smile and then worry crept into her expression. "You're keeping Gavin happy, right?"

With all that happened recently, it was easy to forget that her father's half a million dollar debt brought her here in the first place. She and Gavin hadn't talked about the debt since the night at the club. Another touchy subject to talk to him about. Half a million was a lot of money, money she didn't have. Her temples throbbed with tension.

"Gavin's fine."

"And you're with him?" Mom asked hopefully.

"Yes."

She blew out a breath. "Good. Why don't you go see your father while I get my things together?"

A not so subtle hint that she had daughterly duties to attend to. She went upstairs and knocked on her parents' open bedroom door. Her father's left arm and both legs were in casts. His face still looked mangled. After witnessing what Gavin did to the pervert, she knew her father got off easy. He lifted his head and sneered at her. She half hoped he'd tell her to take a hike.

"If it isn't Princess Lyla," he drawled. "Come to see your boyfriend's handiwork?"

She gritted her teeth and walked forward so he wouldn't get a neck cramp. "No. Came to go shopping with Mom." His nose had been broken and not reset well. It was off center.

"You know how long I gotta stay like this?" he demanded as if she'd done this to him. "Three months!"

Lyla said nothing.

"I feel like a fucking handicap."

Still, she said nothing.

Mean brown eyes narrowed on her. "Living the high life, princess?"

The sarcasm and jealousy in his voice made her want to back away, but she stood her ground. He never wanted her with Gavin, not because of his family business, but because Gavin took her from her father's control. Lyla had done everything in her power to win his approval; she even went as far as getting a job and giving him a portion of her paycheck to gamble away. That stopped once she got involved with the Pyres. Manny showered her with affection she didn't have to work for, and her father's approval became less important to her. Her father resented the Pyre's power and money.

"I'm okay," she said. Her parents knew nothing about the kidnapping, and honestly, she didn't know if they'd care either way.

"I bet you are," her father grunted. "You think about anyone but yourself?"

Lyla blinked. "Excuse me?"

"I don't have a fucking job, and your mother's never worked!" he bellowed, face red with rage. "You ever think how we're going to buy food if I'm bedridden and don't have a job?" When she just stared at him, he mumbled, "Selfish fucking whore."

"Don't talk to me like that," she snapped.

"Why not? You waltz in and out of this family as if we're nothing to you. You don't give a shit what's going on in our lives."

Lyla opened her mouth to shout but heard Mom calling

her name. She slammed the door on her father's stream of insults and stomped downstairs.

"Everything all right, honey?" Mom asked.

Lyla bit back all the angry words that wouldn't make a difference to her mother and nodded.

"Let's go, then."

When they walked outside, her mother came to a stop when Blade gestured them toward the SUV.

"I have my own car," Mom said, gesturing to an old Honda. "I have some errands to run."

"We don't mind," Blade said.

"Come, Mom," she said and took her mother's hand.

One of the guards moved into the last row of seats so she and her mother could sit together. Blade took shotgun, and they were off. Her mother gave instructions to the driver and was clearly embarrassed. Lyla climbed out of the car when they reached the bank and watched as her mother stuck first one and then another card into the ATM machine with a pinched, worried expression. Gut clenched, Lyla accessed her account in Maine through her phone and wasn't all that surprised to find that it had been closed.

She dialed Gavin's number as her mother tried a third card.

"Hey, baby girl," Gavin said.

Lyla took a deep breath. "My money in my account, the five thousand, you have it?"

"Yes."

Why the hell did she think seeing her mother would make her feel better? It made her realize how fucked up her life was. Gavin had all the power, and she had nothing. She tried to tread carefully. "Is the five thousand a down payment?"

"Down payment for what?"

"Dad's debt." She paced as she watched her mother slap the screen of the ATM as if that would change what she was seeing. "I-I know five thousand is nothing but—"

"What's going on?" His voice was clipped.

"I need some money," she said.

Dead silence on the other end. Her heart began to pound, and she tightened her grip on the phone.

"I can get a job to pay you back." Still no response and her eyes stung with tears of desperation. "I know I owe you for Dad's debt, and we haven't talked about how I'm going to—"

"Blade has a credit card. We'll discuss this later," Gavin said and hung up.

Lyla swallowed hard as she pocketed the phone. Her mother hurried back to the car without any cash. Lyla sat silently as they stopped at the post office and then a store. Her mother chose a ghetto grocery store where people sold tamales and black market DVDs out of the trunks of their cars. Blade and the other guards had their hands in their jackets, clearly on edge. As her mother grabbed a wagon, Lyla sidled up to Blade.

"Gavin said you have a credit card we can use?" Lyla asked in a low undertone.

"He texted me. I have the card," Blade said.

Lyla nodded and rushed to keep up with her mother who seemed to be trying to get away from them. "Mom, get whatever you need."

Her mother wouldn't look at her. "I just came for a few things."

"Gavin will pay for it," she said, stomach tight with nerves.

Her mother flushed with embarrassment. "We're okay."

"No, you're not, and you might as well get what you can

while we're here," Lyla said, dreading her conversation with Gavin.

"Really?" Mom asked, hopeful but wary.

"Yes. Get what you need. I don't know when you'll have another chance."

Her mother took Lyla at her word and filled her basket to the max. Lyla grabbed a package of condoms because it couldn't hurt and distracted her mother when they were rung up. Blade didn't blink as he handed the credit card over. Her mother was in a better mood as they loaded up the groceries and headed back to the house. Lyla, Blade, and the guards carried the groceries inside. Her mother filled the empty fridge with food, and it comforted Lyla even though she had to deal with Gavin. Her mother insisted on making lunch for them. The guards were allowed to sit in the living room while she watched her mother put away ingredients and start the preparations for her homemade fried chicken.

Under normal circumstances, Lyla would have been eager to taste her mother's cooking, but not knowing how Gavin would react to this latest incident with her parents made her queasy.

"What's this?"

Lyla looked up and saw her mom holding the box of condoms. Lyla held out her hand, but her mother didn't hand them over.

"What is this, Lyla?" she asked as if Lyla was fifteen-years-old.

She raised her brows. "Condoms. You put them on dicks to save yourself from an STD or getting pregnant."

"Yes, but why would you need these? You're with Gavin, right?"

"Yes."

Her mother's face turned sympathetic. "Is he cheating on you again?"

Arrow through the fucking heart. Lyla was stunned by the pain that simple question caused.

"They're men, honey," her mother said, patting her cold hand. "But if they take care of you and come home to you, who cares?"

Lyla cared. She cared too fucking much.

"But it is better to be smart," Mom continued. "You still have your IUD? You might want to take that out if you want to hook him."

"Hook him?"

Her mother began to roll chicken in flour with quick, practiced movements. "He's a ladies' man. He might move on and then where will we all be? You have to have insurance."

A child as insurance... Lyla rose. "I have to go to the bathroom."

She walked out before her mother could say anything else and passed Blade who had been standing just outside the kitchen. She ran upstairs and sat on the closed toilet lid, hands over her face. When her phone rang, she jolted and reluctantly pulled it out of her pocket. When she saw Gavin's name, she considered ignoring it, but he paid for her parents' groceries, and he might want to discuss how she could pay him back.

"Hi," she said.

"I'm home. I want you here."

Her hand tightened on the phone. "Mom's making fried chicken."

"I'm calling Blade. He's bringing you to me."

Gavin hung up, and she sat there, wondering what the

fuck was wrong with her life. It didn't take two minutes for Blade to knock on the door.

"Lyla? We have to go," he said.

"A minute," she said and took deep breaths.

He knocked again. "He's pissed off. We don't have a minute."

Oh, fuck. Lyla rose and opened the door.

Blade gave her a sharp look. "You okay?"

"Fine." She walked past him and ignored her father's curses when he caught sight of her. He fell silent when Blade stopped in the doorway.

"What are you doing in my house?" her father roared.

"Gavin told you what he'd do if he heard you talk to Lyla like that," Blade said quietly. "I hear you insult her again, I'll finish the job he started."

Lyla ignored them and went into the kitchen to kiss her mother on the cheek.

"But the chicken!" Mom protested.

"Enjoy it," she said and put the condoms in her pocket.

"Remember what I said, Lyla!" she called.

Lyla rushed out of there as fast as she could and got into the SUV, feeling worse than she had this morning. How could she have forgotten that her parents had no income? Yes, it was her father's fault, but how would they survive? She wouldn't let them live on the street. They were the only parents she had. She could get a job and help until Dad was on his feet again.

"You shouldn't let your father talk to you like that," Blade said.

"I don't let him, he just does."

"Gavin won't stand for it."

Gavin might cuss her out himself when she saw him.

"You have no idea what you mean to him," Blade said impatiently.

Lyla glanced at the guards in the front seat who could hear every word and huddled against the door, wishing Blade would shut up and leave her alone.

"I heard what your mom said about hooking Gavin and him cheating on you again," Blade said.

"Will you shut up?" Lyla snapped, finally losing her temper. What was going on in her own head was bad enough. She didn't need everyone voicing their opinions. "I'm not going to trap him, so you don't need to report that to him! God!" What would Gavin think if he heard what her mother said?

"You're different from the others," Blade said.

So there were still others... Lyla blinked back the tears. "Blade, please, shut up."

Her mind raced with ways to pay Gavin back for his generosity toward her family. She would never be able to repay the five hundred thousand her father stole. She possessed nothing of value that she could exchange for even a fraction of the cost. Not only had Gavin paid for groceries, but she also had to ask him for a loan until she could get a job.

When the SUV pulled up to Gavin's mansion, she had to force herself to move. She put her hands in her pockets and walked slowly toward the door. She felt as if she were walking toward a firing squad. Her fingers closed around the pack of condoms as she entered. She closed the door and stood there, listening. She jumped when Blade came in behind her.

"You're supposed to stay outside," she said.

"I have to give my report."

When he tried to step around her, she blocked his way. "What report? About me?"

"Yes."

"What is there to report?" she demanded. "Nothing happened."

Blade walked around her. In a desperate move, she leaped on his back to stop him.

"Please don't tell him," she whispered, mortified.

"Tell me what?"

Lyla froze as Gavin came out of his office. She could feel his energy, and it didn't bode well for her. His eyes were bloodshot from lack of sleep, and he looked pissed. Blade shrugged her off as if she were a flea. She dropped behind him and waited for the explosion.

"We need to talk," Blade said.

Lyla bit back another plea as he walked into the office. Gavin beckoned her with one finger. Slowly, Lyla went to him and wasn't prepared for the hand that shot out to cup her face. She couldn't stop her reflexive jerk backward. His eyes began to blaze.

"We're back to this?" he hissed.

Lyla said nothing.

"Don't go anywhere," Gavin snapped before he slammed the office door.

13

Lyla sat on the couch for what seemed like an eternity, hands clasped between her knees. She would tell Gavin that she had no intention of trying to trap him with a baby. She had proof! She made an appointment with the doctor last night. As for her parents... that was harder. Why would he give money to help someone who stole from him? Her parents were her responsibility. She would get a job and help until Dad healed.

Blade came out of the office. She didn't look at him as he walked outside, closing the front door with a quiet click. Tattletale. She needed to remember that fact in the future.

"Lyla, come here."

Gavin didn't yell. That must be a good sign, right? Lyla rose and tried to conceal her nerves as she walked into his office. He sat behind the desk in the office chair she rode him in yesterday. That felt like a lifetime ago. She didn't have the courage to look him in the eye. She could feel his anger pulsing in the air. She clasped trembling hands together and waited.

"Blade had a lot to say."

Loudmouthed, traitor bastard.

"Do you really think I'd cheat on you?"

Lyla ignored the painful wrench in her chest. "Not right now—" she blurted and stumbled back when he erupted from his chair.

"Not right now?"

"I mean, I meant—"

"Jesus Christ, are you fucking serious?"

"I don't think you're cheating," she said, trying to sound firm, but it sounded unintentionally tentative.

He stared at her. She couldn't read him, but she felt something building and tried to head it off.

"I-I believe you're happy with me," she said, and when he didn't comment, her confidence took a nosedive. How could he be happy with someone with such a fucked-up family? "Or satisfied." Still no response. "I-I know I don't have any right to ask for anything. Thank you for paying for the groceries today. I would have used my own money but..." But he had it. "Dad's bedridden for a couple of months, and Mom's never worked. I need to help them, at least until he's well enough to find a job."

"Why would anyone hire a thief as an accountant?"

Lyla blinked. "You'd stop him from trying to get another job?"

"I'm not going to give him a fucking reference."

Of course he wouldn't. So her father would *never* get another job? She twisted her hands together. "I can get a job, pay you back for the groceries and—"

"No."

She stopped talking, but he didn't elaborate. She raised her eyes and was caught by his predator stare.

"You aren't going to work," he decreed.

"But I need to help. They're my parents."

"Then you ask me for money."

"You'd give me money to pay for their bills?"

A muscle twitched near his left eye. "Yes."

She felt awful even though he could afford it. "Thank you. You don't have to do that."

"I think you're confused about something."

Lyla tensed.

"You think I don't care about you."

She frowned. "I know you care."

"Do you? Because I've been trying to show you that I'm all in, and you're backing away from me like I'm going to hit you."

"I'm sorry." After all he'd done for her, he didn't need this crap.

"Come here."

She hesitated for the barest second before she rounded the desk. She stopped a foot away from him.

"Look at me."

Lyla looked up, and his hands clasped her face. His touch was gentle even though his features were stiff and cut into brutal, unyielding lines.

"If I want pussy, I can get it," he said.

Lyla jerked, and his hold on her firmed. "I know."

"I don't want other women," he continued, eyes boring into hers. "They don't know me, don't give a fuck about me. I know the difference between a slut and a real woman."

His thumb brushed over her bottom lip as he considered her. Her heart pounded in her ears.

"You're right."

When he didn't continue, she prompted, "About what?"

"Back then, the things I did for business still bothered me. It kept me up at night. I didn't want it to touch you, so I used other women. I poured that shit into them. They welcomed it, craved it."

When Lyla tried to twist out of his hold, his hand dropped from her face to her arm. He hauled her close.

"Now I don't need the other women. I don't feel anything when I do what I have to."

Lyla said nothing.

"Three years without you, you think I'd be dumb enough to fuck it up again?"

"I think you need more," she whispered.

"More what?"

"More than I have to give. Right now, you think I'm enough, but eventually—"

He clapped a hand over her mouth and stared at her as if he'd never seen her before. "For the rest of my life, you'll be enough."

His eyes were hungry, desperate pools that wanted to swallow her.

"I never told you I loved you, did I?"

Lyla's heart stopped.

"I never told you that I would die for you, that I adore everything about you. I can't get enough of you. I never will." His voice was strong and sure. "I'm fucking greedy when it comes to you. I don't want anything between us, even my dad, and that's fucked up. But I don't care. I want you to need me, and you don't. You can live without me. You did it for years."

He jerked away and paced, hands in his hair, breathing hard. She watched him, torn between backing away or going to him. She did neither and stayed where she was.

"I hate that you went on without me, that you *could*." Veins popped out on his neck. "You let another man touch you, turned to him for—" He broke off and sent everything on his desk flying. "I forced you to run from me. I know that. Living without you was my punishment, and I suffered, Lyla."

He whirled back to her, his movements jerky and uncontrolled.

"I love you."

It sounded like a threat.

"And I will never let you go, never turn to another woman. You're everything I need."

Tears poured down her face.

"I have men watching you. I call them constantly because I need to know you're still here. I don't care if it makes me look weak. I need to know you're waiting for me. I'm identical to my father in one aspect. When we love, we do it once and forever. I'll never let you go. I recognize what you are, what place you have in my life. I can feel you slipping through my fingers. I won't allow it." He spread his arms wide. "You want to hook me, baby? Take me. Anything, everything. Show me you want *something* from me and aren't waiting to run when my back is turned. I know I don't deserve you, and that most people only get one shot at love. If they blow it, that's it. I forced you to give me a second and third shot. I'll keep asking you for chances because we will never be over. I want legal ties."

"Legal—?" she began, but her voice cut off as his meaning penetrated.

"You're not a part of our world. That's why Dad and I are drawn to you. Innocence, loyalty, purity, and love. You remind me of my mom. You have her spirit. She kept my dad grounded. I lost it when you left. Suddenly, I looked forward to doling out punishments, to sowing fear into the slums. I had nothing to lose, nothing to go home to, and then I found you." His eyes flashed with a rage so potent that goose bumps rose on her arms. "I haven't had a weakness for them to exploit until now. Your kidnapping was a test to see how I'd react. Their orders were to grab you, ask for a ransom, and see how quickly I'd react to get the money together. You weren't supposed to be touched. Someone's fucking with me, and everything in me wants to retaliate, but I have to pass that duty onto someone else. I can be content with those worthless fucks' deaths because I have you. My future flows through you, so I'll pay the price, whatever it is, to have you."

Lyla reached for him, and he came toward her, a wild rush of man, power, and need. He kissed her hard, punishing and cherishing at the same time. His hands roamed over her, digging into flesh, clutching at her clothes. With an angry growl, he set her on the desk. She grabbed his shoulders for balance as he lifted her dress and spread her legs. She had only a moment's warning before his cock sank into her. She moaned into his mouth as he slid slowly but inexorably into her. He didn't stop until he sheathed himself completely. When he yanked her jacket off, the box of condoms fell out of her pocket and bounced on the desk. Gavin pulled back from the kiss to yank her dress straps down and spotted them.

"No," he growled as her dress pooled around her waist and he unsnapped her bra.

"No?" she gasped as he sucked on her pulse and pulled her tight against him.

"No condoms, no IUD." He raised his head. "You should take your mom's advice. Hook me, Lyla."

"A baby?" she asked, mind whirling.

"We're going all the way this time. My ring on your finger, my baby planted in your belly. No half measures. You agreed, baby girl."

"When did I agree to that?" she demanded and bit back a moan.

He gripped her hair as he powered into her, hard strokes that left her gasping for more.

"You agreed to stay with me. Permanently. You think I'd stop at anything but having you bound to me every way possible?"

"But I didn't know..." She let out a short scream and convulsed around him as she climaxed.

Gavin held back as he watched her come apart for him. When she was weak and trembling in his arms, he began to move again.

"You're trying to kill me," she moaned, grimacing against the nearly painful aftershocks.

"No, I'm greedy," he corrected as he lifted her thighs so he could go deeper. He bared his teeth as he thrust. "If you're pregnant, I'd be fucking ecstatic. That loyalty you have toward your parents, I want it. I *need* it."

"You have it."

"No." He bit her bottom lip and tugged but didn't break the skin as he had in the kitchen. "I don't have your loyalty yet, but I will. You're still unsure of me. We'll work past that."

Gavin's hands moved to her clit. She jumped and tried to pull his hand away.

"I can't!" she groaned, head tucked under his chin.

"You will," he decreed. "Come with me, baby girl."

He knew just how much pressure to use. Lyla erupted again, and this time, he came with her, driving himself as deep as possible and then slumped over her, head resting on her chest as she sprawled on his desk. They stayed that way for a long minute before Gavin disengaged and carried her upstairs. They settled in bed facing one another. That awful tension shimmering in the air around him dissipated.

Lyla stroked his cheek and watched his eyes close as if her touch brought him unspeakable joy. Her throat clogged with tears. "I love you, Gavin. Too much."

His eyes snapped opened. "You can never love me too much."

"It scares the hell out of me."

He clasped her face. "Say it."

"I love you."

"Again."

"I love you."

"You'll marry me?"

Lyla bit her lip, and he grinned.

"You love me; you marry me."

"I do love you, but marriage ..."

"Is inevitable. I already talked to a wedding planner."

She tried to rise, but he kept her lying beside him. "Wedding planner? Are you insane?"

His smile had an edge to it. "The day you agreed to stay, I talked to him. He's over the top. He's handled some prestigious weddings. You can meet with him, go over details."

"Details for a wedding," Lyla said numbly. "You don't ask for much, do you?"

"We wasted years. I'm not wasting another month."

"Month?"

"Didn't I tell you, baby girl? We're getting married by the end of the month."

Lyla held up a hand as her stomach pitched and roiled as if she were on a roller coaster. "Gavin, we can't—"

"Of course, we can," he said. "We'll have the wedding at one of our hotels, invitations are being made, and anyone will jump at the chance to make your dress."

"This is too fast!" she exploded, thumping his shoulder with her fist. "Within two weeks, you show up and turn my life upside down. I've been blackmailed, pushed around, seduced, kidnapped, and now ordered to marry you! When is it going to stop?"

"It won't stop until you're mine," Gavin said firmly. "I should have the other side of the business wrapped up by then, and I'm not wasting any more time. I'm tying up loose ends, so we have time to build a life, a family." His eyes searched hers. "Do you want that with me?"

"Holy shit, I'm not ready for this."

"You will be. I'll make sure of it."

Lyla bit her lip. "What about my parents?"

"Give them whatever you want. My money is your money. I'll get you a credit card and put you on my bank accounts."

He had given her an allowance before, but this gave her even more freedom. His trust and generosity stunned her. "Really?"

Gavin flopped on his back and fit her into the curve of his shoulder. "You want them to pay for not being good parents, so be it. Let them be homeless. You want them to be millionaires; I don't give a fuck. I don't respect them. You're you despite their influence. They have no idea how special you are. If they treated you right, I would have rewarded them. Instead, I watched your father skim hundreds, thousands, and then hundreds of thousands. I'm not going to lie and tell you that I didn't enjoy beating the hell out of him."

"Why did you allow him to steal from you?" It was a question that had bothered her from the start. Five hundred thousand was a lot of money. Gavin wasn't the type to miss something like that.

"Your family is your biggest weakness. When I found

you, I'd need a way to hold you here, keep you indebted to me. I let him dig himself a hole and waited to use him for my benefit."

"What if you never found me?"

"I would've found you, Lyla, sooner or later." He shut his eyes and wrapped her close. "Stay with me while I sleep."

"Okay."

Lyla stared out the window at the brilliant blue sky and wondered if she would ever have a simple life. Probably not. Not when she was about to marry Gavin Pyre. She never imagined that Gavin had marriage on his mind, but he always managed to surprise her. His face, even in sleep, was fierce and dangerous. He loved her. She loved him. They were complete opposites, yet somehow, they fit together. Lyla said a silent prayer before she dozed off.

Lyla woke alone, which pissed her off. She had always been a light sleeper, but now it seemed that she slept like the dead. It was dark outside, which meant she had been out for a while. She decided to shower and was in the process of shampooing when her hair snagged on her finger. She yelped and slowly jiggled her hair until it came loose. She lifted her left hand and froze. A beautiful diamond ring winked seductively at her. Lyla held her hand up to the spray and stared at a pale blue diamond set on a thin band decorated with white diamonds. It took her breath away.

"Gavin?" Her voice was weak.

Her hand began to shake. Of course, she remembered talking about marriage, but the ring made it painfully real. Lyla washed the suds out of her hair, wrapped herself in a robe and ran downstairs. She found Gavin in his office on the phone. He quickly ended the call when Lyla flapped her hand in his face.

"You don't like it?" he asked warily.

"When did you buy this?" she demanded.

"Over three years ago."

She was so shocked; she took a step backward. "You bought this... before?"

"Yes, I've been waiting to give it to you for a long time. You like it?"

Lyla eyes filled with tears. "I love it," she managed before she launched herself at him. She wrapped herself around him and hugged him tightly. "You're sure?"

"Yes."

She kissed him and pulled back. "We need to tell your dad."

He grinned. "He might faint."

"We need to tell him tomorrow... and Carmen. Oh, God." Just the thought of their reactions made her chest tighten with anxiety.

"Don't worry about it. They'll be happy for us," Gavin said.

"I know, but you said you wanted the wedding by the end of the month? How is that going to happen?"

"Money," he said carelessly and kissed the palm of her hand. "I hope you know what kind of wedding you want."

"What do you mean?"

"You know, colors, theme, that kind of thing."

She nibbled on her bottom lip. "We can't elope?"

Gavin burst out laughing. The lighthearted sound took away most of her anxiety. She liked seeing him carefree and happy. He was normally way too serious and intense.

"Aside from the fact that Dad would kill us, I want the big wedding."

"Why?" If it were up to her, she would have a backyard wedding. She didn't want to be on display, in the papers, gossiped about. Gavin was high profile enough to garner media attention, which she hated.

"I'm only getting married once, and we have all the resources to make ours legendary. Plus, I want all our business associates to attend."

"How many guests are we talking?" she asked warily.

"I don't know. My assistant gave some numbers to Armand, the wedding planner. You have an appointment to meet him by the end of the week."

"Pushy."

"*Very* pushy," he agreed and tasted her lips. "By the end of the month, you'll be Lyla Pyre." His eyes glinted with hunger. "You ready for that, baby girl?"

"No."

"Too bad." He softened his words by kissing her again. "I have to take care of some business, and then we can eat dinner. The cook is making something. Ten minutes."

Lyla unwrapped herself from him and hurried out of the office. She finished her shower and then paced the room as she dialed Carmen who picked up on the fourth ring.

"Hey, girl," Carmen puffed.

Lyla paused. "Did I catch you at a bad time?"

"No."

"Why do you sound as if you've been working out?"

"I've been working out with Vinny in bed," Carmen cackled.

TMI. Lyla took a deep breath and blurted, "I'm getting married."

Utter silence and then a weak, "No."

"Yes."

A bit louder, "No."

"Yes."

"No!"

"Yes," Lyla repeated.

"Fuck, yeah!" Carmen screamed. "Vinny, they're doing it. Not fucking, getting married! Yeah! No. I don't know. Let me ask her." Carmen's voice was frantic with excitement. "When are you getting married?"

"He wants to get married by the end of the month."

"What? How are you going to do that?"

"A wedding planner. Armand?"

"You got *Armand*? Oh. My. God. This is insane. I'm so excited! Are you happy?"

"Yes." Terrified but happy. "I don't know what I'm going to do."

"Obviously, you have to figure out what kind of wedding you want. I want to see the ring! Send me a picture."

Lyla wrung her hands. "I want to elope."

"You can't elope," Carmen said sharply.

"I know. Gavin won't let us."

"Thank God for that. Okay. Oh, my God. We need to get you a dress, and do you know what kind of flowers—?"

"I have no idea."

"I'm the maid of honor, right?"

"Of course."

"Better be. And Vinny's best man?"

"I think so."

"Better be," Carmen said again. "Oh my God, I'm going on Pinterest. We should shop for wedding dresses tomorrow, so you have an idea of what you want. I'll send you ideas."

The line went dead. Lyla stared at it and then shook her head. She wanted to call Manny, but this wasn't something she wanted to tell him over the phone, and they should tell him together.

Lyla went to the kitchen and saw that the cook prepared salmon and an amazing salad with wine and candles. The cook smiled at Lyla and chatted with her before she left for the night. Lyla was pouring wine when Gavin came in.

"This is nice," Lyla said.

"We just got engaged. We should celebrate," he said and kissed her long and deep.

"You keep that up; we won't eat," she said.

"Fine with me," he said, drawing her closer.

"Well, I'm hungry," she said and pushed him into his seat.

Gavin went easily enough. They fixed their plates while Lyla stared at her ring.

"Carmen wants to look at wedding dresses tomorrow," she said.

He nodded. "Good."

"I have to visit my parents," she mused, thinking about their financial problems and her upcoming wedding. She hesitated and then said, "I don't want my dad to walk me down the aisle. I want Manny to do it."

"Dad would be honored," Gavin said.

Her phone chimed. She picked it up and saw Carmen's text, demanding to see the ring. She took a picture and sent it.

"Why the blue diamond?" Lyla asked.

"Your eyes."

She looked up. "My eyes?"

"The diamond is the same color as your eyes. I knew you wouldn't wear something over the top, but I wanted the ring to be unique."

"It is," she said and when the phone chimed, she told him, "Carmen agrees. Is Vinny going to be your best man?"

"Of course. He's like my brother. Why?"

"Just making sure before Carmen confronts you." She examined this man who she would soon legally be bound to. "You're going to be fine with one side of the business and not the other?"

"I'm training someone to take over. He already knows parts of the business, but certain contacts need to be handled directly."

"Who's taking over?"

"It's better that you don't know."

Yes. The less she knew about it, the better, but, "Why are you so involved? I mean, you play the same role with your casinos as you do with the underworld, right? You're at the top and usually don't get involved in the day-to-day operations. Don't you have, like, a manager or something?"

"I have men I trust under me, but my name is what gives us credibility and strength. I get involved when it goes bad. In this case, I need to introduce the new crime lord and that must be done in person."

That was a part of their lives that would soon be a thing of the past. Gavin loved her enough to give it up. The strength of his feelings for her scared and thrilled her. She would never be able to handle him, but she was okay with that. He was his own person and a force to be reckoned with. It was who he was, and nothing would change him. She tried to imagine a baby cradled in his arms and felt her throat tighten with emotion. God. Gavin Pyre, a father...

"What are you thinking about?" he asked.

"You want to be a father?"

"Yes. My mom had a hard pregnancy, so she only had me. I always wanted a big family. You?"

"I always wished I had a sister or older brother, but I had Carmen, and she was enough. For that matter, we're both only children."

"I'm up for the challenge of a big family if you are."

Lyla tried to imagine kids running around the mansion and smiled. "I'm up for it." He reached for her, and she tutted and scooted backward. "We're eating dinner!"

"We'll eat after," he decreed and hauled her into his arms.

14

MANNY PUNCHED his fist in the air and danced around his dining room after Gavin announced their impending nuptials. Manny kissed his son on both cheeks before he wrapped Lyla in a hug and rocked her from side to side. When he set her down, he clasped her face.

"Thank you," he whispered.

The tears rose unexpectedly and spilled over. "W-Will you walk me down the aisle?"

Manny staggered back as if her words mortally wounded him. "Walk you down the aisle?"

"My dad is…" She shrugged. It was no secret that her father cared little for her. "I want you to do it if you don't mind."

Manny took a deep breath. "It would be my honor."

Lyla hugged him tightly. "I'm so happy."

"This is all I wanted for both of you," Manny said solemnly.

"I'm going to look for a dress today. Carmen's coming with me."

"When's the wedding?" Manny asked.

"By the end of the month," Gavin said.

Manny didn't look surprised. He nodded and clapped his hands together. "We have much to do. Let me know if I can help. This news has made me extremely happy."

They left shortly after, hand in hand. Gavin drove with one hand on her thigh.

"I'm glad we told him in person," she said.

"Yes," Gavin agreed.

"And he's going to walk me down the aisle."

"Did you have doubts that he would?" Gavin glanced sideways at her. "You're his daughter in every way but blood... thank God."

"You never know. I'm just relieved he didn't mind."

"I've never seen my dad react to anyone the way he does to you except my mother." He stroked her thigh with his thumb. "You're good for both of us."

She felt a pang in her chest but said nothing. Gavin pulled up to Carmen's mansion. She rushed out of the house, screaming and reaching for Lyla's door handle before Gavin came to a stop. She hauled Lyla out so she could see the ring.

"I'm so happy!" Carmen crowed, bouncing on her stilettos.

"I see that," Gavin said dryly as he got out of the car.

Vinny came down the steps and gave Gavin a manly handshake and clap on the back before coming to Lyla. He wrapped her close and whispered in her ear, "He loves you, you know?"

Lyla pulled back and smiled up at him. "I know."

Vinny nodded and kissed her before he looked at Gavin. "We'll leave these two together, huh?"

Gavin leaned down to kiss her. She wasn't prepared for

the carnal kiss or the way his fingers dug into her hips. When he pulled away, she searched his eyes.

"You okay?" she asked.

"Get whatever dress you want. Money's no object."

"I hear ya!" Carmen chirped.

"You feel okay?" he asked, and she nodded. "You need anything, you call me."

"Okay."

"A month, Lyla. That's all I'm willing to wait," he warned.

"I'm not contesting it," she said.

"Good." He looked at Carmen. "Take care of her."

Carmen tossed her hair. "Of course."

"Blade will shadow you," Gavin said, gesturing to the SUV.

"Okay."

"Don't let your parents give you any shit," he said in a more businesslike tone. "You don't owe them anything."

She nodded.

"Call me if you need anything."

Another hard kiss and he walked to his car and ducked in while Vinny took the passenger seat. Carmen linked their arms together and led her to the gold convertible.

"I love seeing Gavin like this," Carmen said.

"Like what?"

"Desperate."

"Desperate?" Lyla echoed, offended. "He isn't desperate."

"Any man who gives his fiancée only a month before tying the knot is worried the woman will change her mind."

"I won't," Lyla said.

Carmen gave her a sidelong look. "Good. Because you'd have to deal with Gavin *and* me." Carmen peeled out of the driveway, forcing Blade's tires to squeal as he tried to keep up. "So we have an appointment with a legendary dressmaker. I talked to Armand, and he recommended her. Do you know what type of dress you want?"

"White?"

Carmen gave her a disgusted look. "Girl, you're lucky you have me."

Lyla waved at Carmen before she trudged up the steps to Gavin's home. She was numb with exhaustion. Wedding details swirled around her head. Between Carmen's boundless enthusiasm and the no-nonsense dressmaker, she had no idea what she wanted. She tried on countless dresses until they all began to blur together. This was Vegas. The dressmaker went all out with her creations. When Lyla described what she pictured in her head—something traditional and simple—the dressmaker and Carmen wore identical appalled expressions. Tomorrow they had a follow-up appointment, but she was dreading it. She showered and dressed in the most comfortable pajamas she owned. She went downstairs, warmed up a meal, and curled up on the couch to call Gavin.

"Are you sure you don't want to elope?" she asked when he answered.

"Yes. Are you home?"

"Yes. Carmen dropped me off. I'm eating dinner and then going to bed. When are you coming home?"

"I'm not sure."

"I went to see my parents. I told my mom we're engaged and you're going to take care of their bills."

"You're taking care of it. I couldn't care less."

"I know, but the money is coming from you."

"Lyla, it's your money."

"Okay, well, she didn't like that Manny would walk me down the aisle but—"

"It isn't up to her."

"Yes, I know, and I told her that," Lyla soothed. "Everything's fine. Are you all right?"

"Yes. Hearing from you made me feel better." A pause and then, "Tell me you love me."

"I love you."

"Even though you know what I'm capable of?"

A chill trickled her spine. "Is something wrong?"

"No, I just need to hear you say it doesn't matter."

"I love you no matter what." No response. "Come home to me, Gavin."

"I will. Once I get this squared away, you won't be able to get rid of me. Dream of me, baby."

"I will."

Lyla finished her meal and stared into space, thinking of the strange conversation and their upcoming wedding. It was clear that Gavin was pushing the new crime lord hard. She wouldn't be able to rest until he left the underworld completely.

She climbed into bed and stared up at the ceiling for a long time, thinking how much her life changed in such a short time. Really, life was bizarre. She thought of Jonathan with a distant sense of regret. Now that she was back with Gavin, it was clear that what she gave Jonathan was a watered-down version of love. He deserved better.

Lyla didn't like being in bed by herself. She cursed the fact that Gavin's business kept him out at all hours of the night. Who was the new crime lord? What was Gavin doing tonight that made him uneasy enough to need reassurance from her? Lyla buried her face in the pillow and fisted her hands. Images of the pervert and his partner flashed into her mind, quickly followed by the memory of Gavin covered in the pervert's blood. She relaxed instantly. Gavin would do whatever he had to, and he would come back to her. Nothing would stop him.

───────────

"Lyla, wake up."

A hard hand shook her awake. Lyla opened her eyes and saw Gavin standing beside the bed. She opened her mouth to ask what was going on and saw something dark smeared on the side of his face, neck, and suit. She shot out of bed as her mind registered that Gavin was covered in dried blood.

"What happened? You're hurt!"

"It's not my blood," Gavin said tonelessly. "Get dressed."

"What? Whose blood is it?"

"Vinny. He's dead."

Lyla went cold. "Dead?"

"Get dressed. We need to see Carmen."

"Vinny's dead?" she repeated and shook her head. "No, I just saw him!" This morning Vinny kissed her on the cheek and said Gavin loved her.

"We don't have time, Lyla. We have to get to Carmen."

"Carmen? Oh my God," she whispered. How would Carmen react when she found out that her husband was dead?

"Get dressed, Lyla. Hurry."

She changed out of her pajamas, mind whirling. Vinny dead? She'd known Vinny for nearly a decade. She thought of him as a brother. She braced her hand against the wall as the full impact of his loss slammed into her. Her eyes flooded with tears. Male voices shouted outside, reminding her that she didn't have time to grieve. She had to get to Carmen.

Lyla grabbed a clean shirt for Gavin and ran downstairs. He was on the phone, rapping out orders in Spanish. When he saw her, he slammed the front door open and pulled her outside. Men and cars were everywhere. Guns were displayed openly. The buzz of fury emanating from the men made her feel as if she walked into a war zone. Blade beckoned her to an SUV. She slid into the back seat, shaking hands clasped on her lap. Gavin got in beside her and continued to talk on his phone with an icy, precise tone that was too calm.

When he hung up, he shrugged off his stained suit jacket and the shirt beneath. He reached for a water bottle and wiped his cheek and neck. Lyla smelled the stench of blood, and her stomach lurched. He slipped into the clean shirt. She couldn't stand the suspense any longer.

"What happened?"

"Introduced Vinny to our contact a week ago. When Vinny went to meet him today, the contact decided to test him. Vinny wasn't expecting it. He was shot three times in the chest. Five of my men died."

Lyla covered her mouth, unable to comprehend what he was saying. "The contact decided to test Vinny? Why?"

"They're like wild dogs. They sensed he wasn't strong enough." Gavin's voice began to shred as his emotions came through. "I rushed down there, but he was already dead. The contact took the shipment, the money, everything. I never should have let him go alone." Gavin slammed his fist into the back of the seat. The guard in the passenger seat rocked forward from the blow. "Fuck!"

Something clicked in her brain. "Vinny was the new crime lord?" Lyla asked in numb horror.

"He wanted it. The money, the power..." Gavin shook his head. "I thought I could train him, teach him the ropes. I—"

As his voice faded, Lyla reached out and placed a hand on his thigh. His body was tight and coiled, ready to strike. She resisted the urge to draw away. This was Gavin. He wouldn't hurt her. He didn't acknowledge her touch, but he didn't push her away. She fought back tears. Vinny wasn't strong enough to take on men like the pervert and his partner. Vinny was cheerful, easygoing, and didn't possess the instincts of a predator like Gavin who had been trained from birth to lead.

When they pulled up to Carmen's home, she couldn't move. How could she tell her cousin that her husband was dead? Did Carmen know that Vinny had agreed to take Gavin's place in the underworld?

Gavin grasped her hand and pulled her out of the SUV. Security at the door nodded to Gavin and backed away as he rang the doorbell. Her heart pounded as they heard footsteps and then Carmen opened the door. She clearly hadn't gone to sleep despite the early morning hour. Her inquiring look shifted when she saw Gavin standing there. Her eyes locked on his face and then she backed up, shaking her head wildly.

Gavin reached for her. "I'm sorry, Carmen—"

"No!" Carmen screamed. "No! Don't say it."

"I'll find who did this and—"

Carmen leaped forward and beat her fists against Gavin's chest. "You promised me, Gavin!"

Her shrill scream chilled Lyla to the bone. She hauled her cousin backward just as Carmen hit Gavin across the face. Carmen ripped herself out of Lyla's hold and grabbed the closest thing to her—a priceless vase and hurled it at the wall. Rainbow shards rained down around Carmen, but she didn't pause. Lyla watched with her hands over her mouth as Carmen systematically destroyed her art collection, even beating a metal statue with an iron poker until it was a misshapen blob.

"Blade," Gavin bit out.

Blade walked forward with something in his hand.

"What is that?" Lyla asked.

"A sedative," Gavin said a moment before Blade stuck a syringe in Carmen's neck.

"No!" Lyla shouted.

Carmen whirled and tried to hit Blade with the poker. Blade efficiently disarmed Carmen. The momentum he used to rip the poker from her grasp made Carmen hit the ground hard. Lyla knelt beside her cousin who was breathing hard, eyes dilated with shock and grief.

"He can't be gone," Carmen whispered. "I can't live without him."

Lyla stroked her hair back from her face. "I'm so sorry."

Carmen's eyes fluttered shut. Blade waited a few moments before he picked her up. Lyla led the way to Carmen's room and turned back the covers. Blade set her on the bed.

Lyla glared at him. "You carry sedatives on you?"

"I'm always prepared," he said as he walked out of the room.

Lyla wet a washcloth and wiped Carmen's tear streaked face before she climbed in bed with her. She hugged her cousin who trembled uncontrollably. Carmen buried her face against Lyla's chest and let out a keening sound that ripped her heart to shreds. Lyla murmured soothingly into her hair as her cousin clutched her. Vinny was the closest thing Gavin had to a brother and best friend. They had been raised together. Her heart pounded with dread and fear. What would Gavin do?

When Carmen finally submitted to the sedative and went unconscious, Lyla went downstairs and found Gavin on the phone. Carmen's inconsolable rage and grief left Lyla feeling raw and terrified for Gavin. She wrapped her arms around herself and waited for him to get off the phone. She could taste violence in the air, and it turned her stomach. The sun rose, revealing the destruction Carmen wrought in her museum-like home.

"How is she?" Gavin asked when he turned to her.

"Not good."

Gavin nodded. "I'm going to get them. I'll avenge Vinny."

Lyla had a vivid image of Gavin over the pervert's body —savage and devoid of all humanity. She reached for him. "Gavin."

He stepped away from her. She stilled with her hands suspended in midair. His eyes were a burning copper that revealed nothing. Gavin was morphing into the man she ran from, the man she didn't want him to be.

"This won't stop," she said.

"It will once I make them pay. They'll beg for death before I give it to them."

"Gavin, when does it end?"

"When they end."

She licked dry lips. "You're supposed to be letting this go, not going deeper into it."

"My cousin died," he said quietly.

"Yes."

"It's my fault he's dead."

She shook her head. "No, Gavin."

"He wasn't cold enough to blow their heads off for insulting him. He was too soft. I fucking knew that, but I was so desperate to be with you that I allowed you to cloud my better judgment."

Lyla accepted the blame and the verbal blow. Vinny's death was on her as well. "So you're saying you're the only one who can do this?"

Gavin said nothing. He didn't have to. He would keep the crime lord mantle and turn back into the monster he had to be.

"So we're back to where we started," she whispered, heart splintering.

"You want more people to die?" he hissed.

"What if it's you next?" she shot back. "What if it's someone else you love?"

"I won't give them the chance."

"Gavin, please, don't do this," she pleaded.

"No."

"Gavin—"

"They'll pay. They all will."

Lyla reached for him, and once more, he avoided her. "What are you doing?"

He stared at her, a mixture of need and rage spiking across his features before he turned away. "I don't have time for you. I have to fix this fuck up."

"By killing more people."

He stopped, then turned. "By doing what I have to."

Lyla swallowed hard. "So you're not going to let go of the business?"

"And have someone else die in my place? No."

Lyla felt a slashing pain in her chest. "You promised, Gavin."

"What do you expect me to do?"

"Let it go. Vinny's death should convince you that it's not worth it."

"Grow up, Lyla. If I ignore this, they'll never stop."

"They kidnapped me, and now they killed Vinny. Someone's gunning for you, Gavin! Can't you see that?" she shouted, losing control. Seeing Carmen's breakdown felt like a preview of what she was in for if Gavin died.

"Let them come," he hissed.

"I love you!" Tears filled her eyes and spilled over. "You said nothing else matters but us."

"Look where that's brought us!" he roared.

The force of his shout made her take a step back. She clasped her shaking hands together. "So you're breaking your promise to me." He was ten feet away, but it might as well have been miles. There was no trace of softness in him, no trace of the man she agreed to marry.

"I have to." With that, he walked out the door.

Lyla heard the screech of tires and the murmur of male voices outside. She wanted to rage and scream. Instead, she found a broom and dustpan and began to clean with silent tears slipping down her face. She mourned for Vinny, the only brother she'd ever known and partner for her cousin and Gavin, the people she loved the most. What now?

The front door opened and Carmen's parents stepped into the house. Lyla dropped the broom and ran to them. Her burly uncle wrapped her close.

"Lyla," Uncle Louie murmured as she began to sob, the events of the past hours overwhelming her.

"Where is she?" Aunt Isabel asked.

Lyla pulled it together and took a deep breath. "She's upstairs. They had to sedate her." She gestured to the ruined paintings, statues, and shattered glass.

Aunt Isabel gasped and put her hand over her heart. "My poor girl."

"S-she's devastated." Lyla spent most of her time at Aunt

Isabel and Uncle Louie's house as a teenager. They treated her like a second daughter.

"Did Gavin get the fuckers?" Uncle Louie demanded.

He was a sweet man, which made it easy to forget that he had been Manny's enforcer once upon a time.

"I-I don't know," Lyla said.

"He will," Uncle Louie said with a curt nod.

"I don't know how long she's going to be out," Lyla said, rubbing her throbbing forehead, and then headed into the kitchen. "You should see her. I'll make some coffee."

Carmen's parents went upstairs while Lyla made a much-needed pot of coffee. The doorbell rang. She heard murmured voices but focused on starting breakfast instead of seeing who it was.

"Baby girl."

Lyla turned and saw Manny. The tears came again, and she went to him. He rubbed her back as he held her tight.

"He won't stop," Lyla whispered.

"Let Gavin work out his rage," Manny said.

"By killing people?" she asked, pulling back to see his face.

Manny looked as if he aged since she saw him yesterday. "It's what we know."

Lyla shook her head. "He blames me for Vinny's death, for influencing his decision to pass the crime lord title off on someone else."

Manny sighed. "He's in pain, Lyla. Give him time."

Lyla let out a long breath. "Sit. I'm going to make breakfast."

"Where's Carmen?"

"Asleep. Blade sedated her."

"Carmen's a passionate woman. If she was trained like Gavin, she would be hunting right alongside him."

Lyla shuddered because she knew it was true. Aunt Isabel and Uncle Louie entered the kitchen and greeted Manny respectfully. They made small talk, but they fell into a weighted silence as they all wondered if Gavin had found Vinny's killer yet.

The next few days passed in a roller coaster of emotions. Lyla spent every waking moment with Carmen. She let her cousin rage, reminisce, and grieve. She forced Carmen to eat and even bathed her after outbursts that left Carmen weak as a baby. Through Aunt Isabel's gentle suggestions, Carmen was able to plan a funeral, but it left them all exhausted. By the end of the week, Lyla was bone-weary and heartsick. There was no word from Gavin, which increased her anxiety and stress, but she pushed that away and focused on Carmen. She slept at her cousin's house and even wore her clothes.

The night before the funeral, neither of them slept. They lay side by side in bed, staring up at the ceiling. Lyla couldn't believe how the course of their lives could change so drastically in so little time. The thought of Vinny being shot in the chest haunted her. How could one human being do that to another? In retrospect, it was now glaringly obvious that Vinny would be Gavin's choice for crime lord since he trusted so few. If she'd known that Vinny would take over, would she have put a stop to it?

"How could God do this to me?" Carmen whispered.

"Things happen," she said, focusing on Carmen instead of her dark thoughts. "Did you know that Vinny had agreed to take over that side of the business?"

"Yes, I knew, bu ..."

Carmen began to cry. Lyla squeezed her hand.

"I never thought something like this would happen. He said he could handle it, and I trusted him to be careful, to come home to me."

"I'm sorry, Carmen," she whispered, heart heavy with guilt.

"It's not your fault."

"Gavin's not going to give it up after this," Lyla said quietly. "He doesn't want anyone else to get hurt."

Carmen turned her head on the pillow to look at her. "What are you going to do?"

"I don't know. He hasn't called me in a week. He's gone cold."

"Maybe after he finds who did this to Vinny, he'll come back to you."

"We'll see," Lyla said doubtfully. "They kidnap me and then kill Vinny. What next?"

Carmen decided to keep Vinny's funeral small, but that was nearly impossible because of the Pyres connections in the city. Carmen wore a black dress, veil, and red hooker heels. Lyla stood by her side as they greeted everyone. Uncle Louie and Aunt Isabel stood in the receiving line with them. It wasn't a secret how Vinny died, which created an underlying tension that turned her stomach.

Lyla's heart felt as if it were breaking. A week ago, Vinny was alive, and now they were at his funeral. A week ago, she tried on wedding gowns, and now she was wearing unrelieved black. Lyla looked up as someone made a path through the crowd. Her heart lightened when she saw Gavin. He was alive... and pissed. He hadn't called or stopped by Carmen's house. A part of her wanted to think he was staying away because he didn't want to intrude on Carmen's grief and believed he was to blame, but the wrathful look he directed at her made her heart shrivel into a ball. Clearly, he still blamed her for Vinny's death.

"Gavin?" Uncle Louie demanded.

"I got him," Gavin said.

There were cheers and satisfied grunts from the crowd and the dark energy in the room lessened slightly. As everyone took their seats, Gavin went up to the podium and began to lead the service while Lyla sat between Carmen and Manny. Family got up to tell stories and honor Vinny's life. *Such a waste*, she thought and examined Gavin who stood off to the side as a childhood friend told a story about him and Vinny when they were kids. Gavin looked as remote as ever. He didn't look at her. She called the wedding planner and dressmaker to let them know about the tragedy. She was shocked to hear that Gavin had already postponed the wedding until further notice. What did that mean? Lyla twisted the blue diamond ring on her finger.

After the funeral, they congregated at Carmen's where everyone could eat, talk, and decompress. Lyla didn't stray from her cousin's side. Carmen had a few outbursts, but she quickly got herself under control. It was dark before she was able to look for Gavin in the crowd. She found him in the backyard, staring at nothing. He didn't acknowledge her presence.

"So you got whoever did this to Vinny?" she asked.

"Yes."

"Just him?"

"I needed to make a statement."

"So you killed more than one."

Gavin said nothing.

"I called Armand. He said we're postponing the wedding," she said gently. She wasn't opposed to it, but he should have told her himself.

"I have to take back the reins for both businesses. I don't have time to get married right now."

His dismissive tone raked her raw. She ignored the pain and asked, "What do you want, Gavin?"

"Control."

"Of?"

"Everything. And until I get it, I'm not going to stop."

"Does that apply to me as well?" she asked.

He eyed her impassively. "I won't allow you to sway my decisions anymore."

She beat back the anger. "Meaning you're going to stay in the business and risk all our lives?"

"*No one* will cross me now."

She shook her head. "There will always be someone who wants to challenge you. You're in more danger than ever. Within a week, I was kidnapped, and Vinny murdered. You don't think that means something?"

"It means I should never have let myself be distracted by you!"

Lyla stepped back from the force of his shout. In the house, the remaining guests quieted. He panted as he tried to reel in his emotions, but he was unraveling in front of her. Guilt and rage ripped across his features.

"Just leave me be, Lyla," he said and walked away.

She walked in the house and began to clean up along with the staff they hired. She couldn't stop moving. If she did, she'd break down. When the last guest left, she and Carmen collapsed in her bed.

"It's over," Carmen whispered.

"Yes," Lyla agreed.

"What did Gavin say?"

Lyla swallowed hard. "He postponed the wedding indefinitely and told me that he wouldn't allow me to sway his decisions anymore."

"Dumb fuck," Carmen said and wrapped her close. "What are you going to do?"

"I don't know. He blames me for Vinny's death."

"It's no one's fault but the man who pulled the trigger," Carmen said and let out a long sigh. "I'm not going to lie. I'm glad Gavin killed him."

"I know." She slept better knowing that the pervert and his partner were dead too, but the price Gavin paid was dear. He morphed from a man looking forward to his future back to a man who thought he had nothing to lose. All hope, excitement, and love extinguished. Hate and rage took precedence over everything, including her. Where did they stand now? Another curveball in her life, another bump in their relationship. Did she bide her time until Gavin calmed down and try to coax him out of the darkness? Or should she cut her losses and leave? She couldn't leave, not when her cousin needed her. Plus, she wasn't capable of making any decisions right now, not when grief weighed her down.

"I know I've been difficult. I'm glad you're here," Carmen said.

"Of course." Silently, Lyla added, *It's the least I can do.*

"You and Gavin will figure it out."

Lyla let out a long breath and tried to suppress the urge to cry. She'd shed too many tears in the past week. She drifted into uneasy sleep with Carmen reaching for a husband who would never sleep beside her again.

15

THE NEXT DAY, Carmen urged Lyla to do something for herself. Although she was wan and thinner than she had been a week ago, Carmen looked steady. Blade drove Lyla back to Gavin's where she showered and changed. The house seemed as cold and empty as she felt. There was no sign that Gavin had been sleeping in their bed. She paced for a half hour before she asked Blade to take her to Manny's. She found him sitting by the pool. Wordlessly, he opened his arms to her. Lyla fell into his embrace.

"You've been taking care of Carmen?" he asked.

She nodded.

"That's good. How are you doing?"

Lyla took the chair beside him. "I don't know."

"Gavin's preoccupied at the moment."

"Preoccupied?" Lyla repeated with a snort. "He hates me."

"It's not your fault."

"And it's not his either!" she said passionately.

"I know." Manny scrubbed a hand down his face,

looking older than his years. "I can come out of retirement and—"

"No, Manny."

"Gavin still has a future—"

"And you do too," she insisted.

"I'm tougher than I look."

"Neither of you should be doing this. Gavin should be running the casinos, not killing people for revenge. You should be enjoying your retirement, not contemplating going back to a life of crime."

"I don't want this to affect your relationship with Gavin."

"That's Gavin's choice."

Manny took both of her hands in his. "Don't give up on him. He needs you."

"He's losing himself to these people. I want *him*, not all this crap that comes with his job."

There was a soft popping sound. Lyla turned her head and saw Ricardo topple sideways. Before she could comprehend what she was seeing, men in white masks and black suits glided into the backyard. Lyla couldn't catch her breath to scream as Manny rose and pushed her behind him.

"What do you want?" Manny asked.

Two men grabbed Manny by the arms and dragged him into the house. They didn't touch Lyla, but with a jerk of their guns, indicated that she follow Manny inside. Mind a blank canvas, she obeyed and stopped stock-still beside Ricardo who had been shot in the head. The men dragging Manny threw him on the polished marble in the middle of a circle of men dressed in identical suits and masks. There was an ominous silence on the grounds. Where were Blade and the rest of Manny's security? They couldn't *all* be dead, right? She opened her mouth to scream, but a soft voice caught her attention.

"I've heard stories about you, mighty crime lord."

Manny faced a man who had a gentle, pleasant voice that didn't belong to a killer.

"Funny how you look so harmless, but I know what you're capable of."

"Who are you?" Manny asked.

The man gave a mocking bow. "The new crime lord, of course."

"What do you want?" Manny asked as he braced himself on his hands and knees.

"I want your crown," the leader said, pacing around Manny with his hands clasped behind his back. "Gavin Pyre needs to be taken down a peg. Killing his cousin was just the beginning. It's a bonus to find his little fiancée here. Now I get to kill two birds with one stone."

Lyla raked her mind for a way to get out of this.

"But I think some payback is in order first."

The leader's leg flashed out, and Manny's head snapped back. He fell backward, head colliding with the marble floor with a horrible smacking sound. Lyla screamed and tried to move forward, but a man grabbed her arm in a bone-crushing grip. When she fought him, he shoved her to her knees and held her at gunpoint.

"I'm doing the unthinkable—scaling an all-out attack on the Pyres. No one thought it was possible, but here we are."

The monster spread his arms wide, and the men around him chuckled. Lyla fought the urge to vomit. This couldn't be happening. The leader stomped his foot on Manny's chest. Lyla heard bones break as Manny gasped and tried to get away.

"No!" she screamed, past the point of caring that a gun was being pointed at her.

Her captor used the butt of his gun to stun her into

silence. The impact made her ears ring and her vision blurred. She blinked hastily, unable to rip her eyes from Manny who was being beaten to death. Other men joined their leader and broke every bone in Manny's body. She fought her captor until he slammed her on the ground and sat on top of her. Lyla couldn't breathe. The leader with the sweet voice used the butt of his gun to crush Manny's face as if he wasn't a human being but a clay sculpture that needed to be remade. Bone crunched, and the horrible sound of Manny's screams faded into an ominous silence.

"Please, I'll do anything! Please stop," Lyla pleaded, terror eclipsing all rational thought. "Take me instead."

The monster paused in his torture to look at her. "Don't worry. We haven't forgotten about you."

"He's old. He can't take this," Lyla said, still straining against the guard's hold.

"Do you know what this man has done?"

The man jerked Manny's head back, which flopped lifelessly. Lyla screamed and reached out for him even though she knew the gesture was useless.

"Please, please." She was past pride or fear. She needed to get to Manny to reassure herself that the man she considered her father was still breathing.

"This man has killed more innocents than a serial killer. The Pyre family doesn't care who gets in their way. They don't kill, they *obliterate*. Power hungry, arrogant... They forget they're human and can bleed."

The monster dropped Manny, who fell to the floor and didn't move. When he raised his booted foot, the scream Lyla released was filled with all the horror and helpless rage she possessed. She closed her eyes and struggled like a demon, but she couldn't get free. When she opened her eyes, she saw that Manny looked like a broken puppet. His limbs were bent at odd angles. The man standing above him pulled out a gun and fired. Manny's body jerked. Blood splattered the man's pants and pooled beneath his feet.

Lyla retched. Blood stained shoes came into her line of sight. A black leather glove smeared with red reached out and gripped her hair. A vicious tug forced her head back. She stared up at the mask that shielded the murderer's eyes and poured all the hate she felt into that stare.

"You're so beautiful," the man said and brushed his gloved thumb over lips.

The tang of Manny's blood seeped into her mouth, and she gagged. The man clucked his tongue.

"It's a shame you had to see that," he crooned, stroking back her hair while she trembled in shock. He pressed his lips to her ear. "You're at the wrong place at the wrong time, baby."

Lyla stared into the slits of his mask at fathomless black eyes. The man released her, and she sprawled on her back, staring up at him as he pulled out a shiny blade from his pocket. She tried to run, but a man pinned her wrists above her head while the monster sat on her middle and held the knife aloft. She stared at the blade, knowing this is where she'd die.

"You fucker—" she began before pain ripped through her abdomen.

She didn't have enough breath to scream. Another stab and then another until her body felt as if it was being cut into pieces. She struggled, all to no avail. Her body was on fire. The monster grabbed her face and kissed her through the mask before he shoved the knife into her chest. The arms pinning her down disappeared. Her hand went to the hilt of the knife. The merest brush on the blade made her want to reposition it to end her agony faster. She curled into a ball, knowing there was no surviving this.

Suddenly, there were shouts, scrambling feet, and then gunshots. This mattered little to her. Although her eyes were darkening with black spots, she focused on Manny. She didn't register the fact that bodies were dropping around her. She dragged herself across the slick floor. She was going to die. She needed to be near Manny. The blood spurting from her wounds helped her slide across the floor with more ease. When she reached Manny's broken hand, she dropped her face onto it.

"I love you, Dad." If there was a spark of life in him, she hoped he heard her. Lyla pressed a kiss onto his palm and whispered, "I'll see you on the other side."

Lyla swam through a sea of pain. Death was a series of flickering images and agony. She wanted it to stop so she embraced dark, fathomless oblivion.

_____

Every inch of her body hurt. Even the act of blinking her eyes sent a shaft of pain through her skull. She closed her eyes and drifted. Something soft brushed her fingers. The pleasant sensation distracted her from the mind-numbing agony. She opened her eyes and tried to focus on the shadow at the periphery of her vision. Blonde hair swished over the back of her hand. A person sobbed at her bedside with such fervor that Lyla pushed through the pain. She moved her hand and let out a strangled cry at the unbearable pain. The blonde head lifted. Bright blue eyes awash with tears stared at her. Carmen. Lyla shifted and clenched her teeth against the agonizing pain.

"You're awake, you're awake," Carmen babbled and ran to the door and shouted, "She's awake!"

A slew of people congregated around her bed. Crisp, direct words were said, but she couldn't make sense of them. A doctor shone a light in her eyes and tried to adjust her, which made her grunt urgently.

"Thank God," Carmen whispered and shoved a nurse aside to take Lyla's hand. "I can't lose you too. I just can't. Vinny, Manny—"

There was a wild rushing sound in her head. Memories of the men in masks, Manny's prolonged torture, and then being stabbed... Rage ripped through her. She tried to lever her body off the pillows. Pain tore through her chest. The monitors went crazy, and the medical personnel began to shout. Lyla collapsed as her head swam. She was dimly aware of Carmen squeezing her hand as darkness consumed her.

When Lyla opened her eyes, it took a moment to register that a man sat at her bedside. Dressed in a black suit, Gavin seemed out of place in this sterile setting. As if he felt her regard, he lifted his head. They stared at one another. Gavin looked untouched by recent events. He was cool, calm, collected. It made her lightheaded with fury as memories of Manny's torture flickered through her mind.

"I know you're angry with me," he said.

Her lower lip trembled. She compressed her lips to stop the telltale action, but tears spilled over anyway. Anyone could get angry over stubbing their toe. What she felt toward Gavin wasn't mere anger. The taste of betrayal on her tongue was like acid, eating away at her insides. She wanted to strike him, beat him with her fists until he was bruised and bloody. She would never get those images of Manny out of her head. If her body wasn't so broken, she would have launched herself at him. Instead, she was forced to lay there with him inches away. She could smell his cologne but couldn't feel his body heat, and she was so cold. She should be dead. What was she doing here? She didn't want to be on this planet. It had too much hate on it, too much pain. She wanted to be with Manny, not here with his son who was so closed off; she wouldn't know he was human if he didn't blink and breathe.

"Blade managed to alert me after he was shot. He's in critical condition, but he gained consciousness long enough to send me a red alert code. I got there in time to save you, but not Dad. I didn't get all of them. They're still on the run. Are you able to give me any information? Do you know what the leader looks like? Who they work for?"

She was lying in a hospital bed, unable to move, and he was asking about the monster who did this. Gavin would never stop. He didn't ask about his father or her wounds. She wanted to scream. Instead, she turned her face in the other direction and wept for the man who would never be her father-in-law and for the son he left behind who was a hollow shell of a human being.

"Lyla, I need information," Gavin said without inflection.

After Vinny's death, she told Gavin to let it be. He didn't, and this was the result. His father paid the ultimate price and she... She would never be the same. Witnessing such brutality, she didn't think she would ever be okay. Gavin broke his word. Therefore, she wasn't obligated to honor hers.

"I don't have a lot of time," Gavin continued, "I'm a suspect in a bunch of murders, but they don't have enough evidence. They're looking into my businesses and trying to pin me with money laundering. I'm going to be tied up with lawyers and cops. I need to know who they were."

What more did he need to know? These men were from the criminal underworld and had a personal vendetta against the Pyres.

"Lyla."

He touched her arm. That made her whip her head around, which made her feel faint. Despite the blast of pain, she managed to say, "*Don't* touch me."

Her voice was a bare whisper, but it was there. Her chest was on fire.

Gavin's soulless amber eyes didn't so much as flicker with emotion. "I need information."

"This was payback. He's the new crime lord. Vinny was just the beginning."

There was a charged silence and then, "Anything else?"

"No," she said on a broken whisper.

The door burst open. Lyla smelled cotton candy before she saw Carmen. She looked like a ray of sunshine in Lyla's otherwise bleak world. She used the last of her strength to hold up her hand. Carmen rushed over with tears coursing down her cheeks.

"You're awake," Carmen said fervently, rubbing her face into Lyla's palm. "You can't leave me, Lyla. You *can't*."

Gavin rose. Carmen shot him a frosty look as he walked out, back ramrod straight. Lyla's vision blurred with tears. Carmen leaned down to press a kiss to her brow.

"You were in a coma. I was scared you wouldn't wake up." Carmen swallowed hard and brushed away her tears, which were instantly replaced by fresh ones. "All that matters is you're awake. You're okay. You're gonna be okay."

It wouldn't be okay. It would *never* be okay. Lyla closed

her eyes as tears slipped down her cheeks. She felt as if she
were going to shatter.

"I don't know what the fuck is wrong with Gavin. This is
the first time he's come to the hospital. I don't know where
he's been. Cops are all over the place," Carmen hissed.

Would they find enough evidence to convict Gavin for
multiple murders? He had more than enough blood on his
hands to be put away for life. Lyla didn't have to ask Carmen
to know there had been a bloodbath in the wake of Manny's
death. Gavin would never let it go. If he had been remote
before, he was completely gone now. Lyla brushed her hand
over Carmen's and got her instant attention.

"We need to go," she said.

Carmen searched her eyes. "Are you sure?"

Tears spilled down her cheeks. "Yes. He'll never stop. He
broke his promise. I'm free."

"Gavin won't let you leave. His security is outside
your door."

"You know how to get around them."

"You really want to do this?"

"Please," Lyla croaked. "I can't do this."

Carmen nodded decisively and shouldered her gold
rhinestone purse. "Let me see what I can do."

Carmen shimmied out the door, hooker heels clacking.
Lyla had no doubt that Carmen would be able to get her out
a second time. She used her thumb to slide the engagement
ring off her finger. It clinked when it hit the floor and disappeared from sight. Lyla felt as if a weight had been lifted
from her shoulders. She was done.

CRIME LORD SERIES

Thank you for reading Crime Lord's Captive. Lyla and Gavin's story continues in **Recaptured by the Crime Lord**!

I've written a bonus clip of Manny's mindset before Lyla was brought back to Las Vegas. Join my email list and have it sent to your inbox!

AUTHOR'S NOTE

Hi All,

I hope you enjoyed Crime Lord's Captive. Please leave a review and recommend the book to a friend, it helps me out a lot!

Crime Lord's Captive came out of nowhere. I was writing another series and had vague plans for a psycho ex—enter Gavin. I realized halfway through the book that Gavin didn't fit the series I was writing so I created the Crime Lord Series and Crime Lord's Captive was born.

Manny and Gavin really captured my heart. I was compelled to write these books. All the characters were there, just waiting to get my attention. Once I began, I couldn't stop. I hope you enjoy this series as much as I do.

Don't miss Recaptured by the Crime Lord. It's going to be a wild ride!

Love,
Mia

P. S. I've written a bonus clip of Manny's mindset before Lyla was brought back to Las Vegas. Join my email list and have it sent to your inbox!

BOOKS BY MIA KNIGHT

Crime Lord's Captive

Recaptured by the Crime Lord

Once A Crime Lord

Awakened by Sin

ABOUT THE AUTHOR

Mia lives in her head and is shadowed by her dogs who don't judge when she cries and laughs with imaginary characters. Mia comes from a big, conservative family that doesn't know how to handle her eccentricities, but with encouragement from her fans, has found the courage to put the characters in her head on paper.

Stalk Mia
Website
Email
Mia Knight's Captives (Facebook Group)

f facebook.com/miaknightbooks

🐦 twitter.com/authormiaknight

g goodreads.com/authormiaknight

BB bookbub.com/profile/mia-knight

Made in the USA
Columbia, SC
17 July 2018